A SURPRISE SPOUSE

Eve choked on her wine. Hastily she set her glass down and glanced up in surprise. Who was this man, and what was he doing at her dinner party uninvited? And how had he known her name? Appalled, and at the same time intrigued, she assessed the fine specimen standing just inside the doorway to the dining room.

The room, lit by a dozen or so candelabras, softened the handsome, swarthy face, with its strong chin and patrician nose. The man was dressed in a deep green superfine jacket that outlined his broad shoulders, and his doeskin breeches were tucked into gleaming Hessians and emphasized his taut leg muscles. Although this was not a tall man, perhaps just under six-feet, he was well-built, with hair the color of polished walnut wood, and his hazel eyes were a mixture of colors, mostly amber. He reminded her of one of her father's pirates, but better dressed.

He opened his mouth to speak, and Eve's interest was doused like a fire by water: "My dearest, how good it is to see you again! I could barely wait to reach The Towers and see my devoted wife."

CRITICS CHEER FOR MINDA WEBBER!

BUSTIN'

"Webber again brings readers a comical story full of references to 1940's movies....the story is a fun escape."

—*RT BOOKreviews*

"Minda Webber fills every page in *Bustin'* with her trademark quips and pop culture references."

—Romance Reviews Today

"Webber's books crack me up....They are like kids' cartoons that adults find funnier because of all the bizarre references."

—Book Crossing

THE RELUCTANT MISS VAN HELSING

"Webber delights readers with another laugh-out-loud tale of mayhem among the supernatural ton....This wonderfully witty, wildly clever, gripping, sensual and exciting romp proves that Webber's reputation as an up-and-comer is well and truly deserved."

—*RT BOOKreviews* (Top Pick)

"This sensational screwy satirical sequel will have readers laughing at Jane's capers and Neil's reactions to her antics. The action-packed amusing story line also is loaded with literary references that are fun to follow as these witticisms augment a zany well-written tale that howls for more."

—The Best Reviews

"If you enjoy a funny, yet romantic, paranormal tale filled with monsters, vampires, werewolves and trouble-attracting heroines, then you will most certainly love this book."

—A Romance Review

"Ms. Webber has struck again with her latest offering in this series. The story is lighthearted, witty and pure fun to read....It is an action packed, campy, satirical read that genre lovers will adore. It's a hoot!"

—Paranormal Romance Reviews

The Reinvented
Miss Bluebeard

MINDA WEBBER

LOVE SPELL NEW YORK CITY

LOVE SPELL®

July 2007

Published by

Dorchester Publishing Co., Inc.
200 Madison Avenue
New York, NY 10016

ISBN-10: 0-505-52706-5
ISBN-13: 978-0-505-52706-6

Printed in the United States of America.

Visit us on the web at www.dorchesterpub.com.

DEDICATION

I want to thank my fans, Kathe Robin and the *Romantic Times BOOKreviews* for their acknowledgment of a fledgling author. It can be a scary thing to be published for the first time. I was fortunate and found not only acceptance, but also encouragement and support. Thank you.

ACKNOWLEDGMENTS

I wish to thank Paul, Crystal and Carlos for doing a bit of research for me; Holly Teague for being the first fan that I didn't know personally; Marilyn Webber for reading the manuscript; my editor, Chris, for not wringing my neck on my typos, and for his always great advice; my 2006 night class for coming to my *Bustin'* signing and making me laugh; Scott for his belief in me, *Alien* and a spaghetti dinner; Phil for his belief in me and the corn in his ear; and for one of the best written, best acted and funny sitcoms of all times—*Fawlty Towers*—which has given me years of laughter with jack-in-the-box rats and kippers in bed.

AUTHOR'S NOTE

No pirates were plundered during the writing of this book. No native soil from vampires' coffins was thrown out with the wash. No Frankenstein monsters were chased around insane asylums with burning torches, and no rosebushes were exposed to any indignities. However, creative license was taken once again on historical dates and accuracy.

CHAPTER ONE

It Started with Eve in the Madhouse

The trouble with being a Bluebeard was that everyone associated the name with plundering pirates, peg-legged men, and plank-walking prisoners. They were a salty crew, what with their *arghs* and shouts of *"Give me your jewels."* Their family crest was a skull and crossbones, and no one with any sense wanted to cross paths with them. Eve Bluebeard Griffin had more reason than most to avoid the whole thieving lot, for she was the daughter of Captain Edward Bluebeard, notorious scourge of the seven seas.

"Why must he come here tomorrow, of all days?" she asked herself, her fingers playing with the brief missive written by her father. "Doesn't he have anything better to do? Important things, like forcing his motley crew to swab the deck, or following a treasure map or two?" She squinted, trying to decipher his chicken scratch:

Back in port. Prepare to defend yourself for your mutinous actions—or rather, lack of actions. Love, the Captain.

1

"Doesn't he have any treasure chests to pack? Ocean voyages to take?" Only the silence of her spacious study replied to her distress.

Frowning in frustration, she stared out a large beveled window in the far west wall. Curtains of rich fabric were tied back from the long windows placed between massive oak bookshelves. Most of those shelves were filled with stately bound volumes, books of every kind and size, many with gold-leafed pages that concerned diseases of the mind or supernatural abnormalities. Adorning other nearby shelves were ornaments from the Far East and delicate porcelain figurines from Germany. On the north wall, two more large windows looked into the room. Opened midway, they admitted the sweet breezes and golden sunlight of a day in early fall, the light casting patterns on the hardwood floor.

Through the open casement, the scent of rose petals perfumed the air. Since Eve usually saw patients in this room, the walls were painted a pale green and trimmed in various shades of amber—to calm overset sensibilities and fragile nerves. This was a room that commonly left Eve with a feeling of restfulness, but today her serenity was lost as she envisioned the arrival of her father for their biannual talk. In reality, the "conversations" were one-sided, and filled with a litany of the Captain's complaints. Verily, he would swagger into the room and begin issuing commands as if he were still on deck. Cursing up a blue streak, he would expect Eve to blindly obey, as all good daughters did in 1830 London.

Although it was quite true that she was a daughter, and good, Eve had never done terribly well at blindly obeying. To say her fractious father had been disappointed when she failed to take up the gauntlet and sail the seven seas with him, causing mayhem and madness, was an under-statement. But Eve had wanted a different kind of life, one that would enable her to be captain of her own dinghy, so to speak. Yes, being very much her father's daughter and thus stubborn to a fault, she would accept nothing else but a life free of robbing and looting, a life where people respected not only her, but also her chosen profession.

Even as a small child, Eve had wanted to make a worthy contribution to the world and not just steal worldly goods from unsuspecting travelers on the high seas—or on the low seas, for that matter. Any liquid-located larceny was bad. Several years ago, fortune had smiled upon her in a less than ideal way: Her great-great-uncle, a vampire, had participated in a duel with a young upstart warlock. Needless to say, he had bitten the dust both figuratively and literally. Though he had won the duel, he had sadly miscalculated the sunrise and gone from being one of the great undead to just plain dead. Still, her inheritance had allowed Eve to abandon her father's ship and chart her own course, reinventing herself by remodeling her uncle's old manor on the outskirts of London as an asylum for the supernaturally insane.

Although mostly mortal and not of a supernatural bent, Eve Bluebeard did have a skeleton or two in the old family wardrobe. There was a werewolf or three, and warlocks, though only one vampire now that her great-great-uncle was dead. This rich, diverse ancestry had given Eve a compassion for the supernatural, and also marginal inclusion into the otherworldly world.

Her father, literally an old sea dog, had inherited a few shapeshifter traits, though he was not yet nor would he ever be a full-blooded werewolf. Captain Bluebeard couldn't change shape under the full moon—or any moon—but he did have a terrible growl, a worse bite than bark, acute hearing, and could sniff out a ship in the dead of night. He also aged somewhat slower than humans. Eve had a few werewolf attributes herself, but interspecies marriages to mortals had diluted the Bluebeard blood severely. By the time the shape-shifter genes reached Eve, she was left with merely an acute sense of smell and rather warm blood, often going without a cape until winter's first snowfall.

It had been Eve's paternal grandmother who had passed on the genes. Grandmother Ruby had been a full-blooded werewolf, and had raised Eve after Eve's mother died when she was a girl. Eve had loved Ruby dearly, even though as the years passed the woman had gone beyond eccentricity into sheer lunacy. Werewolves, as Eve learned early in life, could shift shapes only when the moon was full, and in fact they *had* to change form then. But after the full moon came and went, Eve's dear daft grandmother would howl and wander the house in search of her full-length fur wrap that she always seemed to "lose" for twenty-some days every month.

It was from tending to her grandmother in the old woman's final years that Eve had recognized what she wanted to do with her life, which had nothing whatsoever to do with pirates or plunder. Instead, she yearned to help others who were struck with mental instability—especially those who were stark, howling mad. Thus, after her grandmother's death, Eve had dedicated her life to the cause. Helping the supernaturally insane, she hoped to become a "psychiatrist"—a new scientific term for those who studied illnesses of the mind.

In the past, this new field of psychiatry would have

been considered witchcraft, and practitioners would have been burned at the stake. But as time marched forward, so did acceptance. It was the modern world now, and medical science was finally venturing out of the closet. The medical community had discovered that the mind could be diseased like other parts of the body, and with this groundbreaking revelation it had become the general consensus among men of intellect that the insane could be helped to live more normal lives.

Eve had learned that different methods were used by different doctors—like placing hotheads in icy cold baths, or dressing the depressed in straitjackets with silver linings. Fortunately, the days of putting a bowl with a cracked egg underneath a bedlamite's bed to draw out evil spirits had faded into the past. The more modern asylums no longer even threw their mad in pits or left them unprotected from the elements. It broke Eve's tender heart to know that those who most needed kindness had in the past been literally left out in the cold.

Eve herself knew what it was to face bigotry and disdain. When she had entered the University of Vienna to study medicine, she had found herself in an elitist world where males ruled and most men believed females were vain and bird-witted. They believed women should stick to their own professions, stay courtesans, governesses, and wives. Every female was to be mistrusted and ridiculed. And while she'd grown tremendously during her years of medical school, both as a doctor and a person, it had still been devastatingly hard for Eve. Because she was female, the other interns ostracized and belittled her whenever possible. The abuse also came from many of Eve's professors, all of whom were supposed to be highly learned doctors. She had often mused, while she sat along the banks of the Rhine and memorized her lessons, that even getting in the door and taking your coat off in this profession was like fighting on the Barbary Coast.

Yes, Eve had learned that, regrettably, in spite of mankind's new sympathy for the mentally ill, women were still held in subtle contempt. Females, most especially grand ladies, were thought to be creatures of excessive feeling and tender sensibilities—goofy gigglers, meaningless chatterers, and carriers of perfume-filled handkerchiefs drenched with tears. They were a delight to gaze upon and delightful for sport under the bedcovers, but never a man's boon companion or equal. And certainly none had the wit to become a doctor.

No, a female would never be considered strong enough, wise enough, or emotionally stable enough to work at an insane asylum—most especially one filled with monsters. To most men's reasoning, a female psychiatrist in the paranormal field would be sheer folly and quite unsuccessful—would probably be eaten by one of her fiercer patients. But Eve vowed she would not only work at an asylum; she would run one.

Despite harassment, belittling, and the tide of public opinion, Eve had studied hard and prevailed, refusing to buckle under the pressure. With her typical Bluebeard stubbornness, she had not only attended medical school, but had graduated at the top of her class—to the bewilderment of all the males concerned. She had returned to London victorious, with a degree in hand as well as a marriage contract, the latter being much to the surprise of her father. Proudly she was now Dr. Evelyn Griffin, respected psychiatrist for mad monsters.

Eager to start her new life, she had hired staff and hung up her shingle at the Towers, her deceased uncle's now-renovated manor. The first year was difficult; however, the second year had been easier, and by the third season the Towers was becoming well-known in the supernatural community. Even more astounding was the knowledge that Dr. Eve Bluebeard Griffin was charting new territory, proposing that the insane could be cured by talking, in what she termed her "Verbal Intercourse" sessions.

In these conversational sessions, Eve worked very hard at delving into the twisting and turning corridors of her patients' thoughts, trying to unravel the terrors and secrets of each one's subconscious mind. She probed festering memories and night terrors, which mortal and monster alike hid deep within. Whether it was a gargoyle, a leprechaun, or a vampire, their terrors were buried much deeper than six feet under. Eve was the person who lanced these boils, opening the graveyards of secret fear and exposing them to the naked light of day. Only then, she believed, could her patients could begin to heal.

Her task was monumental and extremely difficult, yet Eve thrived on the challenge. Every day and every night was a new adventure where she sailed into the uncharted seas of turbulent minds. And even with a lack of articulate and necessary detail from her patients, Eve held hope that time and determination would free them from their private demons.

Turning her attention from the lush gardens outside her study, Eve began to tap her fingers upon the skull gracing her desk and glanced grimly down at her father's note with more than a little trepidation. With luck, the Captain wouldn't have been into his ninety-nine bottles of beer, which he liked to take down from the wall and pass around. Her wish was probably in vain, though, she realized wryly. He was a pirate captain; beer was like mother's milk to him. As was rum.

Crumpling the note in her hand, she disposed of it in the brass rubbish holder beside her desk. "Tomorrow, of all days. How I wish for a stiff wind to Jamaica and my father sailing there."

The door to her study suddenly burst open, crashing against the solid oak wall. Right behind the banging door stood her butler, Teeter. His countenance stiff, he maintained his usual starched dignity. Teeter was the epitome of an English butler, with one exception. To Eve's dismay, Teeter never failed to enter or exit a room without a great deal of slamming doors—a common complaint against ogres or those with ogre blood. Since the butler's grandfather was an ogre, Eve took Teeter's entrances and exits in stride. She was nothing if not flexible, having learned to be so at an early age aboard the *Jolly Roger*, her father's ship.

When she had first inherited the butler along with her estate, she had begged, pleaded with, and threatened him. But all her efforts to reform Teeter had been to no avail. He had resisted all her efforts.

"Your next patient—one Mr. Frankenstein—is here to see you, Doctor," Teeter said.

Eve sighed as her butler banged his way back outside her study. Good help was impossible to find these days.

CHAPTER TWO

Diary of a Mad Monster

Eve watched her patient enter the room to engage in their Verbal Intercourse session, called fondly by her patients "fireside chats." The nickname was due to the fact that her study held a massive green-marbled fireplace that dominated the east wall and pleasantly warmed the spacious chamber.

Her oversize patient moved to seat himself on an overlarge chair—a chair that had been constructed especially for his large frame when he'd first become Eve's patient seven months ago—and smiled shyly at her. Although he wasn't a resident of the asylum, the patient came once a week to meet with Eve, an arrangement made by his adopted father, Dr. Victor Frankenstein. Dr. Frankenstein had heard of Eve's kindness in treating monsters with quirks, and since most monsters frankly had more serious quirks than he, the Frankenstein monster had been easy to add to her patient list.

Monstrous or not, her patient, this Frederick Frankenstein, was a gentle giant who loved helping blind men cross crowded London streets and listening to violin music. Eve felt that Frederick was a sterling example of "Never judge a pirate by his ship, a madman by his conversation, or a monster by his face." Despite the unevenness of his features and the scars crisscrossing his visage, he was a compassionate soul. To less informed or bigoted people, Frederick at first glance would appear an ugly man, but inside he was pure gold. Well, not actually gold, she corrected herself. Dr. Victor Frankenstein had been quite explicit in the materials that went into the creation. Still, Frederick did have a heart as big as his almost-seven-foot self; he liked everybody, and was always willing to lend a helping hand—or rather, a dead earl's helping hands.

Smiling cheerfully at Frederick, Eve checked her notes.

> *Frederick Frankenstein is not wild and crazy, stir-crazy, non compos mentis, or even slightly dicked in the head. No, Frederick is merely unhinged; perhaps he has a screw or two loose. He has a peculiar habit of eating goldfish. During sessions he's revealed acute feelings of inferiority that are complex in themselves. He often feels as if he isn't as electrifying as anyone else, which, after hearing of his creation, I find to be wrong in many aspects.*

Some members of the ton thought Frederick to be a half-wit, because of his often slow speech, but Eve knew better. His wit had come from Lord Delbrook, and it was very whole indeed. Frederick's feet and legs had once been attached to a very large duke, Hans Holbrecht. His hands were those of an earl, and his aristocratic nose came from a German prince with the family name of Blucher. Unfortunately, the rest of Frederick was composed of criminals and the lower classes. But then, as Eve had learned in her cadaver class, the corpses of good men were hard to find.

The chair groaned as Frederick shifted his massive frame. He smiled apologetically, his lopsided expression stretching the tiny scars across his lower jaw.

"Dr. Eve, it's nice seeing you again," he managed to say, blushing a little.

His blush was nothing new to Eve, since she often had that effect on men, or saw them stuttering in her presence. Many women would have become vain about their beauty, but Eve was not most women. Very infrequently did she think about her appearance, and when she did, she often shrugged it off and went about her business.

Men were not so cavalier about it, however, for Eve was a lovely woman. She had thick wavy hair, of dark reddish gold, which she wore in a Psyche knot. Her eyes were the color of the rain-tossed seas of the tropics. Her face was heart-shaped, with prominent cheekbones, and she had a lush pink mouth with Cupid's-bow lips.

"It's nice to see you too, Frederick. How have you been feeling this week?" Eve returned Frederick's smile readily, feeling the warm glow of knowing that she was creating a trusting relationship between herself and her patient, which would help Frederick relax so he could delve into his fears. She jotted a quick note:

Be sure to have Frederick's chair reinforced. He must have put on some weight. Appetite healthy.

As she studied her patient's chart, she felt not only virtuous, but also a little victorious. Together she and Frederick were creating a new personality. This feeling of power must be what Dr. Victor had felt when he first beheld the monster, and ran around screaming, *"It's alive, it's alive."*

The gentle giant sighed. "Sometimes all I want is a good bowl of soup and to listen to Vivaldi."

"Sometimes all I want is a good book, a brisk breeze blowing in my face, and a nice cup of Indian tea," Eve replied.

"Sometimes I wish I looked like everybody else—anybody else."

"Not everyone can look like Prince Charming," Eve reminded the monster, understanding that he felt less than perfectly put together. He did stand out in a crowd. After all, he was six-foot-eight, with stitches crisscrossing his face and a greenish cast to his skin. Unless you were a troll, that wasn't becoming.

"Who wants to look like an oversize frog?" he asked.

"Nonsense, Frederick Frankenstein! Never a frog," Eve said. She studied him speculatively, a faint smile on her face. "You're far too distinguished for that."

"Distinguished?" He sounded intrigued.

"Yes, distinguished. And you have lovely gray eyes. They are so expressive. You're fine as you are—a very healthy, strapping young man with a kind heart. But you need to come to that realization by yourself. You may be different, but *vive la différence.*"

Frederick contemplated Dr. Eve's words. He desperately wanted to believe her, but life had taught him differently about being different. He was slow to words, slow to anger, and too large. Yet some part of him felt jubilant at this advice from such a wise, pretty woman. Smiling shyly at her, he couldn't keep from wondering about her absentee husband. Why would the man prefer to work with the insane in the Carpathian Mountains when he could be working with lunatics right here? There were certainly enough loons in London without treating foreign madmen. Maybe Dr. Adam Griffin was a bit of a slow-top himself. His logic was certainly faulty in leaving his wife alone. Frederick knew that if he had a wife like Dr. Eve, he'd never leave home without her.

"I don't know. 'Different' is good in birds, jackets, and ladies' gowns, but not people," he said.

"Rubbish! If everyone were the same, what a dull world we would live in. There would be no great discoveries, no stirring music or moving art. . . ."

"But it's so hard at times, Dr. Eve. People always stare. It's not easy being green. I know you're trying to help me get a new lease on life, to help me feel like a new man . . . well, men. But I just feel . . . worn out."

"Rome wasn't built in a day," she stated firmly, hiding her sympathy for the big man. Pity would only undermine her work.

"What's Rome got to do with me? I've never been there."

She grinned. "Rome wasn't built in a day, oak trees don't grow overnight, and confidence isn't something we put on like a hat. You say you feel as if people are always staring at you—"

Frederick interrupted. "They *are*."

"Perhaps. But Frederick, embrace it when people stare. Give them that crooked grin, or dance a little jig like that time you danced at the Ritz. You are Frederick Franken-stein, beloved adopted son of the Frankensteins and cousin to Clare. Your brother-in-law is one of the highest-ranking werewolves in the world, while your aunt Mary is wed to a duke. Your connections are excellent. And inside, you are a kind, gentle man with lovely gray eyes who loves music and sees the good in people even when they aren't at their best. You are special, and you should always remember that."

Frederick blushed and stammered, "Th-thank you, Dr. Eve. It's just that sometimes I want what everyone else has. I want to wa-walk into a ball and have the ladies sigh at me, to want to dance with me. I want to dance with them like a swan, without stepping on their feet."

His words were opening doors in Eve's mind. Frederick was upset about something that had happened this week, most likely at a ball. Again she wrote on her notepad with her quilled pen.

Patient much less animated today than he was last week, and definitely feeling melancholy.

"Speaking of balls, have you been to any this past week?" she asked.

Nodding slowly, his big head bobbing, Frederick explained in a voice filled with regret, "I went to the Graus' ball."

"And?" Open-ended questions were important in a session. They made a patient expound about events or people which sometimes were what had made the patient feel depressed in the first, second, and third place.

"Uh, well, I guess I was introduced to a Miss Beal."

The way Frederick said the name alerted Eve immediately: a *female* was involved in Frederick's latest case of nerves and melancholy. "Did you find her . . . pretty?"

Frederick blushed and ducked his head. "She has puppy-dog eyes, and you know how I like puppies. Her hair is black, with a small white streak, and it's quite tall."

"She's tall?"

"No, her hair. And it's kind of fuzzy, like a lamb's. I like lambs too. And she has a funny smile."

It appeared that Frederick had a slight infatuation with this Miss Beal. Eve hoped the young lady would return his interest. Aside from all the medical strides of the new decade, it was a fundamental truth that a good woman could do great things for a man's confidence.

"Funny, how?" she asked as she wrote:

Tends to put foot in mouth with pretty females—quite a problem, given the size of Frederick's foot.

"A gap between her teeth. I like it. At first her smile made me feel happy inside," Frederick admitted. "But right after that, it made me feel all odd."

"Can you describe that feeling?" Eve asked, making more notes.

"It became hard to breathe, and I saw little dots in front of my vision—like before, when those townspeople in Germany chased me with those torches."

"I see," Eve said, keeping her voice gentle, though her thoughts were anything but. Poor Frederick and his night terrors. He had feelings of fear no self-respecting monster wanted. After all, monsters were supposed to instill night terrors, not be subject to them. Eve wanted to find those nasty villagers and give them a piece of her mind.

"I felt like I was going to fall apart, like my stitches

weren't holding," Frederick went on. "It was terrible. I was so upset, I just left without a word to anyone. Now Miss Beal must think I have monstrous manners."

"Perhaps you could send her some flowers, and a note of apology saying you'd forgotten some previous engagement," Eve advised.

"I would hate to tell her a lie," Frederick argued.

"Then you could tell her the truth—that you found her smile so engaging you didn't know what to say, so you left."

"Maybe so, Dr. Eve . . . but then, if she showed the note to her friends, they might laugh at me."

Since Eve didn't know Miss Beal or what the girl would do, she suggested, "Perhaps your cousin Clare might know of Miss Beal's character."

Frederick brightened. He said, "I will write and ask."

"How is she doing in her confinement?" Eve had met Baroness Huntsley at a ball five months past, and though the woman appeared as eccentric as all Frankensteins, Eve had found her to be a delightful lady with an inquiring mind. She and her husband, *the* Werewolf of London, were expecting their first child in less than a month.

"I saw her two weeks ago, and she was happy as a clam and fat as a pig. Of course, I didn't tell her that part about being fat as a pig."

"Very wise, Frederick. No lady likes to hear she has gotten plump."

Frederick shook his big, slightly dented head. "Oh, no. Clair doesn't care about her weight. Neither does her husband, Ian. Clair just doesn't like people to mention the word 'pigs' around her, what with that unfortunate incident and all."

Eve tapped her fingers on the skull on her desk. Ah, yes, she vaguely remembered some gossip about a misadventure with pigs, ghosts, and a cemetery when she'd first come to town.

"I'm glad to hear your cousin's confinement is going well. Now, about those feelings you experienced at the Grau ball. After you left, did you breathe into a paper bag, as I suggested?"

"Actually it was a horse's oat bag," Frederick admitted.

"Improvisation is good," Eve replied. "Now, did it help with your breathing?"

"Uh-huh."

"Good, good," Eve praised. "Did you count to one hundred and clear your mind of everything but the rolling ocean waves, as I suggested?"

"Yes. But I added fish. Goldfish."

"You were hungry?" Eve asked. Every patient had foibles, and Eve had learned of this patient's culinary fondness by coming into her office one day to find all her goldfish missing from the large glass dome aquarium she'd kept by the balcony doors. That day the fish tank was empty, and Frederick was wearing a stricken look on his homely face. "Well, a sign of hunger is always good, I say, after an attack of night terrors."

Frederick nodded, and Eve glanced at the grandfather clock against the wall. Withdrawing a folder from her desk, she slid out a piece of paper smeared with black ink stains.

"It's time for our other therapy," she said. Inkblot therapy was a brand-new concept encouraging the patient to come forth and give responses to various ink stains on parchment paper. These stains sometimes provided a key to the unconscious. The technique was necessary due to the subconscious mind often being hidden and slippery.

Pointing at the parchment she asked, "What does this picture remind you of?"

Frederick studied the ink spot with intense concentration. Finally he replied, "An electrical storm."

Eve rather thought it resembled the bow of a ship. She held up the next picture. "And this one?"

Again, Frederick concentrated. "I think it's either a gravestone, or maybe my friend Herr Munster's foot."

Since she had never seen Herr Munster's foot, she couldn't disagree, although she thought the dark stain rather resembled a pirate map. "And this one?" she asked, showing one that obviously resembled coins and jewels in her father's favorite sea chest.

"Faces. Lots of cruel faces, staring at me."

His answer was just about what Eve had suspected, and she noted her thoughts on her pad.

Patient's fear of crowds is still prominent in his subconscious mind. Not surprising, when he has been chased half the length of Germany by a vicious, bigoted mob brandishing torches and weapons.

Yes, her work was still cut out for her. She would have to determine a way to help Frederick through his fears of being hunted and big crowds. Perhaps her assistant Pavlov's behavior patterning might provide a method. She would ask the man when he returned from France.

The grandfather clock chimed loudly beside her desk, and Eve stood, her hand outstretched. "Our time is up for today, Frederick. I want you to continue to do the exercises I gave you whenever you feel one of your nighttime terrors coming on. I also want you to practice looking into the mirror every day and repeating, 'I am a jolly good fellow' at least twenty times." She escorted Frederick to the door. "I will see you the same time next Monday. Take care, Frederick, and tell your father, Dr. Frankenstein, hello for me."

Frederick nodded, his big head ducking under the door frame as he slowly began his lumbering march to the front hall.

Tapping her fingers upon her chin, Eve watched him lurch away, his massive shoulders hunched, his oddly shaped head bobbing up and down, and his tremendously big feet slapping loudly on the marble hallway.

There went a good soul, a kind monster, and a complex man of many parts. Too bad most of those parts were mismatched, the cynical side of her thought; people could be so cruel to those who were different. But the more romantic side of Eve caused a faint smile to crease her lips. Perhaps Miss Beal might be persuaded to be Frankenstein's bride.

"What a strapping young man!" her housekeeper, Mrs. Fawlty, said in a voice loud enough for Eve to hear in the study.

Eve followed the voice. As she rounded the corner into the large entranceway, she saw the woman—a tall, middle-aged matron with modishly curled gray hair—scurrying toward her. Mrs. Fawlty's heavily painted face wore an aggrieved expression upon its continuously pinched features. The housekeeper was a woman of excessive nerves, insatiable desires, and uncertain temperament, and she was always in a snit about something.

"It's a shame that husband of yours is in that godforsaken country of Trainstationia, working on those railroads all the livelong days. Who knows what foreign disease he might be catching, and who knows what foreign ladies he might be tupping? They might be giving him an evil eye or something even worse, what with their tawdry Trainstationia ways. You just can't trust them foreign women. No, sirree, I tell you, you sure can't. They'll try to steal him away from you, they will."

Eve repressed a smile. Let them try. Her husband was, after all, the quintessential invisible man, resistant to all lures of the flesh. "It's Transylvania, and my husband is doctoring a mad vampire. Remember, I've told you this before." At least a thousand times in the past two years, Eve thought wryly. But Mrs. Fawlty heard what she heard, and if it wasn't to her liking then it doubtless never reached her brain.

"Well, he doesn't need to be in some far-off land to work his inventions."

Eve did smile then. "It's true, my husband *is* a man of invention," she said slyly. "And his work is very important to him." Yes, Adam Griffin was a creation to rival one of Dr. Victor Frankenstein's. He was almost perfect. No fantasy could be better. "But I trust him. He's a good husband, a good doctor, and a good man. I am blessed and proud to be his wife, especially since he gives me the freedom to go about as I please and do the work *I* love."

"Hmph. Too much freedom, if ye ask me," Mrs. Fawlty said. "A wife needs her husband around to give her a shoulder to cry on and a good tussling in bed." She grinned, showing her buckteeth, meddling ways, and carnal nature. "Nothing like a good tupping first thing in the morning after your cup o' tea. And ye know how men are.

They got their needs, they do. If ye're not there, then somebody else will supply the body. And you're nobody till a body loves you."

Eve smiled again. She trusted Adam implicitly.

CHAPTER THREE

Pirates, Pride, and Prejudice

The next afternoon found Eve tapping her fingers nervously against the skull on her desk, wondering why it always wore such a sly grin. The skull of the notorious Henry Morgan had been a gift from her father when she was fourteen. If only she felt like smiling similarly. Unfortunately, there was no merriment to be had with the Captain's inopportune visit.

"Why must he come today?" she asked again, this time of the quixotic skull. "Today of *all* days." In less than five hours Eve would be hosting a dinner party of select patronage, guests who were some of the top-ranking doctors of the mind. These guests also happened to be the board of trustees for the Supernatural Science Foundation, which provided funding to certain paranormal medical institutes. In short, tonight she would be hosting a gathering of giants.

Giants. These men controlled the purse strings to all sorts of much-needed coin, and Eve hoped to impress them. She desperately needed the funding for her asylum.

Her inheritance was long gone, and many of her patients couldn't afford to pay much at all. The roof was leaking in the west wing, the wallpaper in many of the patients' rooms really could use refurbishing, and food to feed a variety of the mad was maddeningly expensive—which wasn't that surprising since she was treating everything from gargoyles to werewolves. But if funding didn't come in soon, she would be forced to turn away any other supernatural creatures who were seeking treatment. What would become of them if she couldn't provide a safe haven?

For the past fortnight she had worried so much, even going so far as to threaten her staff regarding the preparations for the solemn and supremely important occasion. This dinner tonight at the Towers was to be an elegant affair, with every course carefully selected. Eve had barely managed a wink of sleep last night, as she was more than a trifle concerned with the trifle . . . and the truffles . . . and the good doctors' opinions on her methods of treatment for her patients. She knew she was a fine doctor, and she espoused many of the new treatments for the mentally insane; however, she restricted the newer methods to a degree, believing that each patient deserved a treatment befitting not only their specific madness, but their species. She treated hotheaded merfolk and selkies to cold baths, but did not make other surly shape-shifters dip into icy waters. She had only once done a lobotomy, and only on a gargoyle in stone form who had too much on his mind. Restrictive jackets she used only on vampires with extreme oral fixations and in full bloodlust. Yes, her methods were different, but she was achieving results, and she hoped the other doctors would think so as well.

With great deliberation she had issued the invitations, hoping that the guests—Dr. Sigmund, Count Caligari, and Dr. Crane—might be able to contribute to the treatments of two of her more worrisome cases. But also, more important, she hoped they might provide much-needed funding for the Towers.

The doors flung back against the walls broke into her thoughts as Teeter tottered into the room. "Your visitor has arrived. Mr. Beard is here to see you, Dr. Eve," he pronounced.

Her father often used Mr. *Beard* as an alias, especially when in London, where he was wanted by the English government for crimes against the Crown on the high seas some three-score years ago. And although piracy was not the threat it had been in the 1700s, it was still enough of a concern to make certain Captain Bluebeard had a price on his head of twenty thousand pounds for capture, dead or alive. Twenty thousand was a tidy sum, even if her finicky father thought the amount on his head should be at least forty. That was a grievance he would usually raise after emptying a keg or two of rum.

Stopping her fingers from their repetitive drumming, Eve watched her father enter her study like a clipper ship under full sail, then waited for him to fire the opening volley. He had taught her well: Never fire until you see the whites of the skull and crossbones, and never let your enemies or friends see you sweat—not even when deep in the sweltering heat of the tropics.

This afternoon her father was wearing a blue velvet jacket with a blue carnation in his buttonhole. A large blue diamond earring twinkled from his ear. His blue eyes were large, and the corners were webbed with telltale lines of hard loving and living. He carried a cutlass and two pistols, both probably loaded.

Eve smiled as she stood to greet the wayward salt of the sea, scrutinizing him. His bluish-black hair was tied back in a queue, his beard neatly trimmed. He was a handsome man who still appeared to be in his late fifties, though with his werewolf ancestry he was much older.

The old pirate was dressed to the nines this afternoon, as befitted a gentleman, but a gentleman he was not; he was a wily old scalawag who gave no quarter and did not take mutiny lightly. And for the past twelve years, Eve had been the mutineer in his life. Her financial situation was getting desperate, but she'd never ask the Captain for help. He'd never share any of his ill-gotten gains, not without attaching conditions like babies galore and closing the asylum.

He came to a stop before her desk, rolling on bandy legs as if he were still stationed upon the deck of his ship. Glancing about, hands on hips, he grimly shook his head. "As always, I feel like I've blundered into a madhouse!"

Eve narrowed her eyes. So, this was his opening volley? "You have. But then, you're well acquainted with madness, aren't you? If I remember correctly, your first mate thinks he's a dog and is always barking at whales. Do you still have that same boatswain, the one who thinks he's the prince regent, having everyone curtsy to him?"

Squinting and growling, Captain Bluebeard snarled at her. "He's the best boatswain I've ever had, and you *know* me first mate's a weredog. I suppose ye be putting on airs now ye're all respectable."

Her return shot had drawn blood. Eve hid her smile. "And a fine weredog he is. I've always liked Mr. Collie."

Rolling his eyes, Bluebeard shook his head. "Don't try yer sweet talk now. It won't work," he said, then glanced around the room. "I can't believe me own daughter would choose to close herself up behind these dreary, dank walls. You should be sailing the oceans, with bluebirds of happiness flying high overhead, harboring in crystal-blue lagoons, the cries of gulls and a hearty crew of cutthroats yo-ho-hoing in yer ears."

"More like a bunch of drunken sots yo-ho-hoing about their bottles of rum," Eve retorted, a little stung by her father's scurvy tidings.

"Come now, lass. Ye must miss the sea. It's in yer blood, it is. Ye have a head on your pretty shoulders, lassie. It's past time you started using it, instead of mucking about in people's mad starts. Ye have such a flair with the cutlass, and can navigate a ship near better than meself. Nobody dead or alive can yell, 'Hoist up the mainsail' better than ye. You're wasting away here, Evie! Ye should be surrounded by sea chests filled with booty, the brisk salt breezes blowing through that mane of yours."

Eve frowned fiercely. Bluebeard was using his considerable charm to bedevil her with guilt. "You know, trying to make me feel guilty isn't going to work. It never has. It's true that I love the sea, but I also love my work here." It was so like him to disparage her choices. He wanted her to be a chip off the old block, but she just wanted what she had.

"I've no longing to board a ship and sail away from my problems. I've worked hard for respectability, in both my profession and my personal life," Eve pronounced coolly. "It's what I want, and well you know it. Don't you ever tire of having this same lame discussion year after year?"

Bluebeard shook his head. "I never should have taken your mother to wife. What with her fancy ways and blue-blooded ancestry—gave ye airs it did, and the ill luck of making ye a bit too compassionate for those in need. Yer mother never could refuse anyone or anything in pain. We had more stray cats and dogs on me ship than the ocean has fish." His words were critical but his tone nostalgic.

Eve wanted to roll her eyes. Her father was exaggerating again, something all pirates were notorious for doing when not outright lying. Her father was no better. "Mother had a kind and loving heart," she reprimanded.

"Aye, that she did. But whatever her faults, I loved the woman dearly. She was the best of me and the best of me memories—besides looting."

Eve nodded reluctantly, conceding that the old salt had loved her mother, his sixth wife, as much as he was capable of loving anything that wasn't jewel encrusted or rigged with sails.

"Still, her blue blood did give ye those highfalutin dreams, and of course me own mother didn't help none—filling your foolish head with furball fancies of handsome, honest princes, and virtue as its own reward. Shiver me timbers! Everyone knows thieving provides a better reward, and virtue be for fools with pockets to let."

"There is nothing wrong with honesty or an honest day's work," Eve snapped, a scowl darkening her pretty features.

"Why ever would I want to toil for my supper when I can steal it?" Captain Bluebeard queried in frustration, gesturing with his big hands, flapping like a demented gull run amok. He would never understand women, and he had been married seven times. Scratching his chin, he vowed that someday he would get it right.

He went on: "I didn't mean to make you lose that fierce temper of yours. Although, for being the grand lady ye are . . . I wonder at the gentility of snapping at yer poor ol' dad."

Eve glared at her father. He only played the be-a-lady guilt-trip card when it suited him. Far be it from him to notice her manners at any other time. "I've worked hard to be a genteel lady, with proper manners and grace—a task, I might add, not easily undertaken, given my formative years of swinging a cutlass and robbing unsuspecting ships."

Shaking his head, Bluebeard stared at his poor misguided daughter, at her rising color and tightening lips. "Such a waste of cutlass training, and of teaching me little lass to fire a cannon," he said, fondly remembering. "What a chucklehead ye be. Once ye could hit the boarding side of a ship. Now I doubt ye could hit the broad side of a barn. Why, I have me doubts that ye could even scamper up the ropes to the crow's nest anymore, could ye? Gone all soft in the body as well as the mind."

"No, Da, I've left my cannon-firing and rope-scuttling days behind me," she replied stiffly. The last thing she wanted him to know was that she climbed ropes at least twice a week in the bell tower, whenever the hunchback Hugo escaped from his room.

"Argh! It does considerable harm to me feelings, seeing me only daughter running a madhouse and conversing with monsters with no more sense than their makers gave them or a goose. It ain't fitting for an heir to the Bluebeard heritage. Me ancestors are probably rolling over in their watery graves. What'll happen to me ships when I die? Who'll sail my *Jolly Rogers*—all three of them? I should have had me a son. Seven wives, and none of them provided me a lad. Only your mother gave me a child. And what a child! Instead of helping me with the pirating like a good obedient daughter, you're here helping this scurvy lot. This bunch of strangers. These freaks who should all be boiled in oil."

Eve did roll her eyes this time. Oil boiling was one of her father's favorite threats. Here he went again, on one of his usual rampages.

"Makes me wonder if you're not as knocked about in the head as the rest of these swavies ye've got locked up here—or not locked up here, as they should be. Whoever heard of inmates running an asylum? Ye didn't fall from the crow's nest and not tell me, did ye?"

"If I don't help my patients, who will?" Eve retorted. Despite her extreme indignation, her outward appearance remained coldly polite. She would not let her father get her goat with his trollish attitude; she would strive to be a dutiful hostess, in spite of how infuriated he made her, and no matter his nefarious intentions. "Not every inmate needs to be locked up. Rather, they need counseling and understanding and the freedom to move about. Some of them have fears of locks and closed-in places."

"Ye mollycoddle them, Evie. Ye spend too much time with their hysterical fits and starts. Ye need to be free to come and go, to see the Seven Wonders of the World, not sit here wondering about your patients."

She ruefully shook her head. Her father never releneted in his quest to sever her from her patients. "You know how I feel about the insane. Think of Grandmother Ruby. The mind is a terrible thing to waste, and being lost in the dark, never to find the light of sanity, is a loss beyond tragic—a loss to both humanity and the inhuman."

Unhappily, sanity could be as fragile as a very thin thread of gossamer silk. That line that separated the sane from the insane meant she had to walk like a tightrope to help them. Her patients dearly needed someone to walk it, to share their dark-shadowed worlds with them. Someone needed to help them reveal the things they feared went bump in the night.

"They are like lost children. They need a way home, a route, and someone to help them make the journey," she said.

"If I had me way, all these deranged loons would be walking the plank. Just like me fifth wife, that harpy," Bluebeard muttered.

Eve snorted. Pirates always loved a good tale, especially a fish-tale. She had heard this story more than once, about Bluebeard's fifth wife, who had met her fate in Davy Jones's locker, where her husband had decided to hide while she and Davy were being unfaithful."

"Thought she could monkey about with me, she did, but I showed her different when I made her walk the plank. Watched her fall to her fate below," Bluebeard reminisced, an odd light in his devilish blue eyes.

Laughter burst from Eve. In spite of her irritation with her father, he did have a wry sense of humor. And he didn't mind directing it back at himself. "How fortunate that she was what she was."

"Unfortunate, to my way of thinking—and what a way to discover her perfidy! There I was, a fine figure of a pirate, standing proudly on board me ship, listening to the slattern's loud splash, waiting for a cry of help from the scurvy female . . . and what did I hear? Nothing, I tell ye. Instead of pleas for help I heard another splash, and then I saw a green tail batting at the water and her malicious grin. She saluted me; then next thing I know she flips up that saucy green tail of hers and dives below the surface of the sea! I can still hear her laughter ringing in me ears. Gave me old heart a start, it did. Ruined me plans of retribution, sunk beyond reproach. Like I said, she always was a harpy. I just never knew she was a mermaid."

Eve resisted the urge to smile. She knew her father's pride had been hurt, but that he'd also cared enough about the woman to leave her to the sea and her lover, Davy Jones. The old sea dog should have known better in the first place. Mermaids were never happy out of the water, even if it was on the rolling deck of a ship. Their relationship had been fishy from the start.

"Bested by a fishwife," he groused. "I've never lived that down with the crew."

Eve couldn't help but laugh again. It always tickled her funnybone to see her father defeated, because it was a rare occurrence indeed.

"It was skullduggery at its worst," the Captain remarked, shaking his head. His blue diamond earring sparkled in the light from the large beveled window. Then, shrugging his shoulders, he turned his attention back to his mutinous daughter. "Skullduggery, it seems, abounds in all places— on deck of me ship and in this dusty old asylum. The Towers? Towers of raging idiots is what it is. I had hoped for once in your life you might show some appreciation for what is owed your Bluebeard heritage."

Dismayed, Eve straightened her back and thrust her chin forward. "I told you before that this is the way I choose to live my life. I will not be bound by the pirates' code."

The Captain glared at her. "A plank! A plank! My kingdom for a plank. It's mutiny, surely it is, for a daughter to speak so to her doting old da."

Eve smiled coldly. A lesser woman might have given in to her father's constant harassment, but not she. "Yes, it is."

"Argh," he sputtered, his face red. "Blast it to smithereens! I can't believe me own flesh and blood is so cold-blooded, so unfeeling of her poor da's feelings. Ashamed of me, ye are."

Eve's icy smile faltered, and she hurried over and patted his arm. Was he serious? "I'm not ashamed of you, Da, just of what you do to earn your living. I love you, you know, in spite of the fact that you're a rogue of the first order, and a rapscallion to boot."

The Captain patted her back, the redness leaving his thickly bearded face. "Well, then, if I can't get ye to leave this here mausoleum, then at least give me my second wish. Give me grandkids to dandle on my knee and to sail the China Sea with."

Eve raised a brow. Grandchildren were the last item on her agenda, especially with her husband—or rather, without him. She said, "You know that's impossible for the time being."

"You're speaking of your marriage, are ye not? This mysterious marriage ye contrived in Vienna? This havey-cavey marriage that I was not contacted about, to a man I never met and have still seen neither hide nor hair of?"

Nodding warily, she agreed. Her marriage of convenience was convenient indeed. For her. "Adam is very busy.

32

You know full well that I have explained over and over about him. It's a marriage of convenience." Her father was up to something; she could tell. But what was it this time?

"A connivance is more like it. How's it convenient when the man ain't here to bed ye? Why, it ain't natural! Why on earth would ye go and marry some nobody who nobody ever gets to see?"

Eve hid her wince, his comment cutting too close to home. She turned away and nervously began to twist the pearl necklace around her throat. "You of all men shouldn't contest the fact that he's not titled. I don't care if Adam *is* a nobody. My husband is a paragon among men. I fancy that there is not a male like Adam Griffin in the whole world." And truer words were never spoken.

Bluebeard scowled, repeating with an assurance Eve found quite disturbing, along with a hard glint of determination in his eyes, "He's a *nobody*. It appears you've married a ghost, a nothing, a will-o'-the-wisp."

"You can't say that. You don't know him. He's really quite something," Eve defended staunchly, trying to quell her misgivings about the Captain's comments. He was giving her no quarter, and she really could have used the two bits. "He's perfect—and perfect for me. The perfect man."

Her father threw back his head and laughed. "You wish. Let me tell ye a secret, lassie. There is no perfect man. It's an invention by bored, silly, love-struck ladies." As he said the last, the laughter faded from his voice and his eyes fixed harshly on Eve's countenance. "Or of lassies who think they are better than they are. Daughters who should be giving up fairy tales before pirate stories."

"Your imagination is as unbridled as your tongue. I haven't the faintest idea what you're speaking of. Would you care for a glass of brandy?" Eve asked, pointing to a decanter atop the china cabinet, hoping the old ploy would work.

It failed, and her father shook his head. "I don't be needing any spirits to deal with a spoiled child."

"Oh, fiddle-faddle and fifteen men on a dead man's chest," Eve grumbled. Why couldn't he just leave her alone?

Undeterred by bribery, Bluebeard pursued his course. "You need a flesh-and-blood man, lass, one who'll love and cherish ye. One who'll stick with ye during shipwrecks as well as windfalls." He fixed his fierce blue gaze upon her. "You're ripe for the bedding, Evie. You're twenty-eight come this March. Don't you think it's time to end this farce of a marriage and find yourself a real man? Why, I know Captain Ben Hook is still interested in you. And he said he'd pay me the dowry price. Though he ain't of the Penzance line like we be, the pirates of the Caribbean are not a bad lot. He wants to take to you wife, bad."

More like *bed*, Eve thought grimly, but she kept her rebellious thoughts to herself. Captain Ben Silvers—later dubbed Captain Hook—was a tall, thin man with a dark brown eye and a slightly rakish air. He had an eye patch, and a solid gold hook where his right hand used to be. He was also ruthless and cunning. Ever since she'd turned fourteen, Hook had attached himself to her. When she'd become eighteen, he'd begun to try to win her affections, to bind her securely to him. It had taken all Eve's cunning to elude the crafty rat. She had barely escaped his clutches and a seduction attempt, fleeing to Vienna to go to school.

Perhaps she should have told her father about Hook's less

than honorable schemes. At the time she had been afraid her father would either challenge Hook to a duel or clap his hands in joy at the idea of her getting married. She'd wanted to risk neither event, so she had remained silent.

"You would tie to me to a pirating marauder whose motto is, Any port in a storm or a calm sea?" she asked.

"He's a lusty man who will fill yer belly with fortune."

Eve grimaced. "You make me sound like some Chinese cookie. Besides, I wouldn't want his fortune. I have never been interested in Captain Ben Hook, and well you know it. That rat-faced moron must be the unluckiest person I know."

"Why, that's blasphemy. Ben Hook is a wily pirate. He's got a hoard tucked away in his treasure chests, and his ship, the *Tiger Lily*, is fine, fast in the water and has good, strong lines. He's also got wererat blood in him. 'Tis true he's not a full-blood, but at least he's got some shape-shifting ability."

"I was speaking of his unfortunate habit of losing body parts," Eve remarked. And a rat was a rat, as far as she was concerned, even if he didn't turn completely furry during the full moon.

"Why, Evie, Hook's loss could have happened to any ol' sea dog. It's not his fault that ogre took exception to him trying to steal his gold fillings."

"And his eye?" Eve asked, arching a brow.

"A mere accident in Persia. Could have happened to anyone," her father replied lightly, staring up at the ceiling in an expression of pure innocence.

"Yes. I imagine he won't be peeking through keyholes into any harems anymore."

"That he won't," Bluebeard promised solemnly. "The sultan's threatened to hack off his . . . well, less fortunate parts, should he even show his face there again."

"A wise ruler and a fine judge of character, this Sultan. And you would have me leg-shackled to that!"

"Now, lass, I know Captain Hook is a bit rough around the edges—"

Eve interrupted. "Listen to what I'm saying, Da! I am *not* interested in this one-eyed pirate. He has more mistresses at one time than you have had wives, and that is saying quite a lot. Besides, this conversation is irrelevant. *I am already married.*" She waved her wedding ring in his face and looked away.

"You can just as easily be widowed," the Captain remarked. "I know Hook will oblige me. You're too lovely a lass never to know a husband's touch, and I'm much too impatient not to have a grandchild or two to spoil in me dotage. Now, lass, no more Barbary tales about this absentee husband of yours. Produce him, reproduce with him, or forget about him."

Eve growled. "May I remind you that my husband is dedicated to treating illnesses of the supernatural mind? He is still with one of the Dracul vampires in Transylvania, where he is trying to help the count overcome a rather overzealous bloodlust."

"Yes, yes, you've said that. But surely three years is long enough to cure whatever ails this fruit bat."

"Not when you're of the Dracul line of Nosferatu. Adam may be doctoring him for decades."

"Yeah, he might. Or again, he might not. Fate is a fickle mistress," Bluebeard replied. He tweaked his stubborn daughter's cheek. "As is Father Time. And as you know, fathers know best."

"Indeed," she replied, not daring to speculate what that meant.

"You know it's not nice to try to fool a father," Bluebeard continued. "Trying to pull the wool over me tired ol' eyes . . . You should remember that you have to sail pretty close to the rocky shoal to put one over on yer ol' da."

"So you say," Eve remarked.

"So I *know*."

Eve narrowed her eyes. Yes, the cunning scoundrel was definitely up to no good. But what?

"I see you've kept Plato," he remained, seeing her drumming her fingers on the skull of Henry Morgan.

Nodding fondly, she remembered the day her father given it to her. There were times she missed her years of piracy. The adventure, the cheers of the crew . . . "Always."

"Well . . ." Glancing at the grandfather clock upon the mantel, Bluebeard remarked, "I should be taking me leave soon, since I know you're having that fine dinner party tonight."

"How did you know that?" She stared at him, suspicious.

"I have me ways. Friends in a high place or two."

"Oh," Eve said. More like friends in very low places, where the rum flowed cheap and plentiful.

Before she could question him further, bells began pealing, loudly clashing and clanging.

Bluebeard jumped, startled. "Bloody hell, what's all that noise? You haven't taken to making your poor demented patients go to church, have you? Going and kneeling for hours on end?" There was something akin to horror upon the Captain's weather-beaten face.

"No church, Da. That's just a cranky, bell-ringing dwarf."

The door crashed open with an ominous bang, and her

father reached for his cutlass. It was just Teeter, though, who asked, "You rang, Dr. Eve?"

Sliding his cutlass back into his belt, Bluebeard remarked, "That was close. I felt it was me for whom the bells were tolling."

Glancing over at her butler, Eve sighed.

CHAPTER FOUR

It's a Mad, Mad, Mad World

Around the bell tower, the leaves were falling, but the ill wind named Hugo had been dealt with. Walking down the spiraling steps of the tower, Eve watched as several of her staff efficiently escorted the ranting dwarf back to his room. The victorious Hugo had been in particularly rare form today, swinging through the air like some deranged ape and gleefully ringing the bells. But she had discovered that, this time, the reason the hunchbacked dwarf was ringing bells was to let her know that Fester was once again digging in her garden.

Muttering to herself, she resolutely headed there. "Fester. He must be having one of his paranoid delusions. But is he trying to hide his nonexistent pots of gold or find them?" Really, she thought peevishly, she didn't need any of the leprechaun's shenanigans right now. Didn't she have quite enough on her plate as it was?

If only Fester's pots of gold really did exist, then her funding problems for the Towers would be resolved and she wouldn't be worrying herself sick about tonight's dinner. But her guests would be arriving soon, and she was out trolling for devious dwarves and lunatic leprechauns! She had to stop Fester from his digging, and fill in the holes before any of her guests could fall into them.

Knowing that she had only a few precious hours, Eve hurried from her massive manor home, which was dotted with lichens and overhung with ivy. Its stone was now weathered to a deep grayish brown. Built during the Elizabethan age as a country retreat, it was a massive structure in an L shape, with towering spires and the bell tower from which she had just came. The tower's loud, pealing bells were much to Eve's and everyone else's annoyance, with the obvious exception of Hugo.

The grounds were extensive, with rolling lawns dotted with oak and chestnut tees, and overflowering with rose-bushes and other budding plants. A great marble-and-basalt fountain lay behind the house, and Greek columns were placed elegantly among the clipped hedges and terraces. There was also a hedge maze.

As she passed her head gardener, Totter—cousin to her butler—she gave a quick nod. He was busy clipping an overgrown hedge, but he touched his forehead in respect and shyly pointed to a path through the maze.

"Dat Fester's over dere," he said.

Totter was an excellent gardener, but he had a slight speech impediment. And though he facially resembled his lanky cousin, he wasn't quite as tall. He had more bulk to his physique, which hinted at his ogrish ancestry.

Eve smiled in thanks and took the pathway he indicated, passing brightly flowering roses and traversing the lush hedgerows until she spotted Fester's little baldhead, with its few tufts of gray hair sticking out. The crafty leprechaun was bent over an enormous hole by the hydrangea bushes.

Shaking her head in exasperation, Eve hurried over to him, wondering what to expect. Fester was sometimes quite cranky and other times quite gregarious. With an Irish lilt to his voice but a ruddy face, the little fellow was almost ugly—all but his slanted eyes, which were fringed with thick black lashes and the color of fresh mint.

"Fester, I've told you time and again that these holes are a danger to anyone walking in the gardens. One could break a limb if they fell into your hidey-holes."

Fester glanced up, his eyes all buggy and round. "Well, me bucko . . . they're after it again, I tell ye. I heard them talking through the gilt-framed mirrors in the library this morning. They want me pots of gold. Each and every last one of them! Well, they won't find 'em—I tell ye that now, Dr. Eve! I'm onto their wicked, slick ways, and know their black hearts."

Not the old voices of Parliament through the gilt-framed mirrors again! Eve opened her mouth to speak, but the little man before her began hopping up and down.

"I've foiled them this time, I have! I hid me pots of gold in the house," he said between hops, then stopped to point proudly. "So, you see, this hole here is a decoy. Parliament will think me gold is out here, when it's really inside!"

"I see," Eve remarked, staring at the gaping wound in her garden. "That was rather clever of you." She held her temper by a slender thread indeed. She wanted to beat her head against the proverbial wall. After two years of treating Fester's paranoia, she felt he was getting no better. He was an enigma, a paranoid character with delusions of grandeur along with peculiar conspiracy theory after peculiar conspiracy theory. One of Eve's personal favorites was about Napoleon. Fester believed that Bonaparte was not really dead, and that both the British and French governments wanted gold to finance a secret army to go against him. Those governments were always trying to steal Fester's imaginary gold.

Catering to the leprechaun was all Eve could do for the time being, as a person could argue until she was blue in the face and get nowhere with the wee stubborn man. "Well, since you've fooled them, could I request your arm in escorting me back to the Towers?" she asked politely, but her tone of voice spelled out that she would brook no argument. She would have to get Totter to attend to this hole as quickly as possible.

"Be proud to, Dr. Eve. You never know when one of them British spies might spirit you away and torture you to find out me secrets."

Eve gave a patently false smile and extended her arm. Fester took it, his itty bitty baldhead barely reaching her chin, and as they walked back to the asylum he began babbling more of his far-fetched theories. "I tell ye true, there ain't never been a war with them American colonies, since there ain't really any land called America. It's only British propaganda to trick people into moving to the middle of the ocean, where they set up towns like Venice. . . ."

Through Fester's whole paranoid tirade, Eve kept a smile plastered on her face. Here at the asylum, she had perfected that look. And as they reached the marble fountain, she handed her patient over to Mrs. Fawlty, who took Fester's arm none too gently.

The leprechaun gave Mrs. Fawlty a kiss on her chin, knowing it would set the housekeeper off. Then, turning to Eve he said, "Me thinks our hausfrau is a double spy, pretending to be English when she really is German. She's not after me gold, but me jewels." He patted his pants with a leer.

Smacking the lusty leprechaun on the back of his baldpate, Mrs. Fawlty snapped, "Humph! You should be lined up against the garden wall, shot, and buried in one of your holes, little man. I'm as English as the rain, and well you know it."

Fester laughed. "Don't be too rough with me, my English clover."

"English clover, my foot! I won't stand for your foreign ways. I'll plant you in the garden myself—six feet deep," Mrs. Fawlty warned. "And look how dirty you are, little man. Covered in filth. Now I suppose I'll have to give you a bath!"

Fester squealed in delight.

The housekeeper simply shoved the leprechaun forward, remarking knowingly over her shoulder, "Irishmen."

Shaking her head at the odd pair, Eve picked up her skirts and made great haste to her room.

Dressing and having her hair done in a fashionable style left Eve barely enough time to be downstairs to greet her guests. But she managed. And as she smiled up at them, hope beat like a caged bird in her chest. They just had to help her with her funding, and perhaps offer some advice on two of her patients who were not responding to her treatments as well as she'd like.

The members of the Supernatural Science Foundation entered in fine form: troll, warlock, and wereowl. Two of

the three members—Dr. Sigmund and Count Caligari—
had brought their wives, but Dr. Crane was a bachelor
and attending alone.

After Eve greeted her guests, everyone adjourned to
the blue salon for an aperitif. Eve found herself holding
her breath, watching her six-foot-four butler towering
among the guests, trying to do his duty and serve them
each a glass of sherry.

Normally, Teeter would be a starched shirt, a paragon
of proper English butlerdom. But the winds of change
had recently blown through her asylum, and tonight
found Teeter's hair in wild disarray, his clothing disor-
dered, his cravat askew, and his homely face reflecting abject, stupid misery.

Silently, Eve cursed a blue streak. Apparently her butler and housekeeper had had another of their flaming
rows. Their romance was of recent origin, and was causing chaos in her madhouse. Well, more chaos than usual,
she reflected morosely. She had the overwhelming urge to
vent her temper, to throw a fit to make her father proud,
for it appeared her non-teetotaling butler had totaled a
bottle of something that wasn't tea.

Wanting to tar and feather Teeter, she kept her face
politely composed, hoping that anyone looking at her
would miss that she had mayhem on her mind. Sending a
warning glare at the inebriated butler, she decided that
she really had to run a tighter ship—but she already had
so much to do. Now she would have to add daily disci-
pline for her staff, it appeared. How dared her butler get
tipsy tonight of all nights? After dinner, she was going to
bang a gong over Teeter's head that would put Hugo's
capricious bell ringing to shame.

Wryly, she shook her head, wondering what could occur next to upset her nerves. First her father had discomfited her with his daunting demands, followed by the dustup with the damnable Hugo. One of the gardeners had fallen into one of Fester's holes while trying to fill it in, and severely cut his leg. Following that fiasco, her cook, Sybil, had burned the roast lamb in basil sauce, as well as the Barcelona hens, while the inebriated Teeter had dropped a bottle of port on the dining room rug. When the cock had crowed this morning at dawn, she should have stayed firmly ensconced in bed with the covers pulled over her head.

"Your drinkie, Doctorrr," the tipsy Teeter pronounced, clearly hoping to hide his besotted state. With his very long arm extended, he tried to hand Dr. Crane a glass of sherry. Unfortunately, he tipped the glass while trying to master his feet.

Eve gasped, feeling like a green recruit before her first battle, frozen, helpless to avert disaster. She wanted to cower, or at least to cover her eyes. Yet she kept her eyes open, and breathed a sigh of relief when the good doctor deftly righted the downward-dropping drink. He quickly took it from her butler's hands.

Pretending that she hadn't seen the incident, Eve approached Dr. Crane. "I am so glad you could make it tonight, Doctor," she said. Though he was in his mid-thirties, the slender wereowl's hair was a curious mixture of pale black and whitish silver. The smile he gave was both warm and speculative, with only a faint hint of lecherous intent.

She smiled back, noting vaguely that Dr. Crane was attractive in a bookish sort of way, and that he carried a truly distinguished air. If the rumors were true, he was a fine psychiatrist, if a bit pontificating in lectures, and he

was an expert in the classics as well as the field of the supernaturally feathered *fou*. He was also reputed to have a
taste for soiled doves.

He lifted her hand to his lips and bent low, kissing it
and eyeing her assets with a connoisseur's delight. Eve
managed to gracefully withdraw her hand with her smile
still in place.

"By Jove, my little chickadee, I would have contrived
to meet you sooner had I known how lovely you are." Dr.
Crane gave her another appreciative glance, his big,
yellowish-brown eyes glittering. He cocked his head and
studied her with practiced ease. "I had not thought our
hostess would be so stunning. It's as if Helen of Troy and
Minerva, goddess of wisdom, are combined in your form.
Even male peacocks must envy your splendor. How is it
we have not met? Such a fowl trick, to be deprived of
such an egg. Surely the Fates have been cruel."

"Perhaps your reputation precedes you, and Dr. Griffin
prefers to keep herself tucked safely in her nest," Count
Caligari remarked arrogantly, appearing and bowing to
Eve. She could hear the stays creaking in the corset he
was wearing. She made a curtsy with dignity and grace,
keeping her features politely reserved. She had met the
warlock before, at various medical lectures. He was not
one of her favorite colleagues, this Italian doctor with a
sly intelligence and an inflated sense of his ancestry.

"There's no need to be huffy, Caligari. You're still per-
turbed by my latest book's reviews. You know how they
raved and flapped about my brilliant deductions on hen-
witted chicken hawks."

The count drew his rotund little body up to all of its
five-foot-seven-inch height, a scowl on his features. "Pray
disregard his comments. My books are as well received—

if not more so," he added with an unflappable air. "My latest, *Practical Magic for the Abnormal Paranormal*, won critical acclaim."

"A lot of hocus-pocus, I rather thought." Crane clearly knew the count well, for he was inured to Caligari's condescension. He turned his attention back to Eve. "Now, really. Why haven't I seen you around and about before now?"

"You wouldn't know brilliance if it swept you off your taloned feet!" Caligari ejaculated.

Eve smiled politely at them both, praying to defuse the tense situation. "Dr. Crane, I fear I haven't been in London all that long—a little less than three years—and have been much occupied with running the Towers and treating my patients."

He bowed slightly at her words, and Eve noticed that at least Dr. Crane didn't creak.

"I am glad to finally make your acquaintance," he said, "and am eager, quite eager, to hear of your work." Dr. Crane paused momentarily, then remembered, his round eyes joyous at his recall: "Ah, Verbal *Intercourse* is your theory, is it not?"

Trying hard not to preen, Eve ignored the word emphasis and the gleam of sexual interest in both doctors' eyes, and focused on her growing reputation.

Count Caligari seemed to have forgotten his anger at Dr. Crane's slights. He added, "Yes! A method that I hear is similar to Dr. Sigmund's own treatments."

Dr. Sigmund, upon hearing his name, left his wife's side. He was an older man, in his mid-fifties, with an ancestry that included trolls and endowed him with a bushy head of long white hair, a thick white moustache, and a tall but bulky body. He also had a troll's dark brown eyes—eyes so deep brown that they appeared black. With relish, the noted psychiatrist entered the conversation.

"Yes, of course. I was fortunate to study with Charcow on hysteria and engaging the mind over matter and madness. From reading your hypothesis, Dr. Griffin, I find that your Verbal Intercourse is similar to my own sessions. My Id and TAT therapies are world-renowned, and used by many a modern psychiatrist. I find it quite useful to let the patients converse about themselves and their dreams or fantasies. One can never tell what nonsense or revelations might be revealed from the foggy mists of their ravaged, demented minds. As well you know, the journey from the outer limits of our consciousness to the inner limits of our most secret places can be through a hell filled with fire and brimstone."

"Yes, without dreams where would the arts be today— or music, for that matter?" Nodding, Eve eagerly continued, feeling a need to impress this most famous of all modern psychiatrists. "I have read all six of your books, Doctor, and always enjoy your articles in the *Journal*." She looked enthusiastically forward to Dr. Sigmund's articles, although she did not agree with everything the respected doctor said. Still, she did admire his verve and his devotion to duty. He also was quick to try new methods, and to discount those that didn't work while advancing those that did.

Dr. Sigmund gave a brisk nod, quite used to the homage of the masses.

"Please don't keep me in suspense. Have you read my books also, Dr. Griffin?" Dr. Crane asked, eyeing her delectable décolleté.

Of course I have, Eve thought smugly, keeping her face a

mask of polite interest. To know one's enemy had been a lesson drummed into her at an early age by her father, along with the "*Be Prepared*" pirate motto. Although these men weren't exactly enemies, they were at least opponents. They held the purse strings to the foundation's coins. Coins she desperately needed to help with her work.

"I have, and I was quite impressed with your work on the lineage of the weredodo, citing that constant inbreeding has caused these werebirds to have more feathers than wit."

Ruefully, Dr. Crane shook his head. "Sad but true. Inbreeding has left them with madness, bird-wittedness, and an unfortunate few live births. I imagine we will see the extinction of the weredodo before the twentieth century comes to pass. So sad, the loss of any of my feathered friends."

The conversation progressed into the myriad difficulties faced by wereshifters who were birds, and Eve soon heard the dinner bell tinkle, announcing that the food was ready to be served. As she was about to suggest that they all go into the dining room, the blue salon's doors slammed open against the wall. Dr. Sigmund jumped a little, and Count Caligari sneered.

"Did you ring?" Teeter asked the room at large. "Heavens! Has Hugo escaped again?"

Trying to hide the blush starting up her neck, Eve shook her head. "It was the dinner bell, Teeter!" Repressing the urge to add, *You old fool*, she gave him a look that promised dire retribution later. She should really sack him, but he was good with patients, and nobody was a better gardener than his cousin. And wherever Teeter went, so, regrettably, did Totter, since the two had been raised like brothers by their grandfather.

"Dinner. Shall we retire to the dining hall?"

"Jolly good, I'm quite famished," Dr. Crane said calmly. Noting Eve's dismay, he added, "Pray drop your distress, my dear. My own butler is *dreadfully* correct. Of course, my stable master is a horror—refuses to clean the eaves in the barn half the time. Eaves, where I love to roost on eves of the full moon. I detest messy nests," he groused. "I seriously doubt anyone's home runs like clockwork these days. And as your husband is absent, I'm quite sure you are struggling to stay afloat without him. You must miss a man around the old asylum."

Eve appreciated his helping relieve an awkward situation, yet wanted to kick him in the shins for the remark about her husband. "How polite you are to relieve my feminine sensibilities!" she said. At the same time she was thinking that tomorrow she would lock Teeter in his room for a month with only bread and water. No, that was too nice. She'd lock him the bell tower with Hugo. Her smile widened.

Extending his arm, Dr. Crane asked, "Well, my little dove, shall I escort you to dinner?"

Taking his arm, she nodded. The two of them chatted about the asylum as they led the other guests, following Eve's butler, who lurched into the dining room.

Once they were seated, it wasn't long before the guests' previously stilted conversation became highly entertaining. Eve was greatly relieved as the doctors discussed various treatments and lamented certain patients. Mesmer's hypnosis therapy was discussed and dissected, a subject she particularly found fascinating.

Her guests appeared to be enjoying themselves, Eve decided happily. The doctors' wives were rather quiet, but the food was excellent, in spite of the burned bits, and the conversation was riveting. The seas were smooth sailing, with no skulls and crossbones looming ugly on the horizon—with the exception of the soused butler, who continued to totter about the room, his eyes slightly glazed. Eve's mood lightened, and her blue eyes sparkled.

After the way the day began, Eve had quite feared for the night, but it appeared that her fears were unfounded and she could relax; the ill winds had receded from her sails. If the rest of the night went as well, she would be content. Providing no new disaster arrived, she just might receive some of the funding she needed.

A strong masculine voice suddenly interrupted the conversation. "Hello, my darling Eve."

Eve choked a little on her wine. Hastily she set her glass down and glanced up in surprise. Who was this man, and what was he doing at her dinner party uninvited? And how had he known her name? Appalled, and yet at the same time intrigued, she assessed the fine specimen standing just inside the doorway to the dining room.

The room, lit by a dozen or so candelabra, softened the handsome, swarthy face, with its strong chin and patrician nose. The man was dressed in a deep green superfine jacket that outlined his broad shoulders, and his doeskin breeches were tucked into gleaming Hessians and emphasized his taut leg muscles. Although this was not a tall man, perhaps just under six feet, he was well built, with hair the color of polished walnut wood, and his hazel eyes were a mixture of colors, mostly amber. He reminded her of one of her father's pirates, but better dressed.

He opened his mouth to speak, and Eve's interest was doused like a fire by water: "My dearest, how good it is to see you again! I could barely wait to reach the Towers and see my devoted wife."

A dreadful silence filled the shadowy room, and Eve's stomach clenched in preparation for a disaster of epic proportions. Her ill winds had turned into a hurricane.

CHAPTER FIVE

High Anxiety Is a Lying Impostor

His wife? Eve was flabbergasted. Once she was through being flabbergasted, she was flabbergasted some more. His words were galling, appalling, and preposterously absurd. Suddenly Eve was faced with a wild sense of disbelief mixed with rage. Her senses reeling, she couldn't help but silently ask what in the bloody hell this madman meant. She was no one's wife. Eve's world shrank until she thought she would faint. A madman had invaded her very important party and invented a Banbury tale of biblical proportions.

She swallowed hard past the lump in her throat. A raving lunatic was loose in her house, among her elite guests. A raving lunatic who didn't live here.

She growled in indignation. "Just who do you—"

The presumptuous impostor cut off her words, gliding closer like a predator on the prowl. He stopped beside her with a piratic grin, covetous, condescending, and cocky. "My sweet, sweet wife. How I've missed you." Lifting her hand, he leaned over to press a swift, hot kiss upon her palm.

At first she was too stunned to protest, and then she discovered that his lips were searing and soft—very, very soft. She blinked twice, but the blasted man still appeared a handsome rogue. He moved with the grace of a dancer, and there was deadly power in his movements. Luckily, life in a lunatic asylum had taught her to roll with the punches, just as life on a pirate ship had taught her to keep her balance on a pitching ship. If she screamed foul, then a great scandal would end her party and she would be the talk of the ton. She couldn't explain that this wasn't her husband because she'd never had a husband in the first place; that little admission would be a typhoon of major proportions. She would lose all respectability. Her opportunity to help others would be obliterated, and she would probably lose control of her asylum.

A long moment of indecision passed while Eve ran through her options, all while her guests were quietly conversing and watching the deranged drama unfold. No, Eve couldn't hang this intruder from a yardarm, because she had no yardarm. He also couldn't be shot in her dining hall, not without the guests all going agog.

As Eve was busily thinking, Adam Griffin was appreciating the fine view. The sight of her in all her furious glory actually momentarily mesmerized him. For as long as he lived, Adam knew he would never forget his very first sight of Eve Bluebeard. She was magnificent. Her deep amber-hued gown clearly delineated the supple lines of her body. Her hair, dressed in a psyche knot, was glimmering in the candle light which revealed a myriad of hues of red, brown, and gold. At her neck she wore a three-strand necklace interspersed with emeralds and topaz. Her face was remarkably lovely, even with its current worried expression. With reluctance, he released her wrist.

Eve snapped her hand back out of reach, deep in thought. Her mind had always been an agile thing, as fleet as a ship with a brisk north wind. Yet, tonight she had been broadsided, hit by a large ship and unable to quite find her bearings. Nearby, she could feel the heat of his body as he held her hand. How dared this mad, pirate-looking man kiss her hand?

Forgetting her guests in a momentary fit of rage common to Bluebeards, and unheeding of the scene sure to cause tongues to wag, Eve raised her hand. She wanted to slap the man's grinning face, remove his expression that seemed to dare her to protest his inappropriate actions.

Surprisingly, she found herself being outmaneuvered. The stranger pulled her agilely up and to his side, like in a choreographed dance, and addressed the room in general. "My apologies, but I have lately arrived from Transylvania and haven't seen my wife in some great time."

Slipping closer toward the idiot standing boldly beside her, she stood up on tiptoe to whisper fiercely in his ear, "You're a lunatic." She intended to foil his pretensions immediately. No more wrist kissing.

"No, I'm not," he whispered back provocatively. He knew a reprimand when he heard one, and he knew, smart man that he was, that he had many more coming his way. He relished the challenge.

"That's what all lunatics say."

"Then I must be in the right place." He smiled wickedly at her, then turned back to the room. "Forgive me. My name is Dr. Adam Griffin, and you are . . . ?" Dr. Crane was glaring at him, looking very much as if he had eaten crow, rather than the tasty bit of Barcelona hen he had just consumed.

"You . . ." Eve began softly, not wanting her very important guests to realize that something was wrong in the house of Bluebeard. She made the introductions in a somber tone. The interfering impostor who was standing by her side listened to the introductions of the esteemed assemblage, bowing slightly. Still in shock, Eve's mind again refused to cooperate, its usual razor-sharp edge dulled. Who was this cunning charlatan, and how had he gotten here?

"Are you having an identity crisis?" Eve whispered, halted by more introductions and her mind's inability to absorb this absurd Shakespearean farce. "You aren't—"

"Yes, I know darling, you missed me terribly, as I did you," the fraudulent fiend interrupted. He held up his hand to protest her protestations.

She glared at him, hissing, "Blast it! That wasn't what I was going to say. You deserve a bloody good thrashing. Just wait till my guests leave!"

Clearly undaunted by her fierce mutterings, he leaned down to whisper in her ear, "That's no way to speak to your long-lost husband. Do you want your guests to think you're a shrew, darling? Do you want me to tell them about the marriage ceremony in Vienna that never was? Do you want to deny me, and force me to explain who Adam Griffin really *isn't*? I'm afraid, my dear, your charade is at an end. Mine begins."

"It's my charade, and you have no right to steal it," Eve hissed. "Besides, having a husband is the last thing on my mind." Somehow she managed to keep smiling politely.

Looking to lash out, Eve stepped on the impostor's boot-clad foot. The result was negligible, since slippers with tiny rosebuds sewn on the top just didn't have the same painful impact as her old pirate boots.

He merely grinned at her feeble attempt, noting her narrowed mouth with perverse satisfaction, and replied, "I didn't steal your fantasy; I just stole *into* it. The perfect dream lover comes to life. Many women would envy you."

"I was right. You are utterly mad."

Ignoring her hiss, the man turned toward Teeter. "Teeter, I'm dashed hungry. Set me a plate, please."

"Delighted to serve you again, sir."

Serve him again? Teeter had never met this sly schemer. *Stupid drunken ogrish butler*, Eve thought, shooting the servant a look of pure annoyance.

Glancing at the wine bottles on the cabinet, Adam said, "I'd really prefer a glass of port with my meal. And if your guests will excuse it, I should like to remain dressed as I am."

Dr. Sigmund agreed wholeheartedly—not unexpectedly, since trolls weren't much for dressing up. "Never did like to stand on formality, Dr. Griffin. You've had a long trip and you're hungry." Dr. Sigmund's wife demurred as well, as did Countess Caligari.

Before Eve could voice a complaint, her inebriated butler, beaming moronically, walked to the door to the left of the large china cabinet. Unfortunately, this door led only to the small informal dining room, and not where he needed to go.

"Ahem. Teeter, I do believe the wine cellar door is located near the kitchen," Adam said.

Teeter looked confused.

"I do believe the kitchen door is the one *over there*," the stranger who was absolutely *not* Eve's husband continued, pointing. Eve's jaw tightened in disbelief.

Teeter bowed slightly to Adam. "Of course, sir. Be right . . ." Then he hiccuped and found the correct exit. With starched politeness he said, "Be right back with your port."

With his ham-sized fist, Teeter threw open the door, causing it to slam with its usual force against the dining room wall. Then, turning crookedly in the doorway, he added with an attempt at pomp, "May I be the fi—*hic*—rst to say that we are p-proud to have you home, sir. Dr. Eve has mis—*hic*—sed you something fierce."

Eve's eyes widened, and she found herself being seated back in her place at the table. She was dumbfounded, her mind whirling. How did this rogue know where the kitchen door was, as well as her wine cellar? This was beyond strange, and heading into the totally bizarre, which most likely meant that her infernally interfering father was involved. She would bet a treasure chest of jewels on it. She was going to keelhaul her father and boil this heinous not-husband in oil. How dared either of them trap her like this?

"Carpe diem," she mumbled. But first she had to seize the tricksters.

Seating himself, her husband leaned over to whisper in her ear, "Seize the day. I believe Virgil said it best— fortune to the bold." When she remained stubbornly silent, deliberately ignoring his presence, he added outrageously, "Oh, my sweet, we're in agreement! This bodes well for our future, don't you think? How fortunate we are that great minds think alike."

Glaring at the seductive stranger now seated next to

her, she said in a softly menacing voice, "I'll feed you to the fishes, make you walk the plank!"

"The only plank I'm walking is one that leads to your bed," he replied, hiding his grin behind a napkin.

Teeter suddenly appeared, wearing a similar smirk. "I took the liberty of bringing you the port from Provence."

"Thank you, Teeter," said Adam. "You always know just what I want and when I want it. Remarkable quality in good help."

The butler sighed, his squinty eyes tearing up. "And young love is a fine sight to behold."

Eve stared at both men as if they'd grown four heads. Her butler hadn't met this conniver before tonight; how could he? *Serve him just what he wants? Ha!* She'd serve his liver to the eels!

"Transylvania? It must be lovely this time of year. All that snow," Dr. Crane spoke up.

"Of course," Adam agreed, addressing the whole table. "But I must say that I am glad to be in England again with my beautiful wife. I hate to admit it, but I had almost forgotten what Eve looked like." Turning back to her, he smirked. "You were just a portrait before I came here tonight. And I must say, I'm quite impressed. Also with what you've done with the Towers. Quite the thing, you know." Turning to the others, he added playfully, though with a most sincere expression, "What else is a good wife for but to run the asylum?"

Dr. Sigmund concurred, and his own dear wife gave him a speaking glance.

With lightning reflexes, like a participant in a fast country dance, Adam switched his attention back to Eve. "Have you missed me more than I missed you, or vice versa, I wonder? I will be bold and say I missed you more."

Her eyes hard, Eve maintained an insincere smile. "How could I miss you when you're *always in my mind?*"

"How romantic." Countess Caligari sighed, then looked at her fat, balding husband with mild disgust.

"And Adam Griffin is a man of many faces," Eve continued. Then, in a whispered aside to the impostor: "And all of them are scheming and crooked."

"Temper, temper," he replied in her ear, pretending a kiss. "What would the good doctors think? How would polite society feel about you lying all these years? How would your patients feel to know that their doctor had been telling tall tales, falsifying a marriage, and lying through her pretty white teeth?"

Honesty was paramount in building trust. Measuring her opponent's size and mettle, Eve revised her earlier punishment. Walking the plank over shark-infested waters would be too good for him.

"The plate, Teeter," Adam reminded the servant, lifting an aristocratic brow at the butler, who was leaning heavily against the buffet. "I find I am rather hungry after my long and difficult journey back to my bride."

Eve had just decided nastily that perhaps a little revenge could be served hot, lifting her foot to give the odious man a kick, when her guests' gasps made her switch her attention. Teeter was attempting to make a half bow. Swaying once or twice, the butler's big frame threatened to topple over. He said, "I shall get your plate, Dr. Griffin, as soon as the room stops spinning."

Eve held her breath for the umpteenth time on this horrid, horrid night. The big souse was going to land straight on the table by the stewed prunes!

Eve managed to remain seated, though she wanted to

howl in misery. How had her life become this farce? In one fell swoop, she had found that she had a traitor for a father, a drunk for a butler, and a liar for a husband who was probably also a confidence man, scheming his way into women's lives and robbing them blind.

"What an absolutely dreadful butler—all that banging and lurching about. The things we put up with in servants. I find this quite distressing," Countess Caligari stated, her thin lips quivering in distaste, her small eyes glinting. "I have an employment agency that might help you find someone more suitable. They provide the best servants for all the best houses. But . . . perhaps they are short of staff now." The way she spoke, Eve felt sure that the countess doubted whether Eve's house was good enough for the best servants—maybe even for the worst ones.

"I thank you, Countess. Your sincere offer is most kind," Eve replied. Then, under her breath: "Keelhauling is too good for Teeter. Instead I shall chop him into little bitty pieces and feed him to the fishes."

Having heard his wife's testy comment, the man called Adam leaned over, murmuring to her in a conspiratorial tone, "My, my, such bloodthirst for someone not a vampire. Besides, I thought that was what you were going to do to me—feed me to the fishes. Or have you changed your mind?"

Ignoring his charismatic manner, Eve thought hard for a moment. Slowly she smiled, a smile of pure devious intent. The daft trickster thought he had her leg-shackled and trapped, but he was wrong.

"Ship ahoy!" she whispered. She wasn't her father's daughter for nothing, and *nobody*—even if that nobody became a *somebody*—was going to trick her and get away with it. Besides, hadn't her grandmother always said that necessity was the mother of invention? Eve was far more inventive than most. And soon the affable Adam wouldn't be a fictional husband, but history.

CHAPTER SIX

Adam's Ribbing

Adam couldn't take his eyes off his so-called wife. There was something in her finely shaped features that smote his heart. Her voice was husky and deep, almost too much for such a small package, and her demeanor was both demure and full of militant determination. That wasn't altogether surprising, since her father had relayed that Eve was like a little admiral when she wanted something, demanding and commandeering. What a delight his marriage bed would undoubtedly be! In fact, if his luck held, so-called wedded bliss might be just that. That was, he thought, rubbing his chin, if he could get his new wife to quit shooting daggers with her eyes. If looks could kill, he would have been dead twenty minutes ago.

What a lark his arrival had been. He could still see her eyes rounding in disbelief, her dainty hands clenching into fists. In spite of all her ladylike airs, he had a strong feeling that Eve Bluebeard would have planted him a facer if they had been alone. His pretend wife wasn't shy, coy, or silly, but then a pirate's daughter wouldn't be. He would always know what he was getting with Eve, and that was a refreshing change.

Seconds after spotting his quarry, Adam had decided to stay put permanently, in spite of Eve Bluebeard's wishing him to the very devil. He knew he should be frightened of double-dealing in his deal with Captain Bluebeard, but his nether region and his heart were of a different opinion. The captain had paid him to pretend to be Eve's husband, but he also expected Adam to meet an untimely demise in the not-too-distant future. This death was merely to be a pretend one, with Adam disappearing, leaving Eve free to marry Captain Hook. But that plan was no longer workable for Adam. Instinctively he knew that he had found the home he had been looking for all his life. Neither Bluebeard could force him from this comfy nest now.

Setting down his wineglass, he nodded in answer to another question put to him by Count Caligari and Dr. Crane, the latter having quizzed him quite thoroughly about Transylvania and his latest case. Luckily, Adam had always been a quick study, his love for tomfoolery as great as his taste for high adventure.

"So, you solved this fearsome Nosferatu's bloodlust in less than two years. Remarkable, just remarkable," Dr. Crane remarked, his voice holding notes of contention and disbelief. "May I be so bold as to ask how you achieved this miraculous recovery?"

Adam was about to answer when Eve interrupted. "I'm sure that Dr. Griffin"—she seemed to almost choke on the name—"can share that information with you tomorrow, or another day, after he is rested from his long journey."

"But to cure a vampire of bloodlust is startling!" the

count remarked, lifting his bejeweled monocle up to view Adam suspiciously.

After some moments, Dr. Sigmund nodded, the myriad lines around his eyes crinkling. "That is true, and this could be an important discovery. Most especially with any of the Dracul lineage, since their bad blood often leads to displays of excessive violence. They cannot seem to control their drive to continue drinking every last drop, long after their bloodthirst is quenched. It is due to the strength of their libidos and their oral fixation—a fixation most likely begun in the oral stage of their development as Nosferatu."

"Yes, tell us more, Dr. Griffin, and don't mince words," Count Caligari demanded, spinning his monocle on its chain. "I am agog and shocked. Yes, shocked that such a vampire lineage, which included kings and queens from more than one country, should be so depraved and *abbandono*. Appalling, really, when you think about it, but all vampires crave power. The type of bloody messes the Dracul lineage leave behind are more in keeping with a primitive heritage, however, such as the common riffraff that flood the crowded London streets at night."

Eve wanted to roll her eyes at the count's obvious disdain for anyone not born with a silver spoon between his teeth or the bluest of blood. What would he think if he knew his hostess was the daughter of one of the most notorious pirates in English history—and Irish, for that matter? She would bet her last sextant that the count's horror would be almost worth the disclosure. Almost.

"Go on, Dr. Griffin. I too am agog at how you single-handedly managed to subdue such a ferocious Nosferatu," Dr. Crane urged, his amber eyes gleaming with mocking intent.

Sparing him only a haughty glance, Adam ignored the scholarly doctor's attempt to disconcert him. His motive was quite obvious, as Adam could smell the lust on Dr. Crane even as the owlish man smiled suggestively at Eve again. Obviously Dr. Crane wanted himself and Eve to do more than just flock together.

That thought had Adam repressing a very primitive urge to plant a boot in the addlepated doctor's arse, but before he could utter a setdown to the wereowl, Dr. Sigmund remarked with some asperity, "Dr. Griffin, I have been wondering if this vampire had difficulties in his potty training? Fear of the chamber pot can cause an adult vampire or a human immense problems in their adult lives."

Eyes flashing fire, Eve gave a slight shake of her head. She was clearly warning him to be silent. If he opened his big mouth and spouted nonsense, she could find herself with the committee's censure and no funding. She broke in: "Adam told me he didn't."

"Now, my dear, I know you love to stick that pretty little nose of yours into my business. And you are a great help—so much imagination and passion. And I will be the first to admit that your inventiveness has been my salvation, almost like a birth, leaving me a . . . new man. But I would like to tell this particular tale myself." Nonplussed, he held out a piece of sliced apple, which Eve declined less than graciously.

Slanting his gaze away from her infuriated and fearful one, Adam looked over at the other doctors. Oozing breezy confidence, he finished his early remarks: "My wife is . . . correct. The vampire had no chamber pot fears. Although he did fear certain chambers and what he would do when he first rose from his crypt at sunset."

Glancing at the rapt faces all around, the angry female

face to his side, and the scowling, owlish face across the table, Adam began his tale. Sounding knowledgeable and pompous was just one of the many skills he had recently acquired. Some minutes later, Dr. Sigmund's wife was crying, wiping her eyes on her initialed handkerchief, while Countess Caligari stared in fascination, her greedy eyes devouring more than his fine mind. Dr. Sigmund looked intrigued, while Eve looked like she'd like to lash him to the nearest mast and give his back a striping at the first opportunity.

In spite of Eve's lack of appreciation, Adam knew that the renowned actor Kean couldn't have done better himself. Adam had brought the house down. Aside he uttered, "You should be flattering me."

"Flattery is not what I had in mind," Eve whispered back. She stared at the impostor, seething. This madman, who was not really insane, she didn't think, had just been telling the most outrageous tales about his supposed cure. What a quack! Yet most of her guests seemed genuinely impressed with his ludicrous cures of locusts put in coffins for little meals—small dinners, he called them, to subdue hunger—and violin music to be played when awakened. Next he would have Frederick Frankenstein out at the graveyard listening to the impromptu concert! Furthermore, the utterly caddish crook didn't have a flicker of remorse in his large, expressive eyes.

Twisting her necklace in frustration, she very much debated telling all and sundry that Adam wasn't her husband, that he was in all likelihood really a criminal, a crook, and, last but not least, a pirate crony of her father. But managing to barely hang on to her composure, she sat back in her chair, her attention once again on the conversation at hand.

"It sounds as if your vampire had an internal struggle—a power struggle *sexual* in origin," Dr. Sigmond said as he took a gulp of wine.

Adam's expression perked up even more. He grinned in delight, thinking this mind-doctoring-might be very useful indeed, noting the mulish set of Eve's features. "Indeed! Sexual?"

Nodding, Dr. Sigmund continued with his suppositions in a slow manner, sipping wine as he explained. "Of course, my boy, everything in life is a sexual power struggle. All people—male or female, supernatural or human, whether they haven't a feather to fly with or are as rich as Midas—want to be the leader, the one who holds all the power. Men want to be masters over their own domains and the dominant force in their relationships. It's only natural, since God made man in his own image, and ladies' sensibilities are too flighty for true power or leadership."

Eve bent her head in a politely attentive manner, not wanting to contradict the eminent doctor, even though his remarks were so far off course as to be lost in a sea of stupidity. She'd known this flaw of his all along.

Yes, although Dr. Sigmund did indeed have a brilliant mind and was one of the leading authorities on mental illness in the supernatural, he was still a member of the male gender, with a fallible viewpoint on women. He believed that women were often trials inflicted upon the male of the species, meant to test and improve them. He also believed that every illness of the mind had a sexual aspect. And while Eve believed that some mental sickness came from sexual starts, not every mental aberration revolved around coupling—unless you were an incubus or a succubus.

For a remarkable man, Dr. Sigmund could be remarkably obtuse. He didn't notice Eve's lack of appreciation as he continued with his dialogue. "Yes, people in general, most especially men, crave to be the top rooster in the henhouse, the cock of the walk, so to speak. Naturally, these cocks all want their beaks to be the biggest and their crows loudest of all. These barnyard crows cause all the hens to fall into line. When this doesn't happen, they envy. This envy then twists in their mind, making them sick. Women can also feel this. I call this theory cock envy, also referred to in polite circles as barnyard begrudgement. Problems can occur, causing mental aberrations as well as physical—men running about half-cocked, or with a cock who won't fight at all."

Adam was listening intently, since all this muck about sex and power struggles was highly entertaining to a person of the male persuasion. But he would bet his last groat that his wife was not amused.

Catching her eye, he smiled wickedly, feeling a sudden urge to egg the good doctor on, along with his wife. "Yes, I think you may be right. Over the years, I do believe I have seen evidence of this barnyard begrudgement. I myself have been fortunate enough never to have had cock envy. Probably that's why my marriage works so well. Not that I would crow about it."

"Indeed," Dr. Sigmund replied amiably.

Eve could feel her face heating. Envy his cock, her foot! The man was a chicken—a blight on fair and fowl alike, and a big, fat blighter! He also had a pronounced flair for the bawdy. She wished she could take drastic action by stuffing a gag in this great pretender's mouth.

"How fortunate," Countess Caligari spoke up, her eyes

hot and her tone a little breathy. Glancing at Eve, she smiled slyly. "How very fortunate for both of you."

Eve wanted to beat her head upon the table—or rather, her fake, infuriating husband's head. She'd never envied any cock in her life, much less that of a figment of her imagination.

Catching her eye, Adam grinned and then winked at her, then went on with apparent sincerity, "Yes, we are both extremely lucky. I feel I can tell you in all confidence, that my Eve doesn't have this cock envy, either. I keep her well satisfied, you can believe." The last accompanied a speaking glance at Dr. Crane, who acknowledged it with an unblinking stare.

Take that, you nest-wrecker and rodent chaser, Adam thought nastily. He had known instantly that Dr. Crane was a shape-shifter of the avian sort. By the man's coloring and large eyes, Adam also knew instantly what kind of feathered foe this was, since he had traveled extensively and seen many kinds of monsters. He'd also read the *Who's Hoo* book of wereowls.

"Adam!" Eve spoke up. "I think we've had enough talk of roosters tonight."

The paunchy Count Caligari took that moment to add, "Well, I must say that my wife doesn't have barnyard begrudgement, either."

Eve pinched Adam's thigh, beseeching him with quiet desperation to be quiet, dreading what awful comments would next come out of his mouth. She quickly turned to Mrs. Sigmund and the countess, knowing when to plan a strategic retreat and run for her life. Her face pink with embarrassment and anger, she nodded to the two women. "Ladies, while your husbands view two of my patients, would you care to retire to the drawing room for a glass of sherry or Madeira wine?"

"Thank you, my dear," Mrs. Sigmund replied. "A glass of sherry sounds just the thing, as I fear I am rather weary of hearing about cocks, cocks, and more cocks. If I never hear of another cock it will be too soon. Of course, that doesn't mean I don't want to see one."

Eve barely managed to suppress a gasp of astonishment at Mrs. Sigmund's candid thrust at her husband. She shook her head and said, "Teeter will lead the way, and I'll join you shortly."

Crooking her finger at her cocksure husband, she made a terse request: "Adam, might I have a word with you now?"

He nodded, a wary look replacing his devilish grin. He clearly knew he was in for a tongue-blistering. But shrugging his shoulders gallantly, he accepted the challenge.

"Teeter, if you would escort our guests, Dr. Griffin and I will be in momentarily."

Once the room was empty of everyone but Adam and herself, Eve hissed wrathfully, "If I had my cutlass I would chop you up, you misbegotten son of a sea dog! How could you imply in polite company what you did about your . . ." Eve sputtered to a halt. "And what about that cock-and-bull vampire story you told! Locust therapy? Ha! If you're trying to horn in on—"

Adam touched her cheek. "My poor dear, there is no reason for you to fear for your family jewels. I've brought my own with me, and they are ample."

Eve's mouth dropped open in disbelief.

"Please don't trouble your little head. Ex-pirate though I am, I'll share them with you nightly," Adam continued.

"And in the morning, too. Twice in the morning if it would make you happy." His eyes twinkled. "Anything for my sweet wife. I am not a miser; nor will I ever be. What I have is yours to enjoy whenever you wish."

Eve's face turned from a becoming pink to a brash red, her jaw muscles tightening so that she thought she might have lockjaw. How dared he speak to her like this, this wretched, wicked stranger who had forced himself into her life in a strange and dishonorable manner? Now he was spouting off about what was yet to come!

"If I don't murder you before the night is through, it will be a miracle," She hissed.

"That's no way to speak to your beloved husband."

Without thinking, she swung a hard right at him, but the man was bloody fast and she missed. His grin made her try a second time. She missed again, and he dodged back on the balls of his feet.

"I've boxed in the ring for my supper a time or two, just to let you know. I can keep this up all night—along with other, more interesting and pleasurable things," he boasted.

Eve dropped her fists, feeling foolish, frustrated, and past infuriated. "Just who the bloody hell are you? And how did you know about my pretense? My father put you up to this, didn't he?"

"Why, I'm your *husband*, my dear! Let's save the explanations for when our guests leave."

"Of all the bloody nonsense." Eve sighed. "I don't know you from Adam."

Her new hubby threw back his head and burst into laughter. "You're about to, my darling Eve. You're about to."

CHAPTER SEVEN

You Can Catch More Werewolves with Honey . . . Not to Mention Pirates

As the group made its way to the patients' rooms, Eve held her breath, wondering what outrageous thing Adam would say next. For the moment, he was behaving. Still, she knew better than to trust a placid demeanor, rather like the calm at sea before a storm. A tad impatiently she waited and watched, which made her even more annoyed.

"This is Sir Loring's room," she announced as they entered the large chamber where the vampire resided. A massive coffin twenty feet by fifteen lay in the center. Sir Loring, his fangs slightly exposed in his homely face, was standing beside it. Lovingly he patted some of his native soil, letting the grains run through his bony hands and into the bottom of the coffin. He glanced up, his long, lean face tense.

"Good evening, Sir Loring," Eve began, her voice quietly reassuring. "These are the doctors I brought to visit with you. Remember we discussed their visit earlier?"

Dr. Crane started to close the door, but Sir Loring gasped, dropping the soil in his hands, his writhing fingers rising to create havoc amongst the pomaded gray curls atop his head.

"Don't close it, please. Sir Loring likes a great deal of space," Eve warned. "He is paranoid about closed-in areas."

"Evidently," Dr. Crane remarked, his owlish eyes wide with interest. He stared at the coffin. "I take it that was specially made for the circumstances of his phobia? The workmanship is quite impressive."

The lanky vampire, with his slightly red eyes and long, sharp incisors, fidgeted nervously. "Yes, it is beautiful, a lovely coffin, and it's mine. You can't have it!" He flashed his fangs as an afterthought.

"We won't take your coffin; I promise," Eve remarked. She soothingly patted the vampire on the arm, while Adam took up a protective stance at her side. She glanced at him in surprise.

"Claustrophobic," Dr. Sigmund pronounced.

"Yes," Eve agreed. "Sir Loring can't abide riding in carriages and won't even go near a wardrobe."

"You are only catering to his whims" Count Caligari scoffed. "That coffin is enormous. It's more fit for an Egyptian King than this baronet. I find this placating treatment unusual and *affettivo*—pathetic. Spare the rod and spoil the vamp."

"This is not some childish whim we are talking about, Count Caligari, but a debilitating fear. Once inside a closed-in space, Sir Loring begins to shriek and lose his breath. Er, I think we should continue this discussion outside," she added coolly, noting the increasing agitation of her patient. Perhaps she had made a mistake, and these guest doctors were too much for Sir Loring's skittish nerves. She certainly didn't want to send the vampire into one of his fits.

Outside, in the dank limestone hallway, Count Caligari continued his criticism in the guise of advice. "How can you tell he loses his breath? He's undead. Perhaps you have overreacted to his fear," the count suggested patronizingly.

His question raised Eve's ire, yet she betrayed very little of her agitation. She might not have the age or experience of the Italian count, but she was nobody's fool. Still, the count's criticisms were worrisome. If the good doctors also thought her methods were unworthy, would funding be denied?

She replied with false civility, "Before he came to me, Sir Loring hadn't slept in ages. He was cranky, off his feed, and thoroughly agitated. Once he had his new coffin, he slept for four months. Upon awakening, he was in a much more pleasant mood. Less . . . snappish."

"Balderdash, my good woman! How will he overcome his fear if you cater to his whims?" the count asked again, peering out from behind his jeweled monocle. Before she could answer, he continued with his unsolicited advice. "The mad should never be mollycoddled, but instead punished for their transgressions. Strict punishment results in better behavior."

What a scary man, Eve thought reproachfully. The blood had rushed to her cheeks in vexation. She felt a great sorrow for his patients; after all, one didn't throw out the vampire with the coffin.

"Hmm. I believe it is possible that Sir Loring could

have a mother fixation. His need for her lost love and nurturing transformed with his vampirism into a fear of closed-in places," Dr. Sigmund remarked thoughtfully.

"Why, yes! It is *semplice*—simple, no? Perhaps at his mother's breast he felt smothered when she fed him, like a plump white pillow," Count Caligari suggested, nodding.

Eve narrowed her eyes. Wasn't that just like a man? Everything concerned breasts.

"I don't think that is the answer to why Sir Loring is claustrophobic," she said. "I think it relates to an incident in his childhood when he was locked in a closet for a day and night."

"Was he searching for his chamber pot?" Dr. Sigmund questioned. When everyone stared at him, he shrugged. "Perhaps Sir Loring has a case of coffin envy. Apparently his must be bigger than any others," he amended.

"I'll certainly take that theory into consideration," Eve replied.

She wanted to roll her eyes. If men weren't talking about breasts, they were all up about that other major concern of their lives. Men, she thought snidely; their arrogance and their strange preoccupation with that hanging appendage between their legs were beyond her. Frankly she wondered what all the fuss was about. Dr. Sigmund was way off course in thinking any sensible female would ever envy the ridiculous-looking appendage. In fact, she would rather walk the plank than have that thing sticking out between her legs, leading her about, pointing the way like a deformed compass.

"I think the massive coffin is quite ingenious," Dr. Crane remarked, clearly hoping to curry Eve's favor, and Adam found himself fighting a real urge to box the man's ears. Deciding that a bit of friendly intimidation was in order, he stepped up behind Eve and began glaring at the wereowl over her shoulder. Dr. Crane stepped back a few paces.

Oblivious, Eve smiled at Dr. Crane, and at her behest the small group walked up a slight incline to another room. She fought her annoyance, her thoughts tumbling chaotically in her brain. She was extremely proud of her work. Sir Loring had made remarkable progress since she'd started treating him. Unfortunately, Dr. Sigmund—whom she truly admired—and Count Caligari—whom she found rather despicable—both seemed less than inclined to give her work a glowing recommendation. At least Dr. Crane showed interest in and respect for what she was attempting here at the Towers.

Noticing Eve's bleak expression, Adam moved to stand near her. "My wife has been writing to me regarding her progress with Sir Loring, and I am astounded at how much better the vampire is doing. Before she treated him, he would run screaming from a room if he even saw a coffin inside."

Eve glanced askance at him. She had never written any such faradiddle to him, since she had never written to him in her life. How did one correspond with a figment of one's imagination?

Adam only winked. "Since his family makes coffins, this was killing the old family business, I must say."

Eve pinched him under the arm, and he whispered with aggrieved dignity, "There's absolutely no need for violence, my dear."

She pinched him harder, a steely glint in her eyes. But he ignored her and finished, "Now Sir Loring can not only enter a room with a coffin, but sleeps in one! My wife has worked miracles with her chimney-sweeping cures—or rather, with vampires, we call her sessions *coffin* sweeping."

"Chimney sweeping?" Dr. Sigmund echoed curiously. He studied Eve, a perplexed furrow between his brows. "Please explain, Dr. Griffin. You must relieve an old man's curiosity."

Eve's smile was brittle. Tiny slivers of apprehension flooded her, because she had no idea what this demented stranger was babbling about. Chimney sweeping? If she were one of her patients, she'd diagnose a full-blown case of hysteria.

"Oh, please let Dr. Griffin explain," she said. "He is, after all, the one who helped me craft these theories."

Adam shot her a glance. "My wife is too modest. It was her theory first."

"But you have a way with words, Adam. You tell them."

He acknowledged her avoidance with a wink, wanting to kiss her senseless. He had known Bluebeard's daughter could handle a tricky maneuver or two. He was no doctor, yet he couldn't let Eve be made to look a fool; that was why he'd spoken up. Fortunately, he was blessed with the Irish gift of blarney. "Er, well, it's like this. 'Chimney sweeping' is cleaning the mind of all the cobwebs—rather like sweeping out a chimney, only in this case we are brain sweeps. It's a repeated therapy where the patient talks all night or day, simply conversing for a long, long time."

As Eve listened, she couldn't help but be a tad impressed. This Adam character certainly had a way with words. Whoever he was or wasn't, he was quick on his feet, just like her good old da.

"I see. Then it's much like your wife's Verbal Intercourse treatment," Dr. Sigmund remarked. He gave a nod of his head, pleased at making the connection so swiftly.

Adam caught a glimpse of his wife's fleeting admiration. Even so, he felt some little demon urging him to provoke her further. He found he couldn't resist. "I know, and I must say that my wife's intercourse therapy has always aroused my interest. It keeps me up nights, I must say."

Hold steady, Eve told herself silently; *don't fire your cannons yet.* "Lord love a duck," she muttered to herself. Boiling in oil, walking the plank, fifty lashes tied to a mast, and being fed to the sharks—absolutely none of these punishments was enough for the devious, demented deviant before her. *Just get through the dinner party and then you'll get the answers you need*, she added. Totally ignoring Adam, she marched up to the next patient's door and inclined her head toward the heavy oak. "Here we go."

All eyes swung to the door. "And this room is held by whom?" Dr. Crane asked.

"This particular patient is a werewolf who has delusions. Mr. Pryce sometimes thinks he's a common housefly," Eve explained.

"I can imagine he's quite the *desperate* housefly," Adam remarked with a strange gleam in his eye. "One night you're a four-footed wolf running free; the next you're a flying pest."

Eve knocked on the door, wishing it were Adam's fat head. "Mr. Pryce, we're here to see you. I have brought the guests I spoke to you about."

Opening the door, Eve walked in. The room was disorderly, but the others followed closely behind, their curiosity piqued.

Mr. Pryce, a rather sallow-faced man with thinning

hair, was not handsome at the best of times. At present he was on his hands and knees, his scrawny buttocks thrust up in the air. He made a buzzing noise as he licked a substance off his table.

Wandering over, Adam glanced down at the sticky golden goo. "I see it's true. You do catch more flies with honey. And there's always a Pryce to pay."

Eve sent him a speaking glance, which clearly indicated for him to shut his mouth. He obliged momentarily, since he was fascinated by her patient.

"*Cos'e'questo?*" Count Caligari questioned, and then, realizing he had spoken in Italian, repeated his words. "What's this, a fly?"

"Yes," Eve said, "so it will do precious little good to try to communicate with him."

"Fascinating!" Dr. Sigmund cried as he eyed the man before him like a bug under glass, even if he was a werewolf on a table. "Does he ever talk when he's like this? Does he hear voices, or the call of the wild in this altered state? What's the buzz?"

"The buzz? When he is in this altered state, he only makes that odd humming noise, as you can hear."

"Yes, I see," Dr. Sigmund remarked, staring at the wiry little man on the table. "Not in essence moonstruck. When he is in possession of himself, what has he revealed of his relationship with the chamber pot? What do you know about his potty training?"

Eve shook her head. "His potty training was perfectly normal. I talked with his mother about it."

Adam couldn't help himself. "Is the mother a fly-by-night insect as well?" he asked. He hadn't been so amused since he helped sink the *Flying Dutchman* with the Dutchman aboard. "Does being bugger-all run in the family?" As he looked at Eve's glaring face, the word *mulish* came to mind.

"Of course not! His mother is perfectly normal."

Adam grinned at her reply. For most humans, were-wolfism wasn't a normal state.

They all walked out and back down the hall, and Eve said, "Mr. Pryce is quite a nice man when he is not in his insect delusion, or tearing up the countryside as a wolf. He has few debilitating fears . . . except for the conservatory."

"Fear of the conservatory?" Dr. Crane questioned, arching his neck.

"We have several large Venus flytraps in the conservatory," Eve answered. "I thought of getting rid of them, but I . . . didn't want to pamper the patients' phobias to excess," she added, not altogether truthfully. The last part of her statement had been added strictly for the odious count's beastly benefit. Her mother had brought those flytraps from Greece to celebrate Eve's tenth birthday. The two women had decorated them with tiny silver bells and pink seashells, but the flytraps had eaten them, mistaking the decorations for lunch. Eve and her mother had laughed for hours. Therefore, Eve would never get rid of the flytraps, not even for a patient.

Adam's face broke into a wide grin, and there was more than a trace of laughter in his voice. "Yes, I can see where those plants might be a problem."

"You have the compassion of a goat," Eve hissed at him softly.

He turned and smiled. "I know you are wishing me to Jericho right now, but the trip would take me away from you. And I don't want to deprive you of my company any longer," he replied.

"You're utterly maddening. Impossible! Just wait until I get you alone!"

Adam found the threat terribly interesting. "I wait with bated breath."

He didn't have to wait long. Dr. Sigmund soon took his leave, telling them all that the funding committee would be making its decision in the upcoming weeks, and then all the guests said farewell.

Adam heard the front doors bang closed as Eve ushered him into her study. She slammed that door herself, and turned to face him. A lesser man would have taken flight at the look of utter fury in her eyes.

He grinned, for he was not a lesser man.

CHAPTER EIGHT

Analyze That, Barnacle Breath!

"Blast you to smithereens, you bounder! What in the bloody hell do you want?" Eve demanded.

"I already have it," Adam replied. The little imp within him couldn't help but enjoy the spectacle of vexation that flowed over Eve's beautiful face. Her dark blue eyes glittered like stars in the sky, her cheeks were flushed a becoming peach, and her bosom was heaving. He very much liked how it heaved.

She was magnificent in her fury. Hopefully, he would soon have her beneath him. Perhaps not this night, but soon, very soon. His world had tilted the moment he had seen Eve. She had set his bachelor life to sinking.

"Who told you about me? Who else knows?" Eve questioned, a ruthless gleam in her eye. Her heart was thundering in her chest. Who was this man, and exactly what knowledge did he hold in his grubby little hands? Would he reveal her hoax? Would all and sundry soon know of her deception? She needed to analyze the situation and stop imagining the worst. "Is this blackmail? What exactly are you after—money? If so, you're extremely foolish." No one blackmailed a Bluebeard.

"It's not blackmail, and how utterly insulting an accusation," Adam retorted with disgust. "I have seen and done many illegal things, but blackmail isn't one of them."

"Who told you about the nonexistent Adam? How in the bloody world did you get here?" she pushed, even though deep down inside she knew the answer: her fiend of a father and his infernal interference.

He batted not an eyelash as he answered, "By carriage."

Infuriated, Eve grabbed a porcelain figurine off a shelf and threw it at the brigand. "How did you know to come to the Towers, blast it? How did you know a real husband might not be lurking in the shadows to call you out? I could have a husband waiting in the wings to duel you."

"Ouch." He laughed as the figure caught him on the shoulder. "Play nice. Wives don't throw things at their husbands. And I wasn't worried about being called out to duel—though maybe I should have been. Ghastly prospect, really. All that cold, damp air and people shooting or jabbing at you with very sharp swords. But I wasn't worried, because I knew that you have no flesh-and-blood husband. He's only a figment of your very active imagination. Or so I was told."

"Yes!" Eve shouted. "I know! You were told about me!" And she knew just who the twisted old tattletale was. Her irascible father and his impossibly silly suggestions of grandchildren were enough to drive her around the bend at a maddening gallop.

The fire in the fireplace crackled, and a log broke apart, ominously loud in the sudden silence of the spacious study. Both Adam and Eve knew that the tide had turned and an ocean of revelations was at hand.

He wanted to kick himself in the backside for letting her goad him into revealing himself too soon, but there was nothing Adam could do but watch Eve carefully handling another, heavier figurine. It was a bust, and not the bust he wanted her fondling. The cat was out of the bag, the Bluebeard was out on the prowl, and he might soon be out on his arse.

"Who told you?" Eve asked. She wanted definite proof for when she threw her father's perfidy back in his face. Otherwise, he'd deny it until he was blue in the beard.

"Would you believe a little bluebird wearing a gold earring and a pirate's hat?"

"That backstabbing buccaneer!" Eve swore. "I'd serve my father's liver to the eels, but I hate to give the eels indigestion. I knew it was the Captain. The maddest meddling menace of the seven seas." She threw the heavy porcelain head in her hands, but missed as he dodged.

"My, what a bloodthirsty little vixen I have for a wife," Adam said. "After all that hard work in Transylvania, it appears my wife had greater need of my services here." He gazed at her breasts, greatly admiring the view. At least she wasn't near any more knickknacks to throw, for she plainly intended to do him bodily harm. But what jolly good fun, he thought. He would be the first to admit that he loved a duel at the door of every boudoir. Easy conquests were boring and predictable, and he did so dislike the ordinary.

"What if the good doctors could see your temper tantrum right now?" he asked, glancing down at the broken figurines. "What do you think they would say?"

His words only incited her ire. "That's something else I wish to discuss! How dare you pretend to know what to do with a blood-crazed vampire with an obsessive oral fixation? Your theory of behavior-changing bloodletting of fledglings to relieve fears of the graveyard—pure nonsense!" she snapped, her blue eyes blazing. "And to say that you stuffed that undead coffin with locusts and worms to give them snacks—*snacks!*—to keep their bloodlust in line was positively idiotic lunacy of the first order. And music—violin music and opera singers to sing them to sleep? Rubbish! It's beyond belief. You're telling tales from the crypt, and I won't have it!"

"Ah, the plot thickens. You're angry because I stepped on your dainty professional toes. My theories were absolutely brilliant, and your nerves are too overset right now to comprehend the genius of the scheme. Besides, it was better than telling them to take two cups of rum and call me in the morning."

"Brilliant? Shiver me timbers! It was ludicrous twaddle. How anyone could swallow that cockamamie tale is beyond my ken. And I so respected Dr. Sigmund before this hideous night."

"I don't know. Most of your doctor friends appeared to be fascinated with my little pretense," Adam said, his hazel eyes twinkling. "But by the way, couldn't you come up with a more original name than Adam? Adam and Eve? I feel like I'm in some farce called *Original Sin in the Garden.* Now all we need is the forbidden fruit." He gave her a wink.

Looking to the high vaulted ceilings, as if for divine intervention, Eve said, "You might have ruined my plans, and I could lose my funding. For that alone you should be walking the plank." But inside she was a cauldron of messy emotions. She was furious at her father, scared that he had learned her secret. And she was hurt that he'd deviously used it against her for his gain. And Adam—the man not only made her see red; she felt all hot and bothered whenever he gave her that pirate grin.

"I didn't ruin anything. I only *added* to your dull dinner party with my witty comments and dashing good looks."

"You can't just waltz in here and start ordering me about. I'm not a child!" Eve stamped her foot to punctuate the thought.

"Oh, I beg to differ," Adam remarked. "I have waltzed into your life with a zest that is, I must say, most inspired. It was probably those dance lessons. Of course, they got me into a tight spot in Strasbourg." *Tight spot* was an understatement, he conceded wryly. Due to an empty stomach and an emptier purse, he had been giving dance lessons to the Baron of Eudall's daughters, and the eldest had taken a fancy to him. She had picked up his steps with ease and later led him a pas de depux into a corner, giving sugary, hot kisses and a blatant treatment of his *ront de jambe*. Luck had been in short supply back then—else he would never have been teaching dance to tedious debutantes—and the baron had interrupted the impromptu waltz. Adam had managed to flee Strasbourg with his private parts intact, but just barely.

He managed a faint smile. "Isn't it fortuitous for all that I'm quick on my feet?"

Pointing to the door, Eve ignored the impostor's boastful manner. "Well, Mr. Lord of the Dance, why don't you take your braggart self and waltz right back out of here. I'm sure someone in London must be dying to give an aging roue a chance to two-step. Just do it anyplace but here."

"Shrew," Adam teased, enjoying the battle. He also appreciated his luxurious surroundings. He liked beautiful things, and expressly enjoyed the easy life. Although, his wife wasn't exactly easy. He didn't mind some physical labor, especially when it came to fixing broken things. His wife liked to take broken minds and heal them, which meant that they were a match made in heaven. If only they didn't burn out before the true fire was lit.

"If I left tonight, people would say you drove me to it. They'll say your ill and vicious temper is why I stayed in another country for so long. That I'd rather deal with a blood-crazed vampire than my own wife. I couldn't do that to you, my little jewel."

"Read my lips! I am *not* your wife," Eve spluttered. She dropped her hands to her hips and stuck out her chin. Thieving pirates could be such stubborn louts, especially when they were after booty, but she didn't understand his tenacity. The man was like a bulldog. No matter how she denounced him, defamed him and demanded that he leave, all was to no avail.

Blinking, she noted nastily that he was still there, standing stolidly in her study like some lighthouse perched upon a rocky shore, enduring through the ages regardless of wind, waves, and storms. "Adam Griffin is nothing more than an illusion, a wisp of smoke—bad grog I had on a winter's night," she accused.

"I know that and you know that, but your servants don't. Neither does anyone else," Adam remarked as he leaned against the closet, legs crossed at the ankle, arms in front of him. "And I told your honored guests that I was back, that I would be treating our patients with you loyally by my side—like a good little wife should be."

Eve snarled, "Oh, no. You aren't coming near my patents, Mr. Whatever-your-name-really-is. You aren't a doctor. You haven't spent years studying the diseases of the mind. My patients walk a fine line, and I won't have you pushing them off it with half-baked theories and treatment."

"You're lovely when you're bossy, little admiral."

"Oh, go away."

"Like I said, what will you tell people? Here tonight, gone tomorrow?"

Eve had a ready answer. "I'll tell them that you had an emergency to attend, and had to make haste. Haste to Hades, if I had my way."

Adam snorted. "Now, now. Good little wives don't tell their husbands of just a few hours to go to hell." He lifted her chin with his hand and stared deep into her eyes. While only fools rushed in where angels feared to tread, still, he thought smugly, he was in good company in a madhouse. The place was jammed to the rafters with fools.

"How could you think I would leave you again?" he asked. "I've just returned to you, my darling. We need quality time together, and a quantity of it. We have merrymaking to manage and beds to muss. I say we start now!"

"Argh!" Eve's pirate growl burst forth in full force as she shoved him backward, losing all sense of propriety. "You impossible impersonator! Have you no shame for the sham you have perpetrated tonight? You are a villain of the worst sort, a seeker of booty and ill-gotten gains. And your acting abilities are far from laudable—they're laughable." She brandished a fireplace poker like a rapier, all agility and grace.

But in a lightning-quick move, he took it away from her. "How dare you disparage my acting? Not to boast, but I thought I was rather brilliant as your husband," he said.

He cast a wounded expression at her and placed a hand over his chest. "And I did dress to please you," he added. After a moment he said, "And by the way, I'm not immune to flattery, should you decide to try it."

She glanced at the fireplace poker in his hand. Reading her thoughts, he shook his head.

"I wouldn't try it. I'm bigger, badder, and faster than you are."

"You're an actor? My father hired an actor? We're doomed. Someone will recognize you."

"Now, don't worry your pretty little head. Only once or twice have I trodden the boards—when I needed a quick infusion of coinage. It really wasn't my style, all those dreary road trips into backwaters. Of course, there were legions of fawning women. And I did get raves for my performances. Tonight I outdid myself. No woman dead or alive—or undead—could have asked for more."

"Oh, what utter rubbish! You are far from perfect. *No* man is perfect," she stated emphatically. "Believe me, I lived with men on the *Jolly Roger* for twelve years, and it was far from jolly or perfect!" Eve felt like she was floundering in deep water, not unlike what she often felt when arguing with her father. "I won't have you for a husband. I positively refuse."

"You can't escape. If your fraud is discovered, you'll see no funding. Come now, Eve, you don't really want people to know what a little charlatan you are. You would be ruined, and all your woolly-headed schemes would have been for naught. Admit it. You're truly caught in the net, my dear."

Narrowing her eyes, Eve quietly despised him. Her fall from grace had plunged her into matrimony, and she wished her husband to the bottom of the sea. "Me, the charlatan? What nerve you have." But he spoke the truth. She could not dispute Adam's presence, and she knew it.

So did Captain Bluebeard.

And so did Adam, whatever his real name was. They had hoist her by her own petard.

Adam studied her closely as a myriad of emotions sluiced through her, from rage to hostility to culpability to irate resignation.

"I suppose he paid you well, my father?"

Her husband grinned. "But of course. And aren't you relieved to know that you aren't married to a fool? Of everyone he could engage, you should count your blessings that it was someone who didn't come to you with my pockets—or skull space—to let." Then he quieted, apparently believing he'd yanked her chain enough.

Counting to twenty to regain her composure, Eve drew a deep breath. She wasn't going to let him get another rise out of her; she was beginning to see how he teased her dreadfully just to get her dander up. "That remains to be seen," she grumbled.

Unfortunately, an infernally feminine part of her couldn't help but note how his hazel eyes twinkled and his lips curled up rather sweetly, while he was teasing her. She even reluctantly admitted that he would be quite handsome if he weren't her hoodwinking husband. She didn't want to find him attractive; not one whit.

He spoke again, apparently ready to go another round: "I must insist that next time I choose the guest list. That count was a pompous bag of wind, Dr. Crane is a yahoo if I ever saw one, and Dr. Sigmund is all ego."

Eve sank into a chair, her head in her hands. "I will never, ever forgive my fiendish father," she said.

Adam knelt before her, prying both her hands away from her face. "Come now, love, it's not that horrid a fate. Captain Bluebeard simply wants grandchildren to spoil in his old age." Rubbing her hands with his thumbs he added, "And I'm just the man for the task."

She wanted to yank her hands back, but the gentle rubbing motion on her palms was calming. She, better than anyone, knew what overwrought nerves could do, being both a psychiatrist and a child of a Bluebeard. "He'll be Captain *Graybeard* before I present him with one," she stated firmly. She had no intention of giving in to this slight attraction.

Adam chuckled. "And I was so looking forward to the begetting."

Shoving him hard, she snapped. "Oh, go away and leave me in peace!" She frowned, tempted to offer him a bribe in place of a bride, but she couldn't spare any coin. Every last one was engaged in taking care of the asylum. Besides, no booty she had could match the booty her father had already promised.

"Afraid I can't do that, my sweet. I gave my word to your father, and I am a man of honor," Adam replied. "Although, I must admit that when he approached me I thought he was stark raving mad. But after listening to the Captain's plan, I recognized its brilliance. Pretending to being Dr. Adam Griffin is just what the doctor ordered."

"Honor, my fanny! You wouldn't know honor if it jumped up and bit your arse," Eve growled.

"Ah, but I do. And because of this honor, I could never betray your father. I have reason to be indebted to Captain Bluebeard. Besides, he'd have me filleted if I ever crossed him. Therefore, without further 'I do,' I'm here to stay."

Eve knew her father's vengeful nature, and she wouldn't wish it on her worst enemy, who just now happened to be this handsome impostor. Without a fortune to tempt the so-called Adam, it appeared she was stuck with him. For now. Still, husbands had been known to disappear. And she was too tired to squabble any more tonight. She had concerns to take care of before finally being able to lay her head down on her pillow for the night, so she said, "Without further ado, I've got a patient to see." And she began to leave the room.

"It's rather late to be seeing patients."

"Not when you're a psychiatrist and and the patient is a vampire."

Adam's brow furrowed. He opened his mouth to say something, but thought better of it, saying instead, "Be careful out there."

She ignored his face and words, as well as the hint of concern in his voice. She was just plain weary, and still had a patient to see. Tomorrow she'd start planning the impersonator's departure. She could owtwit this rogue or she wasn't Bluebeard's daughter.

CHAPTER NINE

An Apple a Day Might Keep Adam Away

Upon awakening in the morning, Eve was irritated at discovering her bedding in wild disarray. *Not surprising,* she mused. Her dreams had been vivid and frightening in their content, filled with pirates trying to pillage her ports and kiss her senseless. She climbed out of bed and, instead of waiting for her maid to help her dress, began to slip on undergarments, her mind rolling over possibilities, trying to come up with a foolproof plan for getting rid of the fool posing as her husband. Unfortunately, for all her plotting, Adam wasn't just anybody, since he was in league with her father.

Buttoning up her dress, she shook her head in frustration. Two against one wasn't the best of odds, especially since both Adam and her father were of the pirate persuasion.

As she took the long stairs down to the breakfast room, her mind was consumed with getting rid of Adam. Today was a brand-new day, a day in which she would not let Adam's charming manner or his infectious grin deflect her from her mission of trying to remove him. Furthermore, her mind was quickly sorting through solutions on how to get even with her father. Retribution was a foregone conclusion when your name was originally Bluebeard. The sneaky old scalawag would be lucky she didn't hoist him up his own mainsail!

Eve spied her quarry sitting at *her* breakfast table. His grin made her feel funny. Teeter, his expression correctly dignified and in somber costume, was serving him coffee.

Eve scowled, her appetite fleeing. Even the pleasant aromas of food were not enough to overshadow the unwanted company. Glaring at him, she wished fervently that the infernal impostor would find that he had bitten off more than he could chew and would take himself off somewhere else to digest it.

"Teeter, it appears Dr. Adam is staying for breakfast, so be sure to hide the silver," she said briskly, watching him load his plate with eggs and baked ham. Her husband took a bite of eggs with cream sauce and chewed with gusto.

"Very good, Dr. Eve," the somber—and now sober—butler replied.

Ignoring her sarcastic remark, Adam remarked, "Darling, you look lovely!" Glancing at the butler, he asked, "Doesn't she look wonderful, Teeter?"

"Lovely as a spring flower," the butler agreed, his manner placating and efficient despite of the slight hangover knocking at his head. But, today of all days, nothing would stop him from doing his duty with proper pomp.

"And not just any spring flower, but a rose in full bloom," Adam added, giving her a wink, thinking how wonderful his wife looked in her pale pink gown. It had a lacy bodice and was long-sleeved and cinched at the waist, which decidedly flattered her figure. "I daresay your beauty is such that ships have likely been scuttled and cities laid waste in your name."

"Indeed," Eve muttered between clenched teeth. "What unmitigated gall you have," she added, staring at him, assessing, her mouth tightening. She didn't trust him an inch. He was in high spirits this morning, and certainly didn't appear to have had trouble sleeping, as she had, or trouble with his appetite. Absolutely no remorse or guilt? Wasn't that just like a pirate? A pirate at heart was always a pirate.

"It's amazing the number of thieves in London these days, Teeter," she remarked. "I wish that the Hanseatic League were still in service. They so loved to hang them."

Adam arched a handsome brow, then cocked his head to study her, his face a study of mischievous intent.

Seating herself gracefully, Eve next acknowledged her butler's compliment. "But don't think I have forgotten last night, Teeter," she added. "Your misbehavior remains in my mind"

Teeter cringed, and his eyes filled with apprehension. He nervously ran his finger around his collar. "I must apologize for last night. My ill behavior was certainly not befitting my station."

"I fear this is a case of too little, too late," Eve scolded sternly, ignoring the growing anxiety in Teeter's eyes. "I cannot and will not abide a drunken lout for a butler. You're on Hugo duty for the next month. And if he gets free and heads for the bell tower, then I needn't tell you what your next punishment will be."

"Certainly not, Dr. Eve," Teeter said. Misery filled his dark eyes. Her chastisement had found its mark, and her punishment too. No sane person liked Hugo duty; it was miserable. "But might I say in my own defense that—"

She cut him off with brutal efficiency. "Perchance you wouldn't be trying to offer an excuse? There is none. I expect my butler to attend my guests with dignity and restraint, not have him teetering all over the place, half-soused—no matter his name. Now, go about your duties and consider yourself beyond fortunate that I don't do worse. We'll finish serving our own breakfasts."

Watching the situation unfold, Adam curbed his impulse to laugh out loud. For such a petite woman, Captain Bluebeard's little admiral of a daughter certainly knew how to command. He wondered if the butler knew his ship was sinking.

"My, my, Teeter, is she always this high-handed with the staff?" he asked.

"Of course not, Dr. Adam," Teeter replied loyally, although he did sniff a little, his wounded dignity escaping in that manner.

"*Adam.*" The word was a warning, spoken with asperity and a glare that would have singed a stone gargoyle.

Bowing, Teeter left the room hastily, his shoulders hunched, slamming the door behind him. The paintings on the wall rattled ominously.

Adam winced and said, "You really must insist that he doesn't go around banging doors. He may be in an ill humor, but it plays havoc with the wallpaper—not to mention my nerves."

"Does it, indeed?" his wife replied. "Then I must be sure to raise his pay. And, by the by, he always does that." She happily helped herself to some freshly baked scones and clotted cream.

"Why do you keep him on?" Adam inquired.

"Not that it's any of your business, but he came with the place. He was my relative's retainer. And it's written in the will that he be retained until I can pension him off. That will be a good long while, since he has ogre blood. Still, all in all, he's a fairly decent butler. Well . . . he is at least used to dealing with difficult supernatural creatures."

Adam cocked a brow, inviting her to continue.

"My great-great-uncle wasn't the easiest of the undead to attend, yet Teeter managed quite well. As long as Teeter is sober, he's fine. When he's soused, that's another matter."

"That's an understatement," Adam said in an undertone. "He's an unusual butler, but then this is undoubtedly an unusual house. It's full of the dotty, the damned, and the simply bloody loony."

"We don't refer to patients as 'loony' or 'dotty.' And if you don't find the asylum to your taste, you could always eat elsewhere," Eve suggested sweetly. She shot him a mean little glare and took a sip of tea. "I'm sure there are many other places to loot and pillage." Setting her teacup down, she said, "I wish you a brisk breeze to anywhere you wish to sail. Like purgatory," she added under her breath.

"And leave you alone to fend off mistaken hunches, claustrophobic vampires, and fake wereflies who are really wolves in human clothing? Not to forget bungling butlers and slamming doors. I don't think so. What kind of husband would I be if I left you alone in the midst of all this mayhem?"

"An absent one—the kind I like best!" she answered.

"Don't be tedious, darling. Remember our vows? In

health or in an insane asylum. For richer or poorer—yet definitely richer," he added with slippery charm. The family jewels were already increasing. "Besides, I can slay your dragons for you," he suggested.

"There aren't any dragons here!"

Adam glanced around and cocked his head. "How strange. There appears to be every other kind of paranormal creature."

Eve sighed. "I was right. You're beyond help. And quit talking like that—you know perfectly well that there was never a wedding."

He threw back his head and laughed at her militant demeanor, rigid spine, and clenched jaw. "Ah, but I remember it well. You wore virginal white."

"I wore nothing at all, you fraudulent dolt!"

His eyes lit. "That was later."

Gasping in outrage, she shook her head. He was absolutely impossible! Ignoring his crude laughter, she spread a bit of blueberry jam on her scone. She wouldn't react further. That was the only way to deal with a man so oily he could walk on water.

"I missed you last night, Eve," he said.

"You are seriously deluded if you thought I would allow you to sleep in my bed."

"Oh, but I did. You just weren't in it," he replied. "Are you going to eat these?" he asked, taking a bit of her kippers.

When Eve hadn't made her way to her bedchamber last night, he had crept out to find her. She was studiously writing notes, probably on the successes and failures of dinner. While he would have preferred her company, he returned to her room alone—and enjoyed the best night's sleep he'd ever had. She had a fat, goose-down mattress, with lavender-scented pillows and meticulously clean sheets—after too many long nights in barns, haymows, berths of ships, and upon rocks under the stars, such a clean, comfortable bed was a call for rejoicing. He intended to do everything in his power to make sure he remained in that bed. With one slight adjustment. Eve would be in it with him.

"Where did you sleep last night?" he asked.

"Elsewhere," she retorted, ignoring the fact that there was something deep within his eyes that touched something in her, some sort of vulnerability that appealed. She caught a glimpse of it only every once in a while.

He chuckled, then popped a piece of buttered scone into his mouth. "The staff will talk. My charms will be suspect."

"The staff can go hang, and as far as your charms, they can hang too."

When she was around, they certainly weren't hanging, he mused.

"How testy you are in the morning! I find that a definite flaw. As far as hanging, I'm sure some do in this odd house of yours. Any suicidals here? Perhaps the fly man or the vampire, Sir Loring—or how about that deluded Englishman with the Napoleon complex?"

"Who told you about Major Gallant?" Eve hissed.

"Mrs. Fawlty mentioned his problem, that he often charges up and down the stairs shouting commands and demanding that people call him Emperor. I imagine many would take umbrage at such demands. Still, the housekeeper mentioned that he's a fledgling vampire. That must take the bite out of—or rather put one into—the situation. Either way, I rather think Old Boney might better be served if you let him charge across your gardens at night rather than up the staircase. That way he won't disturb you and me. Of course, he's your patient. I take it you have sense enough to keep him locked up, at least. He's clearly batty."

Eve exploded. "How dare you? What utter cheek to question my methods of treatment! And there'll never be any 'you and I.' Never!" Shaking her head, she held up a hand in haughty anger, the other wielding a fork, with which she speared the air. "Don't say anything else, or I might just make you dinner for an inmate."

Adam knew when to keep silent, when to simply sit back in his chair. Instead of speaking, he grinned, since he was quite out of reach of her fork. His new wife was such a feisty little thing. How he longed to chase her around the break-fast table and kiss her senseless. But pushing aside such lusty thoughts, he managed to look suitably repentant. Or not.

"That innocent look won't work with me," Eve said. "My father uses it all the time. But I'm onto his tricks, and yours too! You've both been scoundrels for too many seasons to be believed."

"You're right," he admitted. "I shouldn't have questioned your judgment on whether you lock in, lock up, lock away—or maybe even better, lock *out*—these bed-lamite characters."

"I don't lock my patients up unless I absolutely have no other choice," she growled. "They're already locked into their own prisons—prisons of their minds. They don't need any other lock; they need keys. But since you have the compassion of a goat and the manners to match, I doubt you would understand."

"But, my little pearl, all you had to do was explain. I understand. Agonies of the mind *are* prisons. And I imagine the pain of knowing that you are abnormal is like dying a thousand deaths every day. These poor creatures. Humiliation, feelings of self-worthlessness and guilt . . ."

Eve didn't like the sympathetic glint in her husband's eyes, or the understanding words he uttered. He understood quite a bit more than she liked—but that didn't mean she was softening in her feelings toward him.

He continued: "Nonetheless, I feel the major might be dangerous in a major way. As your protector, I feel I should put in my tuppence—"

She interrupted him frostily. "Enough. I've had enough. Just who do you think you are? What presumption, to think that you can blithely enter my life, interfering, interrupting, and demanding things? And how can you just drop an old life and enter a new one without any consequences? Don't you have family? Someone who might want you? *Anyone?*" she asked hopefully.

"Everyone has family," he remarked offhandedly, taking another sip of coffee. "But they died when I was a young man. I have been on my own since."

The casual tone in which his words were spoken might have caused her to wonder if his family were of little import to him—if she didn't spend her days and nights listening to what people didn't say. She swallowed her tea, finishing it and feeling a slight lump in her throat. His story was rather sad. He would have had no one to help him grow into an honorable and respectable man whom a woman might fancy for a husband—if a woman were fancying a husband, which, of course, Eve wasn't.

"Friends, then? People who will miss you when you don't turn back up?" she prompted. Finger to chin, she frowned. "Why on earth did I ask that? I doubt anyone could miss your ill advice."

He dropped his elbow onto the table and leaned close, his head in hand, to gaze at her. "Oh, believe me, my sweet wife, some women actually rave about me. There are probably a baker's dozen crying themselves to sleep every night since I disappeared."

Eve glared. She had created this man; she wished it would be as easy to kill him off. Unfortunately, her compassionate nature wouldn't allow that. "Then why don't you do us both a tremendous favor and go find those unbalanced females? Go with an easy heart, knowing that you have left me here in blessed peace."

"Tsk, tsk. I can't imagine this place *ever* being peaceful," he said. "Besides, I like it here."

"In an asylum?" Eve said.

"Each to his own," Adam replied. She started to protest, but he stalled her by raising a hand. "That's what I find fascinating about the Towers—no two days or nights will ever be the same. Or so I would vow." Seeing a look of disbelief fill her eyes, he quickly finished, "I do like a little adventure. That's why I've enjoyed traveling, and have seen much of the world."

"You are an Englishman originally?" His accent was a bit strange, and she had been trying to place it since she first heard his outrageous words last night.

"Born in Ireland, but bred in England during my early years."

"Then, pray tell, if you like to travel so much, why on earth would you want to stay here and pretend to be my husband?"

"Is there ever any *one* reason?" he replied. "For the gold your father gave me. I'm tired of roving the world and never finding a home," he added. He picked up her hand and gave her a scorching look. "Now that I have seen you, my wandering days are over. I am prepared to stay and be a model husband—and immoderate lover. And most important: *visible*. You don't have to carry your burden alone anymore, my dear."

Jerking back her hand, she snapped her fingers in front of his face. She was going to kill her facetious father. "Do you not understand that you are sadly *de trop*? I am a modern woman, and have learned to take care of myself." She pushed her breakfast aside. He was killing her appetite.

He gave a scrupulous glance around the room. "I can see that. But how harsh you are, my love. Wake up on the wrong side of the bed?" He gave a lazy smile. "Perhaps you should have been *in* it."

"Look, you can't just pick up someone else's life and pretend it's your own," she said.

Putting finger to chin, he remarked, "Not normally, no. But then, this is not a normal situation."

"Of course it's not normal! Nothing is normal here, not even my staff. This is an institution for the abnormal," she scolded huffily. Spreading her arms wide, she indicated not just the breakfast room but the whole asylum.

He chuckled again. "I meant the fact that you used to have an imaginary husband, whose imaginary shoes I am now more than willing to fill with my very real fleshy feet. I also have other fleshy bits to fill things with—and quite pleasurably."

"I am not willing to have you fill them, and that is that," Eve argued. She ignored the sensations his words were stirring in her. He *was* very handsome. "I shall tell my father that you are leaving. You can go on your merry way—to hell in a handbasket." Her desperation increased as her body continued to react to his proximity.

"No!" Adam said, slapping both hands down on the table. "And it is not open for debate. I will not leave." Her arguments were beginning to annoy him, especially as he could tell that Eve found him attractive. He knew it by the way she kept avoiding his gaze, and the feverish gleam he caught in her eye.

"No?" Eve echoed. Sadly. She had reasoned last night that his reluctance to leave was because he was in fear of her father. She needed to resolve that worry, which would leave him free to go on his merry, scheming way, causing mayhem and chaos wherever he went. Just not here.

"I think I shall domesticate quite easily," he said.

"In a pig's eye. The only thing domestic about you is your . . . clothes."

"You should see me without them," he retorted. "But then, if I were nude, I fear any thoughts of domestication would go right out the window."

Eve had a sudden image of Adam as naked as the day he was born. This image was accompanied by a sharp sensation in her gut, and her face flushed. She'd had the same vision last night in her dreams. Rubbish, and a dead man's pirate chest!

"You're blushing, dearest," he pointed out.

"Must be the kippers." She pointed a finger at the diabolical deceiver. "You are, without a doubt, the most conceited, conniving buffoon it has been my misfortune to meet, much less be married to—or not married to, or whatever! Now listen to me closely while I explain things to you. I will make things clear with my father, and then you may leave here. I will make sure that he pursues no vengeance. I have some jewelry you can take, and if I receive my funding I'll send you more. A thief couldn't ask for a better deal. You can take your ill-gotten gains and go without a care in the world. What more could you want?"

Leaning back in his gilded chair, Adam studied her, all masculine ire. He hated the fact that she thought he had a sad lack of character, and that he was for sale. He was, of course, but the price was love.

Hiding his anger, he replied, "You. I want *you*." That commanded her attention. "I want a family, a place to belong, and respectability and responsibility. It has been too long since I've known those precious commodities. Besides, Captain Bluebeard would have my liver if I left, no matter what you say or promise. He wants you married to me for life—to *me*, a real man and not some fantasy lover."

Well, that wasn't exactly true, he admitted to himself. The crafty captain had actually hired him for the short term. After he faked his death, Eve would be free to marry again. But Adam had agreed before he had seen her and recognized her for what she was: his soul mate. No one else was going to marry this woman, but him. He just had to win her.

"I don't want you! I don't need you! And most important, I don't respect you!"

Adam's face glowed bright with anger. "Watch where you step, my lady. You're treading on thin ice."

Her anger making her incautious, Eve ignored his warning. She forced the challenge, rising from the table. "How can I respect a man who lies his way into my life? How can I respect a man who was paid to be my husband? What kind of man would do that?"

Adam's features tightened and he stood, towering over her. "Sometimes you do what you have to do to survive.

Sometimes hunger and cold do amazing things to one's scruples and dignity! Have you ever felt so hollow that you could feel your back through your stomach? Have you ever been so cold your teeth won't stop chattering even after you finally find a warm bed? So cold that your feet are like blocks of ice and you can't feel your ears? 'And gilded honor shamefully misplaced.'"

He was quoting Shakespeare. How interesting. "No. I'm sorry," she replied quietly.

It was several seconds before he nodded his head. "Apology accepted. But I've lived in some dark places with scant hope of light. Then, last night, I found a beacon. It was like lightning striking me, for suddenly I knew what I wanted."

He stared at her so intently that she could feel her breath hitch. Finding herself frustrated beyond anything she had ever known—including many battles with her old sea wolf of a Father—she pleaded vehemently, "You can't just step into another life."

Looking around, then pointedly back at her, Adam stated, "But I already have. You can't pry me away, my little jewel, wish me away, or force me to leave. I'm here. So buck up and get used to seeing me at the breakfast table. More important, in your bed. Preferably with you in it." He held out his arm. "Come; we have patients to see."

"Go to hell, whatever your name truly is. I have an appointment with a patient, yes. A *private* appointment."

He took her rejection with good nature. "Then have a nice morning, my love. Oh, and by the way, my first name really is Adam."

Eve's mouth fell open and she gaped. Surely the Fates weren't so capricious. It couldn't be so; the lecherous louse had to be lying.

"Be careful," her husband warned. "You might catch a fly. Or is Mr. Pryce still in bed?" He grinned.

Eve closed her mouth with a snap, her eyes shooting sparks. She hated both the fictitious fiend and her finagling father.

"It *must* be fate," Adam called over his shoulder. "The world is conspiring against you." Then he exited the breakfast room, just in time to avoid a flying cup. Life with Eve meant he needed to be well-off, he decided; it appeared he would be replacing a great deal of porcelain.

Outside the door, he shook his head, irritated. His new wife had quite a mouth and arm on her. Her father had been right when he'd warned that when his daughter wanted something, nothing stopped her. And Eve definitely wanted him gone. But then, Eve Bluebeard had never run up against the likes of him. She wasn't aware of it yet, but the little admiral had just met her Waterloo. He wasn't going anywhere for a long, long time.

The words he had spoken about respectability and responsibility were true; a long time ago he'd had both. A long time ago Adam's heritage had included a title: Baron Hawkmore. But betrayal had ended all that, along with the lives of his parents and younger brother. That tragedy and treachery had killed something soft and good within him—or at least, he thought it had until last night.

Once he had been a man to appreciate the beauty of a sunset on a windswept moor, or the purity of voices lifted in crystalline beauty in a church choir on a foggy Sunday morning. He had enjoyed the bonny sight of a mother strolling with her young sons in the early morning dew, and the laughter of a pretty lass dancing in the thick of a merry crowd. But that man had died a dozen deaths with the passage of time. Adam had learned to trust precious few, and that honor was ofttimes the only thing a man could call his own.

Yes, he had been brought up to believe in duty and honor, home and hearth. That giving love was as important as receiving it. Yet, somewhere along the way this had gotten lost. Perhaps he had taken a wrong turn in the icy winters of despair. Maybe he'd been traveling down hill when he should have been quickly climbing the peaks. He would probably never really know all his wrong turns and missteps, but his path had led him away from what he'd wanted to who he was now. And he wasn't sure who that was anymore.

He had a sense that Eve was a beacon calling him home to his lost self, because, for the first time in over a decade, Adam Pierce Hawkmore had looked in the mirror that morning and welcomed home a stranger.

CHAPTER TEN

Ashes to Ashes and Dust, Too Much Dust

Although she was frantic to confront her father, Eve put aside her anger as she walked into her study. She had to concentrate on her patient, Lady Jane Asher, Countess of Wolverton. Lady Jane had an abnormal fear not only of blood, but of dirt, spiders, crypts, and other things that went bump in the night. Born a Van Helsing and the only female in the clan of infamous vampire slayers, she had found her fears to be a hard cross to bear.

Happily, Lady Jane had escaped her vampire-staking and -stalking duties by marrying a noble Nosferatu. The Romeo and Juliet of the vampire world had fallen madly in love regardless of odds to the contrary. Unfortunately, Jane had been unable to overcome her fears enough for her husband to make her an immortal. And unless Lady Jane could overcome her phobia of blood, it would be ashes to ashes and dust to dust for her after enough time passed.

Her patient smiled cheerfully at Eve as she seated herself on the rose brocade chair. After treating Lady Jane for the past five months, Eve recognized the steel core within the woman, which would help in her cure. She also held great affection for and devotion to her vampire husband. Motivation, Eve had learned, was the key factor in overcoming one's problems.

Eve returned Jane's smile, recalling again the gossip she had heard when she first came to town: dire predictions about a master vampire and a vampire slayer being forced together in wedlock till death did they part. Pessimists had proclaimed that the Earl of Wolverton would be staked before the month was out. Vampire lovers had predicted that Lady Jane would meet a toothsome demise. But their marriage had set the supernatural world on its head, causing vampires to roll over in their graves and vampire hunters everywhere to shake their heads, along with their garlic cloves. In spite of these gossips and manuremongers, the couple had fallen in love and walked happily into the crypt before sunrise, proving all skeptics wrong.

"How is work at the hospital proceeding?" Eve asked encouragingly. She had recommended that the blood-shy countess volunteer her time at a hospital on a thrice-weekly basis for several hours a day. Lady Jane had flinched when the words *surgical ward* were mentioned, but had agreed. Eve felt that if Lady Jane were repeatedly exposed to blood, her phobia would decrease.

Lady Jane smiled. "I enjoy helping with the patients most of the time. So many need a cheerful face or some genial conversation to help ease their pain. Imagine how dull it would be to be stuck in bed for days on end! And I haven't gotten ill at the sight of blood for weeks now, thanks to you."

"No, no. You should congratulate yourself, Jane," Eve said. "You've worked very hard."

She felt like shouting with triumph. When Jane had first started treatment five months ago, she couldn't even stay in the same room with a bloodied patient without casting up her accounts. This new report made Eve cheerfully optimistic. So many of her patients seemed almost hopeless cases. Too often months could turn into years before you saw progress, and from her studies she knew those years could easily slide into decades. If only the brain's problems were like a toothache and you could just pull out offending memories or fears, she mused. But at least for now Jane's nausea had subsided, and the countess was getting better. It was all Eve could do not to dance a pirate's jig.

"How about the fainting episodes?" she asked.

"Well, I am doing quite well with a little bit of blood . . . but when it comes in great amounts, I do still tend to faint," Jane confessed. "But at least I no longer become queasy. Asher is very proud of me—with the exception of the spider incident last month in the family crypt. Actually, he found it hysterically funny until I locked him out of our bedroom for his hilarity."

Eve half smiled. "I'm glad to hear it's going well."

"Yes, although I must admit that the hospital does need more thorough maids. You should have seen the dust bunnies under some of the cabinets," Lady Jane remarked. "I have spoken to the hospital administrator about it."

Eve nodded encouragingly. She knew her patient's disdain for dirt. When she had first met with Asher about his wife's phobia, she'd had several suggestions for after the Lady Jane finally made the transformation from mortal to vampire. The family crypt should be cleaned thoroughly on a daily basis. Asher should be Jane's blood donor, and it was recommended that his native soil—which vampires were required to keep nearby—should be placed in lacy little bags filled also with lavender. And all frolicking in the graveyard would be strictly forbidden, unless he wanted himself and his wife to have a complete dustup.

"I'm sure the hospital administrator appreciated your suggestion," she said. Eve's newest patient—one Mrs. Monkfort, who also hated dirt—would not have merely suggested it, but put her words to action and had the entire ward cleaned. Of course, Mrs. Monkfort was extremely obsessive—to the point of mania—while Lady Jane was only a trifle overwrought.

"I'm not so sure. Ever since the time I fainted at his feet, the poor man tries to avoid me."

"Shockingly poor manners, I'm sure," Eve consoled Jane, adding to her notes.

Patient is particularly sensitive to the slights of others, having lived with an overbearing, autocratic father who found fault with everything she did or does, from badly sharpening stakes to marrying a monster.

Eve knew that in most situations, a mere major would be overjoyed that his daughter had risen so high above her pedigree, but Major Van Helsing had been vehemently disgruntled that his only daughter was sleeping with the enemy. He did not like the idea of a Van Helsing rising out of a coffin to drink rather than stake at sunset.

"How *is* the situation with your father?" Eve questioned, jotting down notations on her patient's chart.

She felt sure some of the woman's fears came from traumatic events in her early life, and with Major Van Helsing as Jane's father, it was no wonder. So far Eve had been unable to uncover any particular event, but that didn't mean there wasn't one. Often life's major events were so horrific that the mind buried them so deep that they lay beneath layers and layers of the subconscious, like a sunken ship slowly being buried by sands at the bottom of the sea. This resulted in the ship's eventually becoming completely invisible to the naked eye over time—just like lost memories.

"If I were still at home, I would be polishing the Van Helsing silver daily. The major was *not* happy when he discovered Asher is a vampire, but since we destroyed the evil Dracul at the time, some of the bite was taken out of him. For a year or so, my father wasn't really overbearing about my husband and me and the whole vampire-and-slayer relationship."

Eve nodded, thinking that Asher and Jane seemed like they had an excellent marriage, and both still acted very much in love.

Lady Jane continued: "But in the past seven months or so he has become quite contrary, as if he fears I'll go over to the dark side. Ridiculous, since Asher isn't even dark. And this whole problem with my being sickened by blood means that I shan't be turned into a vampiress anytime in the near future! Yet still the major blusters and gives me dark looks."

"Much as when you lived with him?" Eve wanted to majorly wallop Major Van Helsing. He was like her own father in many ways, a blustery autocrat who thought he knew best, and who hounded anyone not falling in with his plans. The major had expected Jane to carry on the family name, happily staking her way through life. Captain Bluebeard wanted grandkids and for Eve to sail her life away, pirating and looting. But as mad as her father made her, Eve at least felt he loved her. From Lady Jane's comments, Eve wasn't sure the major even held his daughter in affection.

"Yes. Although Asher is now included in these looks. Do you know my father still believes that the only good vampire is a dead vampire? Thank heavens the rest of my family no longer believes that nonsense! Asher, being Asher, could care less about the glares, but he does feel a bit guilty at the major's disapproving stares directed at me."

"Regretfully, Major Van Helsing is who he is, and has his own fears to live with," Eve said. She sighed. "I doubt your father will ever truly change his opinions. You know the old cliché, that you can't teach an old dog new tricks? Well, I rather doubt you can teach an old vampire slayer, either. He will always judge a vampire by his coffin, and not what lies in his heart. I highly recommend that you ignore any feelings of guilt you suffer for disappointing your father, and not let the man's feelings affect you at all." Eve was reminded again of her father's devious interference. She could hardly wait to track the old reprobate down, and to tell him exactly what she thought of his rotten plan.

She grimaced and continued with her advice: "No, we cannot remake ourselves to suit someone else's image. We must always be true to who we are and what we are, with all our faults and all our remarkable capabilities for forgiveness and talents for whatever," Eve counseled. Her thoughts grim, she made another notation, this time for herself:

Lock Bluebeard in a sea chest and throw away the key.

Lady Jane nodded, an intense expression on her face. Growing up under her father's rule had made her want to please everyone, most especially the major. The major, a man not to be satisfied with anything, had never lavished a single word of praise upon her, making her feel like a failure. That continual feeling had severely crushed her spirit, and if not for her beloved ostrich; her dog, Spot; her dearest friend, Clare Frankenstein; and her brother, Brandon, she likely would have faded away while polishing the family silver.

"You're quite fortunate, you know," Eve reminded her. "You're married to a handsome earl who loves you, and the rest of your family admires him."

"I know. I am quite pleased at how my uncle, Jakob Van Helsing, my cousins, and brother have all taken Asher into their confidence. Why, my brother can hardly wait at times for Asher to come popping out of his coffin to talk to him about things," Jane said. "Although the first few times it happened, Asher said his nerves were in quite a state. A vampire usually gets staked when he wakes to find a Van Helsing standing over his coffin. He doesn't get asked what gift to buy an angry mistress."

Eve laughed. "Yes, I can imagine. Having a renowned vampire hunter perched by your coffin could be quite unsettling."

Jane blushed becomingly. "My husband never minds rising to the occasion when *I* wake him up."

Eve made a notation on her pad:

True love is a wonder to behold.

She smiled and commented, "Dreams do come true." *For some people*, she thought wryly.

Jane nodded happily. "Yes, I am fortunate. A series of misfortunes and my fears ended in a marriage made in hell but a honeymoon made in heaven."

"Oftentimes good can come from mishaps and mayhem," Eve agreed. Although in her case, it was quite different, she thought fretfully. Just look what trying to avoid being married had cost her! Her fake marriage was now being shoved down her throat, along with a tasty yet tasteless blackguard pretending to be her husband.

Glancing over at the clock upon the fireplace mantel, she realized that time had passed swiftly. She reached inside a desk drawer and pulled out several different pictures with black smeared upon them: her art treatment therapy. She handed one to Jane, determined to get to the root of the woman's phobias.

"It's time for the black stains again?" Jane asked approvingly. "I do so love to use my imagination on them. It's like when I sit down to sketch birds."

"Inkblots," Eve corrected kindly. No matter how many times she used her inkblot therapy, her patients got the terminology wrong. She'd even tried to drill the name home using a roar-shock method, but to no avail.

Her patients' inability to remember the name was particularly aggravating, because Eve was rather proud of her thrilling new methodology in treating the mentally ill. It had begun as an accident back at the University of Vienna. For an internship, she had been working at a hospital. One night, tired and worn-out from three straight days and nights of being on call, she had spilled a bottle of ink. At the time she had been taking notes. A patient had commented on the black spots, giving Eve a brief glimpse into his fog-shrouded mind. Soon she was trying the stains on other patients, and eventually discussed it with her mentor, Dr. Kroger. He had embraced the new therapy. Together, they had refined the stains to conform to various images they felt might stimulate the subconscious mind.

"Now, what does this one remind you of?" she asked.

"Asher putting on his cloak," Jane replied. "Did I tell you that he thinks I have the prettiest feet he's ever seen?"

"Odd, I thought the earl would be a neck man," Eve remarked.

Lady Jane blushed. "He loves my neck, too," she admitted. "He's just batty about necks and feet." Then, pointing at a certain spot on the stain, she added, "Yes—Asher's putting on his coat, and that is Spot by his foot."

Eve rather thought the inkblot resembled a pirate sword. "This one?" she asked, holding out the next picture.

"Let me see. Hmm." Jane put her finger to her chin. "This one reminds me of Asher rising from his coffin. He's smiling happily upon seeing me. Waking him is *so* divine. Did I mention that he calls me his little ray of nonfatal sunshine?"

"How lovely," Eve replied stoically. Each to her own desires, she decided. Holding up another mess of black splotches, she asked, "How about this?"

"Asher—waltzing."

Eve twisted her pearl necklace, making notes on her notepad.

Obsessive patient. Whereas a spot definitely resembles a person walking a plank, Lady Jane sees her bloody hus-

band. We need to focus more on her fear of bloodlust rather than plain old lust.

Warily, she flipped over the next picture.

"Dr. Eve, really!" Jane protested. "I can't believe you have a picture of Asher stepping out of the bath!"

Eve almost broke her necklace, twisting it viciously. This was really too much. Young love was a wondrous thing, a many-splendored thing, but not when it barred the way to unlocking submerged and perhaps crucial memories. "Lady Jane, I beg to differ. This particular ink spot is of a crow's nest aboard a pirate ship. I have never had any erotic ink spots in my possession, nor will I. And I certainly would never place in my therapy an ink spot of your husband without any clothes. Perhaps if you look closer at the picture, you might see something else." Her fingers began to tap on Henry Morgan's skull in slight vexation. "Something *not* dealing with your husband."

Accepting the request good-naturedly, Lady Jane lowered her head to again study the ink spot. Her brow wrinkled in concentration. Finally, after several moments passed, she spoke decisively: "You're quite right. I can see that now. It isn't a picture of Asher standing nude in this black blot."

"Inkblot," Eve again corrected.

Lady Jane glanced up and nodded. "You're quite right. This ink splot looks like Orville, my pet ostrich."

Eve wanted to jump up and shout, *Hoist the mainsails, we've got a strong wind at long last.* She was finally getting somewhere. No mention of her patient's dratted husband.

"Yes," Jane continued firmly, as pointing at the picture. "This is Orville, my ostrich, walking in the garden with my beloved Asher."

CHAPTER ELEVEN

All About Eve

While Eve was privately seeing her patient, Adam was busy gossiping with Mrs. Fawlty, who gave him a quick tour of the Towers. The irascible housekeeper was a font of information about his wayward wife; she had been with Eve since the opening of the asylum. Listening to Mrs. Fawlty, Adam began to get a much better handle on Eve, for the housekeeper gave descriptions of her waking life. He quickly discovered that his bustling bride worked with patients morning and night, due to the fact that at least some of her patients could counsel with her only after dark, such as vampires, night hags, and gargoyles. Most of her time was spent in work, though Eve did attend some balls, routs, and plays. But mainly she stayed at the Towers, trying to cure the cretins under her care.

After several cups of tea bettered with brandy, Mrs. Fawlty admitted that Eve could be a mite autocratic whenever she wanted her way—which happened to be most of the time. The housekeeper also confided that Eve could be testy as well, which Mrs. Fawlty believed was the result of EBS—Empty Bed Syndrome. Dr. Eve's bed was empty of all but her sweet self, you see. When Mrs. Fawlty confided this last nugget of information, the lusty housekeeper gave Adam a knowing look followed by a pert wink. Next the housekeeper added that since the master was home, the missus would probably be early to bed and later to rise. Yes—she had grinned leeringly—there would be all kinds of risings. Which in her good opinion meant that Dr. Eve would have a tendency to be singing in the mornings rather than ordering everybody about.

After this rather revealing conversation with the housekeeper, Adam next encountered a leprechaun. He watched a few moments in silence as Fester carved out a hole in the wine cellar with a pickax, and after overhearing that Fester was hiding pots of gold, Adam had searched in high spirits, rubbing his hands gleefully together as he tried to spy the treasure about which Fester kept yammering. Adam had never seen a pot of gold at the end of any rainbow, but he still believed. After all, he was part Irish. If Fester said he had pots of gold, then no doubt he did.

Adam understood that Eve would have him walking the plank if she thought he might filch a pot or two of gold from one of her patients. Still, a man did what he had to do, and he couldn't help his infamous inclination. He had found himself in the situation of having to sing for his supper too many times before.

Casting aside his doubts, he carefully inspected the cellar, looking beneath every wine rack and odd box, all the while stifling the little twinges of guilt he felt. He rationalized his snooping with the fact that Fester was a patient of Eve's, and not likely to be leaving the asylum in the near future. Therefore, the leprechaun really had no need of pots of gold. And Adam would take only one or two of them, leaving the rest for the demented Fester.

Alas, Adam came up empty-handed, not finding any pots of gold. Not even one measly doubloon. It brought him to the unhappy conclusion that Fester, like Eve, had an overactive imagination.

Adam might have been more disappointed in this quirky turn of events if he hadn't decided to converse with the leprechaun to see just how delusional Fester was. Fester turned out to be highly entertaining, and extremely knowledgeable about government conspiracies. Adam was particularly impressed with the conspiracy about the Corn Laws, which Fester believed were an attempt by Parliament to cover up the huge circles found in cornfields. The leprechaun then added vehemently that the government was keeping the common masses from discovering that elephants resided in England, where they liked to play a game much like the one called ring-around-the-rosy. Furthermore, these elephants were going to be used to march over the Alps when England invaded Switzerland for its chocolate. It seemed that England had a shortage of chocolate, Fester had ended grandly, and Parliament didn't want the common masses to panic.

Being the gentleman that he was, Adam had nodded approvingly at the appropriate spots, hiding his grin. As far as conspiracy theories went, Fester's lacked common sense but had panache. He gave the inventive leprechaun a pat on the back for effort, and even helped him fill in one of his "gold holes." Then he had advised the daft dwarf to try his hand at writing.

Having had enough of fool's gold and lunatic leprechauns, Adam went in search of his beautiful bride. He yearned to bask in her company. He found Eve walking to the main entranceway with a pleasingly plump lady with remarkable greenish-silver eyes.

"Darling, there you are!" Adam said cheerfully as he approached, taking his bristling bride's hand in his own and kissing it tenderly. He disregarded completely her frigid demeanor. "Even though I saw you only a short while ago at breakfast, I find myself missing you, my little jewel."

Noting her patient's stunned expression, Eve quickly drew back her hand. She didn't want to introduce Adam to Lady Jane, but saw little choice. She would rather her patient meet her pernicious pretend husband than have Jane think she was involved in some scandal. After all, who—even a person with a Nosferatu husband—wanted to think of her doctor embroiled in some tawdry fly-by-night affair?

"Countess, this is my . . . husband," Eve said, her teeth aching to gnash in vexation. She sent him a withering glance. "Dr. Adam Griffin. Adam, this is the Countess of Wolverton, Lady Jane Asher."

Adam bowed, then politely kissed Lady Jane's hand. She exclaimed, "Oh, Dr. Eve, why didn't you tell me that your husband had arrived home? How exciting for you! I would have skipped my session today if I had known. I'm sure you two lovebirds long to be together, alone, and not deal with others' troubles—today of all days."

"You are as astute as you are charming," Adam answered agreeably.

"No, I didn't mind at all," Eve stated firmly at the same time. Seeing Lady Jane's confusion, she hastily amended, "Adam loves to tease, but I fear you'll think he's impertinent. Which he is, but that's another discussion. The discussion under discussion is that I truly enjoyed our session today, and wouldn't have postponed it for anything."

Adam sighed dramatically, a smile on his handsome face. "'Tis true, Countess. My wife would only have worried if she hadn't seen you today. Her patients' welfare means a great deal to her. That's why I fancy her as I do. Such a compassionate lady, and such a fine, dedicated doctor."

Giving him a secret evil eye, Eve said, "My husband is a doctor as well, you know, and understands the profession's demands on time. I was glad to have our session today."

"But a husband is not just *anybody*," Lady Jane quickly pointed out. "A husband is a great part of a wife's happiness and duties—the latter which some spouses make seem like treats and not duties at all. I think your husband may be like my husband in that respect." Her eyes twinkling, Lady Jane smiled at Adam.

He grinned. "Truer words were never spoken. What a sensitive woman you are—and what a fortunate man your husband is," he said. Then he added with a dramatic shudder, "However, since I have been away from my beloved's side for so long, I fear my dearest feels she isn't even married. I am very much beginning to believe my winsome wife has grown so independent of her doting husband that she feels she has no spouse at all."

Eve glared at him behind Lady Jane's back, while the countess smiled knowingly. "I can tell how happy you are to be reunited with your wife, the sign of a happily married man. I still wish, though, that I had known you were due back from the Continent."

"It was unexpected," Adam explained. "I do so love to surprise my devoted wife."

"You can say that again," Eve muttered. Only Adam's sharp ears caught it.

"How wonderful for you both," Lady Jane said. "Together again after such a long separation. It must seem as if every day is a brand-new world."

"Oh, happy days," Eve agreed, with only a faint hint of mockery. But espying Adam's mirth-filled expression over Lady Jane's head, she had to count to ten to suppress her desire to boot her hysterical husband out the front door.

"Since your situation has changed, Dr. Eve, you simply cannot refuse my and Asher's invitation to Vauxhall Gardens on Thursday," Jane spoke up. "I've invited you to the gardens several times, and you've refused each time because Dr. Griffin was away. Last time you told me that you couldn't come because the romance of the gardens reminded you too much of Adam and your honeymoon." Jane clapped prettily. "Now that Dr. Griffin is here, he can escort you. You can re-create your honeymoon! I won't take no for an answer."

Which she didn't, no matter how many times Eve tried. The Countess of Wolverton clearly got the results she wanted when she desired; Eve had no doubt it was due to her Van Helsing heritage. And she could also tell from the determined glint in Adam's eye—and his vociferous acceptance—that she had little choice. They were going to attend Vauxhall Gardens with the Ashers.

As Lady Jane exited the front door with a smile and it closed with a bang, Eve turned to Adam. "Sirrah, you forget yourself! How could you accept?" she snapped waspishly, her chin out and her back rigid. "Why did you say we would attend?"

"I had little choice," Adam replied with a grin. "You kept inventing excuses. Besides, Lady Jane's request was just what the doctor ordered." For him. He would get to spend more time in a romantic setting with his beautiful, belligerent bride. "We wouldn't want the world to think our marriage is in trouble before it's really begun. Remember, we're supposed to be a happily married couple."

"Oh, you are just impossible!" Eve hissed, wishing that his little dimples didn't make her feel rather shaky inside. "You brigand. You delight in putting me out of countenance!"

Staring at her, he shook his head, his eyes riveted to her lips. "I'd much rather get you out of something else. However, I have an ulterior motive. The Countess of Wolverton is quite well-known. I encourage the connection. She thinks we're united in wedded bliss, and thus so will the funding committee—if they don't think so already. They should. Your patients are joyous at our matrimonial state, as are your servants," Adam explained patiently. "It's good for your business. Now, my little admiral, tell me what Lady Jane was speaking of when she mentioned all that about gardens and our honeymoon? Was that where we held it?"

"Rubbish, rubbish, and a rubbish pile! We never had a honeymoon, you stupid, stubborn-as-a-mule pirate."

"The countess seems to be under the impression we did," he retorted.

Eve sighed, realizing that the very attractive but infuriating man standing in front of her would fail to leave her alone until she confessed this tiny white lie she had told to decorate the story of her fictitious marriage. But "I don't trust you," she said.

He cocked a brow and shrugged. "Remember you have no choice. And, by the way, though I have been a pirate and a rogue, I am both trustworthy and loyal."

Eve looked up at the high vaulted ceiling, searching for divine inspiration. Her life was in shambles. She should be marching this rake by swordpoint to the top of the Towers and making him walk off. Instead, she found herself explaining her little fibs. He listened patiently, his head cocked to one side, an amused glint in his eyes.

"I merely mentioned to Lady Jane that we spent our honeymoon in the Hanging Gardens of Babylon."

"I see," Adam said, a grin spreading across his face. He shook his head wryly. "Although I do believe that the Hanging Gardens were destroyed during biblical times."

"Oh, well . . . I'm a doctor of the mind, not of history," she snapped.

"Apparently the Countess of Wolverton is neither," he replied, then threw back his head and howled with laughter.

Before Eve could let loose a string of curses that would do her scalawag of a father proud, her medical assistant, Pavlov, arrived with baggage in hand through the open front door. Pavlov had been in France for a short trip to attend the wedding of a close cousin who happened to be one of the undead.

"*Bonjour*, Dr. Eve, it is good to be back," the young Frenchman said earnestly.

An ugly dog following Pavlov spotted Eve and leaped toward her. His fat speckled tongue hanging out, the dog charged up to her, then immediately plopped down and rolled over at her feet, waiting to be petted and adored, his body wriggling. Adam wasn't able to recognize the breed. Its color was a blend of spotted black, red, and gold. It had long hair around the face, and a tail that curled upward, which at the moment was wagging furiously like a demented flag. It was the ugliest mutt Adam had ever seen.

Bending over it, Eve began to stroke the mangy mutt. She greeted her assistant by asking, "Pavlov, how was your trip?"

"Paris was lovely, the wedding such an *affaire de coeur*—and my family was quite happy to have me there for a visit," her assistant replied. He pulled his faithful companion to its paws and then straightened his pristine velvet gold jacket with a flourish. "But now I am eager to get back to work. I have missed the Towers. In spite of all its quirks, it's become home. I hope you have missed me just a bit, *oui?*"

Adam watched this exchange, a little chagrined to note that the young Frenchman was not an unattractive man—although much too young for Eve and much too foppish, what with his gold jacket, lime green vest, and the dark curls all over his head. Just who was this preening peacock, and what was his relationship to his wife? Surely he didn't live here with Eve. Surely Adam's baffling bride wasn't involved with such a foppish fellow and his ugly mutt. He wouldn't stand for it!

Firmly grabbing Eve's hand, Adam pulled her to his side and staked his claim. "She has been much too busy to miss you, now that I am home. And just who in the bloody hell are you?" There was no mistaking the possessive quality of his question, or the mocking threat in his eyes.

Taken aback, the man questioned hesitantly, "Just who are *you*, monsieur?"

"Dr. Adam Griffin. *Her husband*," Adam retorted, ignoring Eve's attempts to loosen her hand from his. She was his wife, and she had better become quickly adjusted to the fact. She really had no idea how lucky she was to have him for a husband, pretend or otherwise.

"I'm her assistant," Pavlov answered, noticing Eve's flashing blue eyes. Ignoring the muscular frame of the man, he asked bravely, "Dr. Eve, is this true? This is your *mari*? Am I finally to meet Dr. Adam Griffin? *Oui*, he is finally here in the flesh?"

"Oh, he's here, all right," Eve said, as Adam squeezed her fingers in warning. "Interfering flesh and all." The last was said in a whisper.

"*Non*. But you are not happy," Pavlov guessed, a bewildered look on his face. Dr. Eve rarely spoke of her husband, but when she did, she was always respectful and cheerful. She was not so now.

Eve started to reply, but realized that she didn't want her assistant to discover the true state of affairs. Pavlov was a brilliant assistant, and he had been very helpful in her work. His behavior patterning had great merit. He also had a humorous bent, and had trained his faithful canine to sit in a chair at the table and eat whenever a dinner bell was rung. It was quite amusing to watch, as long as the demented Hugo didn't get loose. Sometimes the hunchback would ring the bell and no food was served the long-suffering dog—a good dog who always sat patiently waiting in his chair.

"No, everything is fine, Pavlov," she said. "Dr. Griffin and I had a difference of opinion over something at breakfast," she added as Adam squeezed her waist and pressed her closer. His actions had her feeling rather tingly.

"Ah, a lovers' quarrel?" Pavlov remarked thoughtfully.

"If you were French, I would advise you to kiss and make up."

Adam perked up. "I'll take that suggestion, even though I'm not French," he said. He pulled Eve into his arms before she could react, and kissed her greedily. Her mouth tasted of honey, and her lips were soft. She was heaven on earth and sun-kissed raspberries. She was perfect.

Caught up in the kiss, Eve found herself too stunned to protest. The heat from Adam's body and the warmth of his lips seduced her senses. This kiss was quite different from any that she had ever received. As he kissed her, she temporarily became insane. Regardless of her best intentions, Eve found herself heatedly returning the embrace. She wanted his lips to devour hers. This fiery feeling was akin to her burning up in flames, becoming a phoenix reborn. She had experienced nothing like it in all her twenty-seven years on earth or at sea.

Pavlov cleared his throat, interrupting. Embarrassed, Eve pulled back, but Adam held tight to her, his smoldering eyes regarding her with amusement.

Pavlov said, "By the way, Dr. Eve, where is Teeter? He is the butler, *oui*? Shouldn't he be opening the door—or at least Mrs. Fawlty? Aren't they being rather lax in their duties again? I have bags that need to be taken upstairs, and I also purchased some new lab equipment. It's in the carriage and needs to be attended immediately."

"I heard that," a harried-looking Mrs. Fawlty snapped as she crossed the marble floor. "So, you're back from your foreign country with your foreign ways, eh, Pavlov? Humph. I see you brought that foreign nuisance of a dog back, too."

"I beg pardon. My dog is part English setter," the assistant replied.

"Well, be getting on with ye to your room. You'll have

to carry up your own bags, since Teeter is chasing that daft dwarf and his marbles, and the footman is filling the hole in the wine cellar where Fester was digging," Mrs. Fawlty chided. "And you know I'm too frail to be carrying your bags up meself."

Pavlov shook his head, murmuring, *"Quelle dommage. But in this fou place, what else can I expect?"* He wore a slight hint of disgust on his face as he picked up his heavy bags and began hauling them up the main stairs, complaining every few steps.

"You'll have to excuse his manners, Master Adam. Pavlov's. French, you know," Mrs. Fawlty whispered with disgust before scurrying away.

Eve finally managed to break out of her husband's heated clutches. She snapped, "You despicable, depraved, and dangerous dastard! Don't you ever kiss me again!" Then, sucking in a sharp breath, she fled the great pretender—and even better kisser. She really hated having a husband, with the exception of his kisses. Those she'd quite enjoyed. So her betraying father was going to pay for his folly with blood.

CHAPTER TWELVE

East of Eden, and Way Beyond

Though Eve left in a decided huff, Adam didn't take it personally. She had every right to be angry. But he knew that part of her anger hinged on the fact that she didn't understand how he could help her with the unhinged. Although at the moment he didn't know a whole bloody lot about her insane business, that didn't mean that he couldn't learn. Adam had realized long ago that life was a balancing act, especially whenever he took on a new role. And being a doctor would be only slightly more unbalancing than trying to get Eve with child. Which was the only way the cunning Captain Bluebeard would forgive his double-dealing and be content at having a grandchild, even if it was Adam's.

Adam shrugged. All life was basically a risk, and this risk was well worth the gain. For over a decade he had floated along like a piece of driftwood, willing to let life's currents take him from shore to shore. No more. Eve had met her match, and so had Captain Bluebeard. They just didn't know it yet. And so had the patients in this house of the deranged.

"Time to get down to business," he said. A visit to the loony ward was in order.

As he approached the arched entranceway to the patients' ward, he ran into Eve's assistant. Behind the Frenchman was his ugly mutt, bushy tail wagging and wearing a goofy doggy smile.

Pavlov nodded at Adam, curiosity evident in his expression. "*Bonjour*, Dr. Griffin. I had not thought to see you again so soon. Are you going to start evaluating patients now? *Non*, I thought you might want to rest after your long trip."

Adam knew opportunity when it knocked—or, as the case might be, when the dog licked. The pooch had slurped on his hand. Leaning down, he patted the homely beast on its massive head and said, "I thought I would take a quick peek around and immerse myself. I think I should study each patient's history before I begin treatments."

"*Oui*. I'd be happy to introduce you to some of the patients and their *folie*—madness—if you'd like." Seeing his dog delivered into ecstasy by Dr. Griffin's deft touch, Pavlov added, "Let me introduce you to my furry assistant, Junger. He's part mastiff and part English setter—with a hint of corgi, I believe."

Adam nodded as Junger sat up straighter and then happily lifted his paw to be shaken, at which point Adam grinned. The dog was certainly no beauty, but it did appear well trained and intelligent.

"Junger helps a great deal in my research."

"How?" Adam wondered aloud. Did it chase the loons about the place, or find them if they became lost?

Pavlov started to walk down the limestone hallway. "Well, I am working on a therapy about managing behavior, and I practice on Junger. I hope to help patients over-come addictions to rum and opium by retraining their impulses. Can you imagine trying to stop drinking when all you desire in life is a drink? Impossible! Drink becomes everything—lover, friend, all your desires. My therapy, I call behavior patterning. I hope someday it will help many. Perhaps even those with strange compulsions such as repeatedly washing their hands or reorganizing their wardrobes. Dr. Eve hopes to be able to use my research for vampires with oral fixations. Currently I am trying to get Junger to associate pleasure with the sound of a bell, to reinforce good behavior and punish the bad. Addiction can be so . . . tragic."

Yes, Adam had seen firsthand the wicked wages of ad-diction. They not only stole life; they stole hope as well. Though he wasn't fond of this little Frenchman, his goal did sound impressive. "Very worthwhile, I'm sure. Have you met with much success?" His opinion of the little frog was changing slightly. In fact, if Pavlov wasn't interested in seducing Eve, he could grow to like the little fellow.

"I've only began working with the dog. Junger now eats whenever he hears a bell. Unfortunately, with Hugo Lambert ringing bells day and night, Junger has put on a bit of weight."

Adam didn't try to hide his amusement. "I'd like to meet this Hugo character. He sounds like a noisy, nasty little plague—a character straight from Bedlam."

"*Cela va sans dire*. That goes without saying. He is *fou*—crazy, Hugo, but he's asleep now, and trust me, we don't want to wake him up." The Frenchman actually shuddered at the thought. "Hugo was picked up off the streets when he was eight for picking pockets. From there he was sent to an orphanage, where the monks let him ring the bells, making him their unofficial bell ringer. He became obsessed with bells, so the good monks sent him here. This turn of events was fortunate for Hugo, but unfortunate for us, since this old house has a bell tower."

Adam chortled at Pavlov's expression, while the assistant continued with his complaints. "Hugo's also obsessed with marbles. He likes to drop his down the bell tower steps when we are trying to put him back in his room."

"Does he lose his marbles often?" Adam asked.

Pavlov sighed. "At least once a week, the demented old dwarf. He's a master at picking locks and escaping the inescapable. So we're oftentimes bombarded with bells."

"I see. He's a menace," Adam said.

"*Oui, exactement.* But he's *our* menace." Pavlov sighed. "Dr. Eve treats all her in-house patients as eccentric relatives. She—*Merde*, what am I saying? You know your wife and her work. I know she writes to you faithfully at least once a month to tell you of her problems and solutions. At least, I have seen her writing the letters in her study. . . ."

Adam jerked his head in a brisk nod. He might not know Eve Bluebeard, alias Eve Griffin, well yet, but he intended to know her very well as soon and as often as possible. And in the biblical sense.

Pointing to a door, the Frenchman opened it briefly. Adam stuck his head inside and saw a large stone gargoyle perched upon a massive stone fireplace mantel, albeit a rather short fireplace. The mantel was three feet from the floor and quite thick. The large and oddly constructed fireplace took up almost half the space in the room. There was only a small bed and chair, and an encoignure rested in one corner with several books and a large candle set upon it.

Pavlov closed the door, and they continued their journey. "Mr. Carlen, as you can see, is a mad gargoyle. Since it's daylight, he is in his stone form at present. Yet when it is night and the stone becomes flesh, Mr. Carlen remains as if stone. *Catatonic* is the word they are using now for his malaise."

"What does Dr. Eve think causes this catatonia?"

"Dr. Eve thinks it has something to do with fear—a very great fear."

Adam pictured the rather odd fireplace, and suddenly he knew. "He's afraid of heights!"

"*Oui.* Mr. Carlen has vertigo."

Adam shook his head, recalling various gargoyles he had seen atop towering spires in France and Germany. "Hmmm. I surmise that for a gargoyle that would be a tad upsetting."

Pavlov nodded.

He next halted outside a very clean door, which looked like it had been scourged again and again, what with missing wood chips and the smell of lye wafting from the old oak. Indicating the door, Pavlov explained, "This patient is Mrs. Gina Monkfort. She's our newest. Dr. Eve is still evaluating her, but already we know that Mrs. Monkfort has an obsession with cleanliness. She even washes her own *water!*"

Adam cocked a brow, but Pavlov shrugged. "What can one say? They do claim cleanliness is next to godliness. So she's a saint," Pavlov finished emphatically.

"Is that why she's here? She washes water?" Adam asked.

"Only a small part. She's a widow, once married to a wereboar, for over seventeen years. I gather from what Dr.

Eve has said that Mrs. Monkfort's husband was rather a piggish fellow. Always snuffling around the house with his piggy hooves all muddy, snuffling at the clean linens and leaving dirt all over. Dr. Eve concluded that Mrs. Monkfort has stored up rage over her husband's messiness. When he died, the rage came out as an obsession to have everything always as clean as possible. Mrs. Monkfort can't handle the disorder of dirt, and seeks to control her environment."

Knocking on the door elicited a voice calling out, "You may enter if your hands are clean and you've washed behind your ears."

Adam entered the room and assessed its lone occupant. Seventeen years of wedlock had left their mark, and all beauty lay in the past. The woman's gestures were erratic and encompassed massive amounts of cleaning, always keeping her fretful hands busy. Today the widow was dressed in black, though crocheting a monstrous white lace blanket that looked like a gigantic spider web.

Nodding politely, Adam watched the widow don glasses and check him over from the top of his head to the soles of his boots. Her gaze was in no way seductive, but studious.

"I'd like to introduce Dr. Eve's husband, Dr. Griffin," Pavlov said.

Mrs. Monkfort sat down and wrinkled her nose at Adam, still inspecting him like a bug under glass. Finally finished, she put a distressed hand to her mouth. "Oh, my, you have dirt on your boots! I must clean it immediately." And so saying, she rose and went over to one of several large buckets of water.

Glancing up at them with a moue of distaste, she

137

asked, "Do you know what's in this water? I do. It's disgustingly horrid, nasty, and dirty."

In a soothing voice, Pavlov addressed her. "The *eau* is fine, Mrs. Monkfort. Mrs. Fawlty cleaned it especially for you this morning. Besides, you know what Dr. Eve has said about your cleaning constantly. Have you been a bad girl today?"

Mrs. Monkfort lowered her head. "I . . . couldn't help it. My door was reeking, so I did what I must. After all, I am a lady."

Pavlov shook his head. "So you cleaned your door. Anything else?"

Sneaking a peek out of the corner of her eye, the woman frowned at the short Frenchman. "Maybe."

Adam found the dialogue strangely fascinating. There were more screws loose in this place than he had originally thought. If the Towers were a clock, time would stop. "I think I see. Water is a wellspring of hope, is it not?" he said.

Raising her eyes to meet his, she nodded. "Yes, it is. *You* understand why I cleaned my shoes and the maid's shoes."

"And?" Adam probed gently.

"I might have cleaned Mrs. Fawlty's too," she admitted reluctantly, staring off into the distance, a guilty look on her face. The silence finally compelled her to speak. "Oh," she said crossly. "She had such dirty shoes! They had smudges on them, and flour, and were just reeking of grime."

Again Adam probed. "Anyone else? Confession is cleansing to the soul," he said.

Letting out an exasperated sigh, she nodded. "Yes, I

138

suppose it is. And I am clean, sparkling like a star." Noting Pavlov's little frown, she admitted, "I also cleaned that nasty little leprechaun's shoes. And don't frown at me, Mr. Pavlov, because Fester had been out digging in that messy, dirty garden again, and you know how dirty dirt can be."

Pavlov shook his head and looked at Adam. *"Comprendez-vous.* Fester is forever digging holes here, there, and everywhere. Which reminds me, Mrs. Monkfort, you must take care. Don't take a walk at night without a lantern or you'll end up falling into one of Fester's pits."

Studying Pavlov, Adam again began to wonder if there truly was some hidden gold. He would use his considerable talents to solve this puzzle sooner rather than later.

"That grimy little leprechaun should be kicked out of the Towers for bringing in all that nasty dirt. He's insane, you know," Mrs. Monkfort confided sagely, her head bobbing like a broken jack-in-the-box. Holding up her skirt she added, "See how my slippers sparkle? Not a bit of pig drool on them. Did I mention I also scrubbed the hallway? It was a veritable dirt hill out there. Of course, that was before I came."

Pavlov seemed torn between trying to reprove or soothe her. He finally decided on the latter. *"Oui.* I must say our shoes and hallways have never looked so nice."

Adam bit his lip to keep from chuckling. The weird widow smiled happily and picked back up the large white spiderish-looking mass she was crocheting.

Making their good-byes, Pavlov and Adam hurriedly left, closing the sparkling clean door behind them. Eve's assistant frowned. "I don't know if Dr. Eve will able to break Mrs. Monkfort of her obsessions or not."

Smiling sympathetically, Adam remarked, "In the words of James Boswell, '*Spree meliora.*'"

Pavlov smiled, working out the Latin. "I *do* hope for better things. Thank you, Dr. Griffin. I too shall pray for that poor deluded woman." His expression was rather somber as they walked down the hall to another set of rooms. "Mr. Jack Rippington's room is here. A fascinating case. Rippington used to be a barrister in London, where he earned the reputation of being crazy like a fox. Not surprising, since he is a werefox. Tragically, when a young kit, he fell deeply in love with a vampire named Rose. She was staked. This loss caused him to acquire some rather peculiar habits as he grew."

"What kind of problems?" Adam asked.

"Prickly problems, which made his family send him to us. He had embarrassed them rather infamously at a ball. He's known now as Jack the Rip."

"What is the little peculiarity that landed him here, and why the odd nickname?" Adam pressed, not wanting to beat around the bush any longer.

Pavlov sighed. "The nickname really says it all. He . . . rips off his clothes and exposes himself . . . to rosebushes."

Ouch, Adam thought. A sticky business, trying to cure a man who flashed his prick at pricker bushes. "The man must be mad."

"*Cela va sans dire.*"

"Quite so," Adam remarked. "'That goes without saying.' Quite so."

CHAPTER THIRTEEN

The Good, the Bad,
and the Good and the Mad

The skies were an ominous gray that perfectly matched Eve's mood, as did the aging buildings she was passing. Although Eve had seen a hundred docksides while growing up in ports around the world, they always depressed her. The taverns were shabby, and the patrons a dirty and uncouth lot living in abject poverty. Garbage always lined the streets, and the sewage smells were enough to put a person off her food.

Again Eve cursed her father for his interfering ways, and for having to seek him out in one of his favorite haunts. When she found him, she didn't know what she would do, but she did know that the coming confrontation would not be pleasant. Especially if she unleashed her formidable temper. "Loose lips sink ships," Eve muttered, remembering this fact well, since her father had drummed it into her as a child. He'd always advocated a united front for the Bluebeard family, no matter how bad things got. Of course, he was usually the one causing problems. "I shan't pull out his blue beard or curse a blue streak and threaten his liver. I shan't call him an infernal interfering boil on the arse of humanity," she reminded herself.

By her side, her butler nodded. He'd driven her here in the asylum trap. "That's right, Dr. Eve. I wouldn't think you should."

Eve gave an inarticulate grunt. "Don't get mad, get even," she muttered.

Teeter glanced around, taking in the rough-hewn cobblestone path. "Get who?"

She rolled her eyes. "No one. I meant, I shouldn't be angry; I should get even with that callous conniver who calls himself my father. He'll rue the day he crossed me!"

Teeter replied anxiously, his Adam's apple bobbing, "I wouldn't threaten to break his bottles of rum or lock him in a treasure chest and throw away the key, like you did the last time."

Eve glared at her butler. Then, continuing her search, she found her ire increasing, but no Captain Bluebeard.

"My father is like a hammerhead shark—hammering away until he gets what he wants," she complained. "Doesn't matter what he destroys in the process. Like my very fine life. Oh, no! He wants me married, pirate-booted, and pregnant, the old-fashioned reprobate. To his mind, a woman's made to stay on a ship for her master's pleasure, bearing his children and cleaning the poop deck. Perhaps wielding a cutlass in times of emergency. For him, one female is much like the others. Hence his seven marriages. He's a barbarian, the ripe old cod!"

As the afternoon wore on, Eve discovered that the

captain wasn't at the Barbary Coast Pub, the Sword and Crossbones, or Thatch Blackbeard's Den of Scurvy. Finally she located her father at Lafitte's Pride, a regular nest of pirates with a few landlubbers thrown in for good measure. Materlinck, both the bartender and an aspiring writer, waved her through to the back, where her father was holding court by telling outrageous tales of his high-seas adventures.

The smoky room teemed with rough characters. Some wore eye patches, others earrings, and a few sported peg legs. There were scarred faces, grizzled beards, and smelly bodies, and a continual din of grumbling voices. Through the hazy atmosphere and the window's faint light, Eve spotted Captain Bluebeard sitting by a grimy hearth, with his back against the wall—the only way her father sat in a room full of cutthroats—a smile on his face. He was smoking his corncob pipe.

Turning to Teeter, Eve noted her father's condition. "At least he isn't castaway yet. I wish you to stay here by the bar." Seeing her butler's pleading eyes, she relented. "Yes, you can get yourself an ale."

Teeter's delighted grin spread from ear to ear, which had her hastily adding, "*One* ale. Only one. I need you to drive us back. Read my lips. No new taxies."

The grin fled as quickly as it had appeared, and the ogrish butler peered down his very long nose at her. Eve ignored his wounded expression and marched over to her father, pushing through the mass of disgustingly dirty humanity.

Catching sight of his daughter, Captain Bluebeard grinned. His dark blue eyes lit with joy, his lips twisting into a knowing smirk. The cat was out of the bag, the vampire out of the coffin, and the pirate off his ship. *Ship ahoy!* His daughter's prow was true and straight, and she was approaching at ramming speed.

Captain Bluebeard's smirk only made Eve's blood heat to the boiling point. "I'll personally kick his Tortuga," she muttered, but halted abruptly when she reached him. Ignoring his disreputable drinking companions—his crew were beyond three sheets to the wind, were more like eight sheets into a full-blown hurricane—Eve let loose her own personal nor'easter. "What skullduggery have you set loose in my asylum?"

Bluebeard chortled. "Skullduggery, you say? Just exactly what are you accusing me of?"

Eve didn't fall for the look of indignation that quickly covered her father's rugged face. The old scalawag was playing it for all he was worth. "You really should tread the boards on land, not on sea. Don't fash me, father. As if you didn't know! You can forget the protestations of innocence. You haven't been innocent since the day you were born. Knowing you, I bet you swiped the cookie of the baby next to you!"

Planting a large hand on his chest, Bluebeard groaned, playing to the audience of blasted buccaneers seated around the table. "To think me own dearest daughter speaks to her da like this. Doesn't trust me. Just breaks me heart, it does."

Eve stamped her foot. "If the eye patch fits, wear it!"

"Evie, my love, shiver me timbers. How cold is a thankless child!"

Glaring at her father's companions, Eve snapped out her next words: "Do you louts think you could pretend to be gentlemen for once, and leave me to speak with this old scalawag alone?"

The three pirates hastily departed, Ol' Peg almost getting his wooden leg caught in a spittoon. Drunk or not, none of Bluebeard's sea dogs wanted to get in the middle of this father-and-daughter talk; the Bluebeards' bites and their barks were equally bad.

Pulling out a chair, Bluebeard nodded for Eve to sit down. She obliged warily, plotting her options. Then temper won out. "How dare you presume to invent a husband for me when I've already invented one myself! It's utterly despicable! I want Adam whatever-his-name-is out of my life tonight! And I do mean *tonight!*" She lowered her voice to keep the tavern's crooked customers from overhearing, she didn't need to be blackmailed by this scurvy lot. Though, with the din of the crowd and the fact that most were so drunk they wouldn't remember much of anything, she wasn't too worried.

The Captain squinted. "Is someone pretending to be your husband? Why, I'll run him through, I will."

Eve scoffed. "That look hasn't worked on me since I took my hair out of pigtails."

Bluebeard fought down his pride. Instead of praising her courage he complained, "It's just unnatural for a daughter not to fear her da." But Eve had a good wind, all right, no doubt about it.

"It's unnatural for a father to pay a man to pretend to be my husband," she retorted, clenching her fists. She needed that money much worse than did the wastrel who was being paid to be her loving husband. In fact, she wanted to beg her father for some of his treasure right now, but knew she never could with the terms of surrender. They would be too heavy: Close the asylum and marry that hateful Hook.

"A pox on yer fears, daughter. Ye should trust me!"

Girding herself for more battle, Eve let nothing show on her face. She wasn't her father's child for nothing, having his fierce determination to be victorious. She would stay afloat without Captain Bluebeard's plundered, pirated, sunk-shipped treasure.

Her father said, "You gave me no choice, lassie. Wedded bliss is a fine state, a holy state between man and woman. Marriage is forever and, well . . ." He hesitated before nodding. "Marriage is blissfully blissful."

"How droll! How can you say that when you've been married *seven* times?"

The captain remained unrepentant, ignoring her scorn. "Well, now, it took a bit of practice. But I got it right with your dear mother."

"Humph," Eve grumbled, shaking her head.

"Now see here, missy, no need to get on your high horse. 'Tis true—marriage is a fine state with the right companion. It's not me fault that six of me wives were she-devils in disguise."

Eve snorted inelegantly. "None of your wives were demons."

Bluebeard shrugged. "Nay, ye're right. They were worse. Me first wife was a witch. Mean-tempered, with a wart on her as—" Realizing what he had been about to reveal, he quickly said, "Never mind where the wart was. Just know that she was a stomach-churning shrew, always spewing curses and stinking up me ship with her boiling cauldron and mumbo jumbo. Me second wife was made more for the bliss bit of matrimony, but she just didn't have a strong constitution. Of course, it wasn't her constitution that got her in the end, just her poor eyesight."

Eve nodded, for she had heard the story a time or two when her father was in his cups.

"Aye. Imagine mistaking a crocodile for a stepping-stone," Bluebeard reminisced. "We were married only four years. I never should have taken her to Africa."

"At least not without her spectacles."

"True, true. But then, she was a vain woman, even on nature walks," he replied, pursing his lips. "So she died looking better than she saw."

After a moment he frowned, recalling his third wife. "Holly was a true beauty in every respect, but she couldn't keep her nose out of me treasure chests. Could sing like an angel, and could wield a cutlass better than most of me sailors. But she was a hard-hearted wench who loved gold more than me. And the rolling of the sea made her queasy."

"Should have been hanged from the yardarm," Eve remarked sardonically.

"She was," Bluebeard replied, and then added with a contented sigh, "In Port-a-Prince, after putting her hands on the governor's chest.

"Now, yer mother was the best of the lot. Six was me lucky charm. Yer mother was a real lady with a heart of gold. She was me real treasure. Loved me with all her heart and never played me false, even if she couldn't tell north from south or hit the broad side of a barn with a cannon. Still, I loved her dearly."

Eve's anger died a little in the face of her father's adoration.

"She was my pride and joy—just like you are," the crafty old pirate added. He loved his daughter, warts, nuthouse, and all. "That's why I picked a handsome, fine husband for you. A good solid Irishman, with a touch of piracy, a touch of the English, and a seducer's touch as well. His father was a baron, ye know."

"No, I didn't," Eve said, "and I don't care. Besides, I think one pirate in the family is enough." That Adam had been into pillaging the seven seas with a bunch of cutthroats was another point against him—a big, fat point. "And I find him neither fine nor handsome," she lied.

Bluebeard pinched her cheek. "Never try to lie to a liar, lass, or cheat a cheater—or outman the man of the sea. They'll give you no quarter."

Eve glared, hating the fact that her father knew her so well. "I didn't say he was *ugly*, now, did I? This Adam character might be fairly attractive, for argument's sake, but I'm not in the market for a husband. As you well know!"

"Of course not, Evie. You already have one." Her father laughed.

"Da, if you don't get rid of him, I'll have him thrown in prison for pretending to be someone he's not."

Her father glared at her. "I don't think so, lass. I have a friend or two in some pretty high places."

"Of course you do," she snapped. "But that won't stop me from declaring him an impostor. Adam is looking at a fall."

"Adam won't be arrested for pretending to be anything, for he's the very man ye married in Vienna. Or so I shall say. Already those busybody doctor friends of yours think he's yer husband. How will they feel about giving their coins to a woman who says her husband isn't her husband, yet who pretended he was her husband when he was pretending to be that same husband?"

Shaking her head, trying to decipher that sentence, Eve finally got the gist, and the jest was unhappily on her. Dr. Sigmund and Count Caligari would never give her their foundation funds if they realized she was a liar and a fraud. It was all as she'd feared. "You bloody-minded, conniving, conspiring crab!"

The Captain's face became a mottled red, and he fought the urge to turn his grown daughter over his knee and paddle her bottom as if she were still a child. "You're one to talk! That's like the pot calling the kettle a Bluebeard. Look who's the calculating chit, pulling a spouse out of thin air with nothing more than her overactive imagination."

"Well, I certainly learned from the best!"

The captain stood, pointing a finger. "Adam stays as your husband. If ye so much as breathe a word to anyone that he isn't, I will personally see that the good mind doctors find out the whole story. Ye will be ruined in the scientific community. Ruined in any society, scientific or otherwise—except on a pirate ship, which is where ye belong anyway, so don't tempt me!"

Eve's chin quivered, but she held back her tears. "You hard-hearted barnacle! For how long am I supposed to play house?"

"I want grandkids, lass."

She shot him a look of pure horror. "Sleep with him? We're not really married!"

"Now, don't get your sails in a knot. I have a plan," he confided craftily.

"Why am I not surprised?" she muttered, her eyes aching with the sting of sorrow, yet her demeanor rigidly polite.

"Adam is to be your husband for only a while. Then, unluckily, he dies and you're a widow—free to marry a flesh-and-blood person!"

"*He* might have something to say about dying just to please this plan. I know I do. I don't like the lying lout, but I won't let you murder him," she retorted abruptly. What a waste! Not many men were so dashing that they could make a lady's toes curl by kissing her silly. "When did you become so bloody bloodthirsty?"

The captain rolled his eyes and shook his head, his weathered face revealing his annoyance. "I'm a pirate. What do you expect? But I wouldn't do him in. Since he's yer pretend husband, it will be a pretend death. But we'll have one fine and dandy funeral for him."

"A real funeral?" She was beginning to get mixed-up.

"Of course, real. A fancy funeral for a fine man, so that all will know ye to be a poor widow."

Eve stomped her feet, then stood with legs apart, hands braced on her hips. Ironically, so did her father.

"Let me get this straight," Eve managed to mutter through clenched teeth. She had gone beyond vexation into pure rage. "You've made me accept an impostor as a spouse so that you can pretend to kill him off so I can be a fraudulent widow?"

"You'll be a widow for only a short time, lass. Then I'll see ye married good and proper."

"I see," Eve said in stunned disbelief. Her deceitful da was even more devious than she had previously thought.

Plopping back down in her chair, Eve slowly shook her head. "We have a room in the Towers if you're interested, because you've gone barmy, I declare! Madder than any patient of mine," she growled, her eyes shooting sparks. "How could you?"

"Not mad, just crazy like a fox—even though me bloodline's pure werewolf. Still, I'm canny as a wolf, and you should be overjoyed. Since Adam isn't as fine or as

handsome as ye like, ye can marry me boon companion,"
the old salt suggested, waiting to see if Eve would take
Hook, line, and sinker. He knew he had to continue to
advance while her guard was down.

Eve just blinked. Her father intended her to marry
the nefarious Captain Hook? "I think I'll keep Adam,"
she replied sarcastically.

Bluebeard shook his head. "No, lass. Adam is a fine fellow for an impoverished impersonator, but I want a real
pirate for a son-in-law. See, it's just like I always told you,
lassie: every cloud has a silver lining—and if one doesn't,
you just steal it."

"Never. I'll never, ever marry Captain Hook!" Giving
her father one last baleful look, she turned sharply on her
heel, shoved her way through a dirty dozen or two, and
stalked back to where Teeter had just ordered his third ale.

Grabbing the mug from him, she downed the strong
brew in less than a minute, without choking once—an
advantage of having lived on a pirate ship.

So, her father wanted her married to Hook, and by
crook. But she wouldn't marry the heinous Hook, and she
wouldn't sleep with Adam. She would be captain of her
own destiny. Maybe not tonight or tomorrow, but soon.
"Well, as soon as I can come up with a plan to upset the
old pirate cart," she muttered to herself.

Teeter started to argue as his mistress drank the last few
drops of his ale, but seeing her harried expression, he decided that his two previous mugs were quite enough for the
time being. He would raid the wine cellar later—perhaps
with Mrs. Fawlty, if she were in the mood for high romance.

Eve cursed and set down the mug. Her father had just
trimmed her sails without a shot being fired. "Blast him
and all men to smithereens!" she growled, shoving Teeter

out of the tavern and into the darkness of coming night.

"Where's our bloody carriage?" she asked sourly. Twisting the pearls around her throat, she realized that in her anger she had forgotten her father's cardinal rule: "Early to rise and early to strike makes a pirate healthy, wealthy and wise," she repeated. Well, it didn't rhyme but it was true. Her father had struck swift and early, his aim deadly accurate, and now she was trapped in a pretend marriage.

CHAPTER FOURTEEN

The Good, the Bad, and the Truly Mad

The horse-drawn carriage took both Eve and Teeter back to the Towers after her unpleasant visit with her father. Any other night Eve might have taken a moment to appreciate the spaciously noble building and its lush location. As an inheritance, it was grand. The house had been set upon a slight hill, and had a fine view of a meadow and woodlands. Its lofty walls and soaring spires had been raised when Elizabeth I was queen. Now the walls were dark gray with age and mellowed by centuries of weather, and covered in a variety of deep green ivy and flowering plants.

Walking inside the asylum, Eve found it more than odd that the place appeared deserted. Before she could become thoroughly worried, however, a loud disturbance outside caught her attention. Eve discovered as she opened the balcony doors that sounds of merriment grew louder. Perplexed, she stepped down the terraced steps to find a fairyland. Under the soft golden glow of the moon, and hundreds of colored Japanese lanterns, Eve watched her patients and servants mill about the yard with plates of food in their hands, or tap their feet to an orchestra.

"Why is there an orchestra here?" she asked. It was true that music soothed the savage beast, but it wasn't even a full moon yet.

Eve narrowed her eyes in disbelief as she took in the scene before her. Between tall Greek pillars crowned by heraldic beasts or Nosferatu or wereanimals, she spied curious faces laughing and frolicking. Everyone appeared in a rather boisterous and rowdy mood. It was a little after nine at night, and it seemed the madhouse had moved into Eve's garden. She didn't know whether to frown or smile. So often the insane were trapped in silent, ugly worlds, but tonight was certainly different—as evidenced by the chaotic sounds of laughter and mayhem.

"What on earth is going on?" she asked as Teeter came to stand beside her. Glancing up at his homely face, she could tell from his expression that he was as clueless as she. "Who ever heard of a nighttime picnic for the insane? Who ever heard of any picnic for the insane? Who ever thought up this particular folly should have *their* head examined!" She hoped her paranormal patients didn't decide to eat the servants.

Teeter volunteered a comment nervously. "Madam, the lunatics might escape into the night. If they do, they'll turn London upside down with their strange behavior. What will we do?"

Eve's face clouded as she assessed the situation. So far, everyone appeared to be in fine form, behaving themselves. Did she dare break it up and become the bad guy? No. "I guess we wait and see. And, speaking of duties, I see Hugo." She pointed to the bellicose bell-ringing dwarf. His face was cast mainly in shadow, but she could see his weak chin and the slash of his mouth.

"But we weren't speaking of duties," Teeter complained.

Eve almost smiled and let him off, but a punishment was a punishment, else a ship would go to rack and ruin and a madhouse would be run by its inmates. "Come now, Teeter, it's not so bad. Hugo is playing quietly with his marbles. And see? Sir Loring is watching as well," Eve cajoled. "With avid interest," she added. Upon closer inspection, she had noted that it was not Hugo's marbles that had mesmerized Sir Loring, but rather the dwarf's fat little neck. "Go and tend Hugo now. And see that Sir Loring is fed immediately."

As he left, Eve directed her attention to finding the culprit who had devised this foolishness. To her direct right Mrs. Monkfort was standing on the large marble fountain. Eve assumed that it was so that the widow wouldn't get her feet dirty. Mrs. Monkfort was busy admonishing Mr. Pryce not to land in the potato pie with his grubby little wings. "There's a fly in the ointment, which gives me heart palpitations," she was saying. "Where are my smelling salts?"

Eve raised her eyes to the heavens, hoping heaven would grant her a bit of peace from this day from hell. Her insane patients were having a picnic outside? Yet, to give the devil his due—in this case Adam?—most appeared to be behaving remarkably well. With the exception of Mr. Jack Rippington, who Eve reluctantly noticed, was currently sneaking up on a pair of innocent rosebushes with his pants undone. Fortunately, Pavlov was a mere few feet behind him, evidently having been given Jack the Rip watch.

Sighing in relief, Eve continued her earnest search of the area for the viper in her garden, a particularly tricky little serpent whom she knew was responsible for this nighttime folly. Her enemy was crafty and quite deviously charming, what with his sharp wit and twinkling hazel eyes. And she absolutely would not remember his kiss. He had to go—and the sooner the better. She couldn't have him usurping her authority and ordering picnics with orchestras and champagne without so much as a by-your-leave.

Turning her head to the left, she found him. His powerful build stood out among the members of her staff, and he was jauntily telling some story that had everyone chuckling.

Hurrying over, she nodded briefly at her staff, then pulled on his shoulder to get him to bend close. She hissed in his ear, "I'd really like to throttle you. You make me so hot!"

"The feeling is mutual," Adam replied. Eve brought out the little devil in him. In fact, staring at her, he felt as if a runaway carriage had hit him, and his little devil was looking to get in something holey. "You must stop glaring like that, my love, or people will start to talk" he said. "We wouldn't want to give them something to talk about."

"You cretin! Did you give the orders for this picnic?"

Some of the people in the small group moved away, looking surprised by her cross tone. Adam, however, seemed unfazed. "Of course, my love."

Grabbing him by the arm, she dragged him a distance to a large oak tree. Under it, more in shadow than light, they were isolated by soft darkness from the surrounding crowd and provided the illusion of being alone in a sea of soft lights.

Although she longed to shout and jump, Eve kept her voice low. "You are overstepping yourself again. You had no right to throw a picnic for my patients."

"Don't be a gudgeon. How can I be overstepping my bounds when I'm your husband?"

"Stop saying that. You're not real. I made you up, remember?"

"Aren't you a little old to have imaginary friends? Besides, I'm as real as the next man—and a lot more fun to play with."

"Never!"

"Never," he warned, his voice between a growl and a purr, "say never to me. I love a challenge too much to resist making you eat your words."

"You should be flogged and hung from the quarter mast. You have no right to even be here. I won't live a lie!"

"You already have been," Adam reminded her. "My little pearl, you don't have to do everything alone anymore. You need a husband to warm your bed and your heart. You need help. It's so much more pleasant when you share the burdens of everyday life along with the pleasures."

Eve drew herself up to her full five-foot-two inches with an indignant gasp. "How dare you, sirrah! I fear you have a sad lack of character. I have absolutely no interest in the married state. I know *exactly* what I need! After all, I'm the doctor!"

Adam sighed, shaking his head. Women could be such . . . well, *women*. But while Eve might not care for him now, she needed him. That much was obvious, after only a night and one day. Her patients needed him, too. Eve had too much on her plate, and the asylum's inhabitants needed another quick mind—a less serious mind—to ease their burdens. Eve could cure them, but he would make them laugh. "You're a bossy little thing, aren't you?" he said.

"I prefer to call it instructive," she replied, trying to lessen her temper, for she knew the value of a cool head when under attack. Especially when the attack was one of hot charm, skill, and witty seduction.

"That you are," he agreed with a wicked smile. And passionate—a nature he intended to capitalize upon. "Just think of instruction in bed."

A charged silence hung in the air between them, and in the soft glow of moonlight and lanterns Eve's eyes widened. Adam's face stood out in stark relief, ruggedly handsome. Staring at him, she had to forcefully remember to ignore the way he made her feel, the quickening of her pulse and the butterflies in her stomach. She drew on her previous anger. "How *could* you order up a midnight picnic without consulting me?"

"The patients seemed depressed, so I thought this might cheer them up."

"Of course they're depressed. It comes with the territory," Eve argued. "They are insane!"

Adam lifted a brow. "Territory?"

"Their madness," Eve whispered. "Mad people are often melancholy. Often their terrors are such that they can't speak of them. And some patients are sad because they know they're mad and want only to be normal. Wouldn't you get tired of living in dark shadows and endless pits of despair? Not to be melodramatic—I get enough of that around here as it is."

Glancing around, Adam regarded the patients. "They don't seem sad now. For once they are forgetting their sorrows." He smiled engagingly. "By the way, how was the visit with your father?"

"My father is the devil's tool," she snapped. "And just how did you know I went to visit him?"

Adam pointed to his head. "I would have done the same. Tell me, how did the old reprobate take your scold?"

"None of your business," she replied.

"It's a rare female who can keep a secret from her husband," he suggested mischievously. "Besides, I know your father. He told you the marriage stands. He quite likes me, you know."

"I can't imagine why. But then, the Captain has never been known for his good taste—with the exception of marrying my mother."

"You'll have to include me in his good taste now. I wouldn't want you to feel disadvantaged in marrying me. I wouldn't want you to feel disappointed."

"Oh, I'm disappointed, all right. You're still here."

"Making merry with your patients and finding ways for them to have fun," he agreed. "See?" He pointed.

Eve glanced over and found, to her surprise, that her lovely fountain was now brimming with ripe red apples. Next to the large marble edifice were some patients and staff, including Jack Rippington, who was at least now standing with his pants buttoned. Rippington was actually smiling for once, and looked interested in bobbing for apples.

"My fountain has apples in it," Eve remarked stupidly, feeling rather dull-witted. "And Jack is there. Not by any rosebushes."

Adam shrugged with that devil-may-care attitude that Eve found distracting. "I thought it was better for all concerned that Jack the Rip should be bobbing for apples and not bobbing for roses—or any other females of this picnic. Furthermore, every Eden should have apples. Besides, you know what they say—an apple a day keeps the doctor at play."

As Rippington bent to bob, Mrs. Monkfort suddenly pointed a finger at Mr. Pryce, shrieking, "He's returned! The fly's returned, and he's masticating on apples! Nasty flying creature. We're cursed! Cursed by the fly." And before anyone could stop her, she began swatting him with one of her numerous handkerchiefs until he buzzed off. As others replaced Mr. Pryce, Mrs. Monkfort shook her head, trying to recover. Staring into the fountain, she said, "I know what's in that water. Do you? It's repulsive. I wouldn't duck *my* head in it."

"Bobbing for apples?" Eve said. "At a picnic?"

"I told you, I thought it would keep them busy. You know—fun and games," Adam teased. Then winked at her. "Or maybe you don't. You're much too serious, you know."

"Oh, I think I could come up with one or two games," Eve remarked, a sly smile on her face.

"When you look like that," said Adam, "I don't think I want to know."

"I could suggest tar and feathers to them. And I know just who should be tarred."

"I'm sure you do," he agreed, almost wincing at the memory of a time he'd seen a man tarred and feathered in Penzance. The unfortunate victim, Sullivan, had looked like a half-plucked turkey for weeks. "Generally I would be happy to be at your disposal, and feathers would be fine, but the tar I must protest. Not my style at all. Besides, they are too busy bobbing."

Eve's attention turned back as Hugo submerged almost

completely in the water, but he came up with a nice red apple caught between his crooked front teeth.

"See, the midnight picnic was a fine idea!" Adam crowed. "They need to laugh, just like you do." And kisses—his Eve needed thousands of kisses. He could barely restrain himself from giving her one right that minute. However, he wasn't in the mood to have his face slapped.

"How in the world did we manage to entertain ourselves before you barged into our home?" she asked sarcastically.

He bowed. "I live to serve. Besides, I feel it's rather more than obvious that I have a certain finesse and leadership skill."

"Rubbish! Next time ask the doctor about her patients before you go ahead with any of your harebrained schemes," she said. She was unwilling to concede that Adam's picnic was coming off splendidly. Perhaps her patients did need to make merry, but this audacious man was just too smug for his own good. She didn't care that the dimples in his cheeks were unfairly appealing. And she was too wise to be taken in by his performance as a devoted spouse. The man was, after all, a dangerous deceiver, a great pretender.

Looking smug, Adam placed a hand theatrically over his chest. "Isn't it lucky, then, that I am a doctor."

She blasphemed once, then again for good measure.

"All by your invention!" he continued. "Keep that in mind, sweetheart."

She was quite the little handful, but he would be devout in his attentions. Even seeing her cursing him to the high heavens—and the nine levels of hell—Adam fully believed that a mixture of teasing, thoughtfulness, tenacity, and a tumble in the asylum, a tumble in the garden, and a tumble in the bell tower—or anywhere else, for that matter—would eventually win Eve over. Yes, they would settle down in this cuckoos' nest and raise a fine, attractive brood.

"Argh! You're driving me around the bend!"

"Shall I get the carriage, or the high-perch phaeton? Any particular route you wish to be driven? Shall we go fast or slow? I do like both methods—depending on the occasion, of course."

She stormed away, all ladylike pretensions vanished, her heart beating rapidly. He was a master of the lurid phrase. He was dangerous. Therefore, she would eventually roust him, rout him, and rally her defenses against him, by using her wits and her wile. "Or my name isn't Eve Bluebeard Griffin," she swore resolutely. Then she thought a moment. "Well, it *isn't* really Griffin." She was honest to a fault.

CHAPTER FIFTEEN

Mad About You, Mad at You

The night sky deepened to a dense black, with light from only a scattering of stars and the glow of the moon. As Eve made her way around and visited with her patients, she searched earnestly for any signs of mania or violent behavior. Instead she found laughter, betting, and light flirtations, and only discontented grumbling from those who usually were of a stern and unhappy nature. Relaxing her vigil, she sat down upon a marble bench beneath two massive oaks. A half dozen lanterns above her lighted the trees, while she watched the picnic in progress. She shivered slightly, though she did not know whether from the cooling night breeze or the acknowledgment that she had met a worthy and sly foe in Adam.

"I have more important things to think about than him," she muttered. "Like Mr. Carlen."

Eve was happy to note that for once the gargoyle wasn't in his catatonic state. Although he was a cold man at the best of times—rather stone-faced and denigrating—tonight he was alert, and even now was speaking warmly with Major Gallant. Their conversation was for the common good, since he was keeping the major occupied. Major Gallant hadn't yet charged around the garden. Rather, he was standing with his hand in his jacket, wearing his ridiculous hat.

To Eve's right, Mrs. Monkfort was surveying the ground around her and muttering about dirt while wringing her hands. Hugo was tossing marbles in the air nearby, while the wily Fester was snatching at one or two of his marbles and grumbling. Something about a black witch who was in league with the House of Lords? Eve thought she heard Fester remark that the witch had cursed the marbles.

Eve shook her head. Searching for the why and how a patient slipped away into a netherworld could be likened to searching for a hidden treasure, with only an aging map with missing pieces to guide the way. And yet, the search for this buried treasure was probably one of the most important searches in the world, as well as being one of the hardest and most frustrating.

Watching Eve from the shadows, Adam smiled faintly. The antics all around faded into the background. He felt at peace, here, because there was an odd kindness, and comradeship as well. Dedicated in his youth to overcoming betrayal and obtaining worldly goods, he had forgotten the wealth of home and hearth. The peaceful contentment of knowing a loving household had faded into a vague memory.

But in the blink of an eye his world had changed. Strange that he would find happiness here, of all places: yet he had known the moment he had seen her, just as his father had known the moment he spied Adam's mother.

Like his grandfather before him, and his great-grandfather before. All those men had felt something upon meeting the only female in the world for them. It was bred into Adam's bones, the heritage of all Hawkmore men to instinctively know their mate. He felt blessed this good night, because he had a wife called Eve, a home, good friends, and a worthy occupation—all lay before him in a deranged and daunting splendor.

Yes, it was bizarre that he should find himself quite comfortably entertained and content in a lunatic asylum, but so be it. Fate was a fickle mistress, with a highly developed sense of the absurd. But he truly liked many of the people he had met. He regretted the fact that he would have to double-cross Captain Bluebeard—being both a man of common sense and honor—but there was no hope for it. Once a Hawkmore male found his mate, nothing stood in his way—not even a cutthroat pirate like the captain.

He looked his fill. The softness of the lantern light accented the beauty of Eve's heart-shaped face. It set the reddish highlights aflame. She appeared some pagan fairy princess come to earth in the dark hours before dawn, and if he had some fairy dust on hand then her anger and distrust would vanish before he could snap his fingers. Sadly, there was never a true fairy around when a person needed one, for they were a secretive and elusive lot.

Adam strolled over and sat down next to her. Once seated, he pressed his luck by moving his long, muscular leg next to hers on the marble stone bench.

"What are you doing, stalking me like a shadow? I didn't ask you to sit down," she complained haughtily. "And tell me that's not your thigh crowding mine."

Her rudeness didn't bother him; he had been insulted too many times to count in his past misadventures. So he said, "What refreshing candor. But it leads me to believe that you have a fear yourself, Doctor." He stroked his bottom lip.

"What utter nonsense. What fear?"

"The fear of intimacy."

"How ridiculous," she scoffed, then quickly added, "Move your leg; it's too close."

He laughed at her discomposure as Mrs. Fawlty strolled up, Teeter at her side. "Ah, young love," the housekeeper said. "So fine and so lusty." She gave both Adam and Eve a crooked grin. "Are ye up to something naughty, Dr. Adam?"

"Oh, indeed," he replied with roguish intent, the dimple in his cheeks showing. "A doctor does what he must, and a husband—well, his work is *never* done."

"That's a fine thing. You're right back where you belong—in yer wife's bed. Ye'd best stay there."

"Wild werewolves couldn't keep me away," Adam promised. "For no other woman can compare."

Mrs. Fawlty nodded happily. "See that you keep him, Dr. Eve. Them wicked foreign women know things, so you'd better keep on your toes. German women are some of the best cardplayers—especially when they play without clothes. Frenchwomen are the best kissers. Now, you take them Russians? They fair heat up the sheets, so I'm giving ye some advice me old ma gave me, Dr. Eve. Don't go to bed mad, or any other place. And you might try kissing a bit more. Men like that, ye know."

Hearing a stifled chuckle beside her, Eve elbowed Adam discreetly in the ribs. As the older couple strolled away she said; "Don't you dare laugh."

"Do you think I'd laugh at you? Laugh *with* you, definitely, but not at you. And don't worry about Mrs.

Fawlty's comments. Those wicked foreign women didn't tempt me when I was in Transylvania. I was faithful to you, my darling. My marriage vows were never broken."

Her eyes narrowed. "What utter rot," she replied.

"I dreamed about you last night. And I know I will again tonight," he said. "You are temptation itself."

"And you're full of blarney. Just like Fester. Don't think I don't know that," she answered. He was a charming liar, but a liar nonetheless. Yet he held a fascination for her rather like a rabbit did for a snake. He was an enigma, complex and capable. He also had expertise in using his good looks and husky laugh to best advantage.

But no, he was the enemy and a puppet in her father's plan. She would not be locked into any marriage, even with a man as attractive and intriguing as this.

"It's the truth, I'm telling you. You could drive me mad quite easily—mad about you, mad for you, mad without you, and mad that I hadn't met you sooner."

In spite of her many misgivings, Eve had to admit Adam appeared to fit in well here. It was as if he'd lived at the Towers for years. She frowned discouragingly, hoping he would leave her be.

He leaned back negligently, studying her, his face highlighted by lanterns and the moon. "Do you know how pretty you are when you smile? But I bet I haven't seen you smile more than twice since I've been here."

His words took her aback. "I'm a psychiatrist."

"Psychiatrists don't smile?" Adam asked with an amused expression. "Or laugh? Is that the hippocrytical oath?"

"Hippocratic. And of course they smile . . . we smile. But sometimes one forgets. After all, psychiatry is a serious business. When a doctor loses a patient, he loses a life, but when I lose a patient he loses his mind—and that's a terrible thing to waste," she said. "My patients end up living in total mental darkness, and sometimes in total fear. They feel guilty, sad, angry. . . . Most know they aren't normal, and that is a heavy burden to bear."

Adam cocked his head to one side, pleased. Eve was finally opening up to him. "I always thought normal was just a varying degree of insanity. Is anyone truly normal? Can we define it?"

Eve glanced at Adam, surprised to find herself explaining about her work. But his expression was very focused, and she knew that he was listening—really listening—unlike most people she knew. "I think some are more normal—or what society would term normal—than others. Sometimes the sane can become crazy, it is true, but the truly insane live in reverse—with their madness a daily habit and lucidity found in flashes. The shadows and mist that fog their minds are so difficult to discover. . . . I often feel like I'm sailing a ghost ship into uncharted waters. Somehow I must lift that fog in spite of the difficulties, and help my patients find themselves."

Her sincerity touched Adam in a place that had grown jaded by years of living to survive, years with women who had fornication on their minds while cheating on their spouses or lovers, or making a few coins. This petite woman in front of him was different, as his mother had been. When these women devoted themselves to a cause, it was completely.

"Do you know, Eve Bluebeard Griffin, that you are an admirable woman? A woman who knows her own mind and her strength. And best of all, you share yourself with those around you. In today's modern world, a woman still has to struggle with great obstacles to achieve her aims.

You do. This same strength you bring to your patients. So, never fear you won't succeed, because I believe that you always will."

Eve didn't know how to take the compliment. Was Adam teasing her, mocking her, trying to flatter her into the bedroom? She'd be a fool twice over if she didn't notice the heated looks he had been giving her all evening. Actually, they'd been scorching looks, as they'd been since she first met him.

Ruthlessly she crushed all feelings of warmth for Adam. She would not be taken in by his manly charms. Adam was turning out to be many things, some quite opposing. He was bad, he was good, a pirate and a prince. He was a schemer, yet he had his own code of honor. He'd revealed a sharp wit along with a deceitful nature, but his words were often tempered with tenderness and generosity. "My father disagrees. He feels I'm wasting my life on land."

"Captain Bluebeard sails uncharted seas, so why shouldn't you sail into the minds of your patients?" Adam asked.

"The Captain wants me at sea," Eve remarked gloomily.

"But he wants grandkids more. Trust me. Give him a few, and see how his tune changes," he added.

Leaning closer, he grinned, his dimples becoming more prominent. Picking up her hand, he kissed it slowly, letting her see the fires of passion in his eyes. She felt her breath quickening at his close proximity and heated stare.

Adam's grin deepened as he noted Eve's reaction to his nearness. She might be difficult and carry more portmanteaus than the royal family, yet in spite of her faults she was a fitting daughter for the Captain, and a fine wife for himself. She would make strong babies—*his* babies. "I gallantly place myself in your hands to be of service," he said, "for the servicing." He couldn't resist teasing.

"Oh, you wretch," she began, and yanked her hand away.

"Oh, no, you don't," Adam said. He snatched her hand back. A flash of resentment filled him at her judgmental tone. Tapping the ornate gold band on her finger, he subtly reminded her just with whom she was dealing.

She opened her mouth to protest, so he leaned down to kiss her senseless. His lips met hers with a fierce possession, hot and demanding.

Adam's kiss, Eve saw, was different from that of the black-hearted Hook. Adam smelled regrettably delicious, and unknowingly she had been lonely for just this—the touch of a lover, strong fingers caressing and worshiping her, kisses that made her forget all her troubles. These kisses doused her anger and sent her emotions swirling like the wide Sargasso Sea. She felt entirely right in his arms. In fact, she felt perfect, as if she had been designed for him alone.

At first Eve fought, shoving at his shoulders and keeping her lips closed to his passionate assault. But now she relaxed a bit, and Adam gentled their kiss, slipping his tongue into her mouth. She was so soft and fragrant in his arms, and her lips were hot and sweet. He hadn't lied to her or tried to charm her when he told her that he was mad for her. His senses were crazy for her taste and feel. She called to him on such a primitive level that he felt like running away with her, ignoring all and sundry for one night in her arms.

For Eve, disaster had struck in the form of these eminently kissable lips. Her blood began to hum as the world faded. Strangely, she felt herself growing breathless, the kiss drawing her inward. It was a bold journey into swirling emotions and liquid-hot feelings. She was tumbling head over heels, awash with passion. Gathering her willpower, she tried to halt her treacherous emotions, but that was as useless as trying to stop waves crashing upon the shore.

Instead of cursing the liberties he was taking, Eve now nestled closer, pressing her bosom against his rock-hard chest. His lips were hot, demanding, and oh, so sweet, with a hint of wild cherries. He was all male, predatory as his hand began to pick the pins loose from her hair, letting the thick, shoulder-length waves fall free. His other hand moved down her back to mold the tops of her buttocks. He groaned. So did she.

Somewhere in the back of her mind, Eve knew she should be outraged. Instead, she felt the place between her thighs grow wet with need. She felt a hunger in her stomach, and lower an ache that was bittersweet, needy, all clamoring senses urging her to mate. It was disturbing and earth-shakingly potent.

She clasped Adam's back harder, dimly aware that his kisses were dangerous as opium. He could become an obsession, with her appetite only whetted by his attentions, growing greater in need, she realized with dismay.

Warning bells began to ring in her mind. Or were they really ringing? Reality had returned in a rush, and Eve pushed Adam away.

He glanced at her, his eyes still hot with unrequited passion yet a touch of confusion. He had kissed many a female, but never had one rung his bell quite so literally.

"What's with all that ding-donging?" he asked, his arousal aching and feeling quite neglected.

"Hugo, the demented dwarf," she replied, her eyes trying to focus past the fog of sensuality in which she was drifting. She took a step back and threw a quick left hook that Captain Kidd had once taught her.

Adam caught it square on the nose. Holding his face, he glared at her. "I should put you over my knee! You enjoyed that!"

Before she could reply, some of her patients began to come undone at the pealing of the bells. The bonging in the cool night air caused Major Gallant to bow once, then charge up the terrace stairs with an imaginary sword in hand, yelling in his faux French accent, "They're blowing the bugle. Charge, men, charge! We can't let those Englishmen win the bridge!"

Not far behind, Mrs. Fawlty was bringing up the rear. She chased down the major, who was heading straight for the bell tower. The harassed housekeeper merely scowled, saying as she passed, "Sure to be, your name's Dr. Adam and hers is Dr. Eve. But I tell you true, this ain't the Garden of Eden."

Eve picked up her skirts to hurry after them.

CHAPTER SIXTEEN

Silence of the Lambert

Eve scowled as she hurried toward the bell tower and the batty dwarf in the belfry. Adam had sprung up as well, and caught up to her, while Mrs. Fawlty, ever the busybody, tackled the major. Teeter, who was following fast on the housekeeper's heels, stumbled over the pair, and the patients and staff cheered them all on to the accompaniment of the bells.

"It's a good thing your loony bin is located in the country, more or less, since town neighbors would be up in arms over this ringing at all bloody hours of the day and night," Adam panted as they ran.

Eve remained silent. This husband-and-wife deal was for the birds.

"Why does Hugo feel the need to ring bells constantly?" Adam asked.

"Besides the fact that he's insane?" Eve snapped.

"Besides that."

She reluctantly explained: "The monks in the monastery where he grew up were busy with other duties, so Hugo spent much of his time as the bellboy. With his deformity and surly temperament, he ended up a crotchety, hunchbacked dwarf. His mother spoiled him, giving him everything he wanted while she was alive. Therefore, Hugo feels as if the world owes him, and he rings the bell to call attention to that."

As they passed the massive fountain, Mrs. Monkfort waved, then returned to her thorough cleaning of the statues. Mr. Pryce was rubbing his legs together behind Mrs. Monkfort's back.

"Hugo can be charming upon rare occasions, but he is mean-spirited when he doesn't get his way. He even cheats."

"Cheats?" Adam asked, glancing back and seeing Mrs. Monkfort drop her sponge as Mr. Pryce buzzed her. This tickled Adam's funny bone, and he found himself chuckling.

Eve narrowed her eyes at him. "Cheating, like any dishonesty, is never a laughing matter."

"I apologize. Please continue," he said with a playful grin.

Eve's eyes narrowed further, for his handsome face appeared even more devastating in the faint moonlight. "You do know, Adam, that I'm not some dim-witted debutante looking for a husband, nor some loose-skirted floozy searching for a tricky, tempting rake?"

"Ah, so you find me tempting! My, my—I am coming up in the world."

"You only had up to go," she responded.

He laughed. "So, how does this cranky dwarf cheat?"

"It's not important."

"You brought it up."

"Oh, very well. We vote on dinners once a month. It cheers the patients to have a say in their daily lives. The most votes decides a meal. Or at least it should—except, Hugo has a habit of breaking into wherever I happen to hide the ballots. Then he marks them all to his favorite meal. An appalling one. At first I didn't understand what was happening, but after the last two polls being such a disaster, I investigated. I found out then what the little devil did."

Curious as well as amused, Adam had to ask. "What is this appalling meal?" Surely it wasn't all *that* bad.

Eve's nose wrinkled in distaste. "Boiled cabbage and herring."

She was right: the combination was appalling. Adam grimaced. "So, we have a mean-spirited, cheating dwarf who has a taste for breaking and entering?"

"With bells on," she said in resignation. "Yes, that about sums up Hugo Lambert. Unfortunately, his father was a thief with an amazing ability to unlock any lock. Hugo evidently learned from him. His father was also a powerful warlock who seduced a Gypsy, Hugo's mother. When his father married another, his mother gave her lover *mal de ojo*."

Adam nodded. "The evil eye."

"You speak Spanish?" she asked, surprised, as they drew nearer the bell tower.

"In my travels I picked it up."

"When you were a pirate?" Eve couldn't help asking, curious about this strangely odd and attractive man by her side even though she knew that he was a shrewd schemer and certainly could in no way be construed as a romantic interest. All speculation was definitely against her best scientific judgment.

"No. I wasn't a pirate in Spain. Although it's true that I have been a pirate and a poet—and a prankster, a pugilist, and a pauper, a butcher, a baker, and even once a candlestick maker," he added with a shrug. "But in Spain, finding myself on the horns of a dilemma, I was a bull-fighter for an extremely short while."

"You? That sounds like a cock-and-bull story to me," she said. "But with you, one never really knows." Arriving at the gate to the bell tower, she ventured a further question, wondering if he would lie: "Have you ever long worked in honest employment?"

He sent her a brief look of aggravation. "Why, of course, my dear. In many ways I am an honest man. I must say that I've enjoyed such employment as well as the dishonest. After all, life's an adventure whether you're a king or a pirate, a vicar or a vampire." He returned their conversation to the subject of the dwarf. "I take it the evil eye somehow affected Hugo, from what you said?"

"Yes, the Gypsy's curse carried over to her son. That curse, I fear, damned her son to madness."

"Have you tried to find a cure for the curse?" Adam asked as they opened the wooden door to the belfry.

"Of course," she shouted, to be heard over the loudly clanging bells. "I even consulted Dr. Jekyll of Edinburgh. But he failed as well."

Adam was impressed: Dr. Jekyll was the premier authority on ancient curses.

As he stepped inside, he noted that the circular bell tower was lit with flickering tapers. The erratic light glinted off the dense stone walls, casting shadows everywhere. He winced and covered his ears, as Eve did hers, since the bells were deafening in the enclosed space. They both scampered up the spiral staircase.

Although it was only a minute, he felt as if it had been at least an hour before he stepped into the uppermost tower room. Wall sconces lit a large area where two massive bells swung back and forth. Taking his hands from his ears, Adam noticed that the noise here was less intense. Part of the sound was carried away by the open architecture, as all four sides were open to the air, with only thick stone columns to support the roof. Adam watched as Eve shook a fist at Hugo, her posture rigid. The hunchbacked dwarf did not see her. He was swinging jauntily on the ropes attached to the undercarriage of the bells, cackling gleefully. Two large handkerchiefs were stuffed in his ears.

"Hugo Lambert, you get down this minute!" For such a little female, Eve had a booming voice. Hugo, however, his body wrapped around a thick hemp rope, his deranged little face merry, thoroughly ignored her. Eve shook her fist, then slipped off her slippers.

"What are you doing?" Adam yelled, frowning.

"Climbing up there with him to try to talk him down," she shouted.

Grabbing hold of her arm, he shook his head. "Too dangerous. I'll go."

"Nonsense. I've been doing this for years—climbing crow's nests and whatever else."

"My wife shouldn't place herself in such an undignified position. Especially when I'm an expert on climbing too," he argued at the top of his lungs.

Cocking a brow, she appeared amused. "Let me guess. A . . . mountaineer?"

"Close. I had a tree house as a child," he yelled, stripping off his jacket. Besides, I'm bigger. I won't allow you

177

to risk that delectable neck. The bells aren't going to toll for you—not if I'm around."

So saying, he shimmied up the rope, his muscles showcased by his black trousers and white shirt, bulging and straining as he climbed.

Watching Adam wrap his legs around the rope, Eve stared unabashedly at his broad back and the tautness of his buttocks in those buff breeches. The cad really was too attractive for his own good. She sighed. Couldn't he be blessed with bowlegs and a scrawny back? Of course not.

As she watched, Adam shouted something at Hugo that she couldn't make out. Hugo stopped swinging for a moment, studied Adam, and then smiled, his crooked yellow teeth showing. Without further ado, the dwarf scurried down with Adam close behind.

Slightly stunned, Eve watched Hugo bow and hobble out the door. Adam let go of the rope and dropped the last few feet to the ground, his shirt damp with sweat. Oddly, she found the sight erotic.

"Whatever did you say to get him down?" she asked begrudgingly. She had never gotten Hugo to quit ringing his chimes so quickly. And the silence inside the bell tower was absolutely marvelous.

He bowed formally, grinning. "How do you think? I bribed him."

Rubbing her forehead, she grumbled in exasperation. "I should have known."

Adam chucked her on the cheek, laughing. "Your eyes speak volumes. You're irritated."

"How did you bribe him?" Right now she didn't like Adam one bit. Even if he did have a fine backside, maybe even the finest she'd ever seen. However, her practical side won out. If Hugo could be bribed, she certainly wanted to know how.

"Why, with boiled cabbage and herring, of course."

Eve stamped her foot in frustration. "That's so simple! I can't believe I didn't think of it," she said.

Adam glanced at her thoughtfully as they walked down the spiral staircase. "I wonder, can you be bribed?"

His eyes were dancing mischievously, but also seemed rather serious.

"I am made of sterner stuff," she replied. "So forget nosegays, chocolates, or any of the hearts-and-flowers stuff. I was raised on a pirate ship."

"How about some nice, fresh fish?" he joked.

"Not in this lifetime," she snapped. "I'm not that fond of fish."

"Surely you want something. Perhaps my devotion, my heart . . . ?" The words seemed to echo in the tower, along with their footsteps on the stone stairs.

"You were paid to be here," Eve reminded him curtly. His gaze was much too serious, his words too romantic. She didn't want to feel so warm inside. Yet she could feel heat stealing through her, like after she indulged in a fortifying glass of brandy. She didn't like feeling special because Adam admired her beauty and her wit. She was a doctor. She didn't have time for emotions. His words of adoration and love were merely words, with no real substance. What fool fell in love like this, just because he made her patients laugh? Perhaps she found his wit amusing at times, but that didn't mean she was willing to risk her heart. Her father had done precisely that seven times, and only got it right once. Then her mother died, and the captain had almost gone mad with grief. Her grandmother had loved her grandfather dearly, only to unearth that he had a vampire mistress. Right after her grandmother's grim discovery, Eve's grandfather died, leaving Ruby to lose herself in her creeping madness. "This isn't real. We're merely playing house," she said. "And by the way, I'd thank you not to engage in the game so ardently."

He grabbed her arm and turned her toward him. Taking her hand, he placed it on his chest. "I'm real, Eve. Feel the way my heart beats for you. I've never felt this before. You make my heart sing. You make my head ring. You make every—"

"Stop! That's just Hugo's bells. Besides, a rogue is always a rogue, and a pirate is always a pirate."

He grinned. "I'm wild about you. How could I not be? It's not every female who could invent a man as debonair, handsome, talented, and adorable as myself—and then end up with him."

"You would have me forget your deception?"

"Life is too short. If all you do is work, someday you'll wake up and find that life has passed you by. That love is only a four-letter word. You need a man who fires your blood, who drives you mad with desire, who flies you to the stars when you make love. I am that man."

His soulful look nearly melted her heart. She could almost believe him, here in the moonlight where romance hung heavily in the air. But staring back into his twinkling eyes, she chided, "It'll take more than poetic words to win my affections. I'm not like my father, falling in love at a glance through rum goggles." And with those words, she slipped through his fingers and off to her study.

CHAPTER SEVENTEEN

A Fool and His Money— and a Grumpy Leprechaun

Several days later, Adam was helping Fester dig for his pots of gold in the wine cellar at the Towers; he needed some physical activity to divert his lusty thoughts from his wife. At times he was cursing himself six ways to Sunday for being gullible enough to believe. Did Fester really have any gold? Maybe if he bribed the leprechaun with the location of the Blarney Stone, he could find the real answer to the question. Plunging his shovel into the dirt, he mused that perhaps his ship would come in with a crusty little Irishman at the helm.

Although Adam was in excellent shape, it was fortunate that only a thin layer of slate covered the cellar floor. This looking for lost pots was hard work, and he groaned as he began yet another hole. "I must be crazy," he muttered again, stopping to wipe the sweat from his brow.

Fester kept digging. "You'd be in the right place, then, Dr. Adam. But somehow I don't think it works that way."

Realizing he'd spoken aloud, Adam said, "What doesn't work what way?"

"Doctors can't be crazy. If they were, who'd treat the patients?" Fester studied his hole a moment, then turned to glance at where Adam had dug a four-foot pit.

"From the mouths of leprechauns," Adam couldn't help saying, and resumed digging.

"Ye need to dig a good two more feet there," Fester chided him gruffly.

"You're positive this is where you hid your gold?"

"Well, not positive, but possibly," Fester said. "It was a while ago, I got to admit. More than a wee bit ago. Back then I wasn't thinking too clearly, what with the king's men being at me back. I still remember the feel of their icy stares and their hope of trying to ferret out me secrets, ye ken?"

Stopping his digging once again, Adam fixed an eagle eye on Fester's baldhead. "Just how 'possibly'?" He hoped he hadn't been wasting his morning and his good clothes. But then, what did he expect? He had spent a lifetime chasing rainbows, watching his life roll by and his dreams float away like puffy clouds on a hot summer day.

Throwing another shovelful of dirt to the side, he remembered the old saying, *The early pirate gets the treasure*—though the one who could read a pirate map was even more likely. Just once in his life, Adam wanted to be early rather than late.

Moving to avoid a faceful of dirt from Fester's shovel, he asked for the umpteenth time that morning, "Just how possible is it that your pots of gold are here?"

"As possible as can be. I had to put them somewhere safe. This wine cellar seems as safe a place as any." Scratching his sharp little chin, he added distractedly, "If I remember correctly, the place was owned by a vampire fella at the time. I figured his wine cellar was as good a hiding place as any, since the undead may like their wine, but blood's more to their taste."

Before Adam could probe deeper into the leprechaun's memories, Eve stepped into the wine cellar, her eyes shooting sparks. "Just what is going on here? What tricks are you up to now, Dr. Adam?"

Leaning on the handle of his shovel, Adam replied, "What does it look like? We're digging for gold." She looked beautiful, as always, and mad. As always. He knew she had been avoiding him the past few days, but that was all right. He was letting her get used to his presence, just like a wolf would do when finding a new pack. Instead of moping about, Adam had immersed himself in learning all he could about the various patients and treatments, like any good doctor worth his salt. He had hoped to impress her and help with her work.

"In my wine cellar?" Eve was outraged. "Fester, you know better than to dig in the house! I've warned you time and time again!"

Fester hung his head and looked guilty, contrition weighing heavily on his features.

Swinging back to Adam, she blasted him with words, her finger jabbing him each time she drew a breath. "And you, his partner in crime. How utterly shocking, you impossible man! Who do you think you are, encouraging him in his delusions? I should have you hanged from the quarter mast." Her finger hit squarely in the center of Adam's chest with surprising force. Adam oomphed.

"But, Dr. Eve, you don't have a quarter mast," Fester began, only to be cut off by an infuriated Eve ringing a peal over her patient's head. It almost sounded like Hugo had gotten loose.

"Go to your room, Fester, and stay there! I'll deal with you later." She gave the order like the little admiral she was. Fester wisely recognized the authority behind the command, and did as told. He left the room, his head hung low.

Eve tried not to feel guilty at Fester's dismay, but did anyway. How could a cranky old leprechaun look so helpless? She sighed. Didn't she have enough problems in life without her cellar looking like a bloody graveyard? Her sane, ordered life had been turned completely upside down.

"Eve, I can explain," Adam began, cautiously trying to defuse the situation, but found himself interrupted by a fiery blue-eyed harridan.

"You scheming seducer of innocents! You pillaging proliferate pirate! How dare you add to his delusions! How dare you dig up my cellar looking for buried treasure! Isn't it bad enough I have as many holes in my garden as you need to play golf? Isn't it enough that Fester thinks everyone is after his gold? Now he has to worry about his doctor, who really isn't a doctor at all, but a thoroughly disreputable thief! For shame, to steal from a mad leprechaun. And to think just two days ago you were pretending to have such a compassionate constitution. How utterly depraved can you be?"

Sticks and stones he was used to, but name-calling still bothered him. He didn't want to lose any ground in this game of love and war, and besides, he had meant what he said; he did care about her patients. He also cared about their gold.

"I only wanted to help. Fester seemed lonely. I wanted to ease his burdens a bit. Not to mention he's getting a bit old for all this digging alone. This cellar floor is fairly hard, and he's not a young leprechaun anymore."

"You dare to mention my floors? How could you dig here?" Glancing down, she fought back a scream of frustration. It was bad enough putting up with Fester's folly, but now she had to worry about Adam encouraging Fester's delusions. "And as far as Fester being lonely, that's one for the old Blarney Stone. Fester's never met a stranger he didn't like—except in Parliament. Blast ye to smithereens, Adam. You wanted his gold. Isn't my father's treasure enough?" It hurt that after being paid to be her husband, the impossible impostor was still a gold digger. "Well, the old saying is true. If you lie down with sea dogs, you're bound to get fleeced."

Adam had been watching her carefully, and he noted the flash of vulnerability in her eyes. He backtracked, taking another tack. "I may be digging myself a deeper hole, sweetheart, but the only treasure chest I'm interested in is you." Her chest was indeed priceless, and he could see it as she stood there, bosom heaving. The flesh inside her rounded décolleté rose and sank in a dance that made very hot blood pool in his groin. He had only to look at Eve to want her fiercely. She had only to open her mouth to make him think of silky, cool sheets, hot, sweaty skin, and the musky scent of lovemaking in the air.

"Compliments won't work, Adam. And keelhauling is too good for you. You should be marooned on a desert island. You pirates are all alike. You're never satisfied, always wanting more." It burned her breeches. How could anyone who looked so magnificently male and dashing, even with dirt on his sleeves and cheek, be such a scallywag?

Eve's outrage only made Adam want her more. She was all fierce passions and primal desires, a woman any man should be proud to call his own. Lust overruled his good sense, encouraging him to tease her. "Are you casting stones at me?" he asked.

"What a delightful idea. Let me go find a nice fat one."

Ignoring that, he shrugged on his jacket. "If you won't share your treasured chest with me, then perhaps you'd like to see something I'd like to bury. It's just a matter of where to put the family jewels."

Her face reflected confusion until she realized the meaning of his words. Disconcerted all over again, she spluttered for a moment, her face turning red all the way down into the neckline of her gown.

"You . . . you pompous, conceited crook! You randy, roguish rake! You're beyond impossible! Hell will freeze over and pirates become members of the House of Lords before I let you . . . let you . . ." And yet, she was tempted. She was still a virgin at the advanced age of twenty-seven. Of course, she was also a doctor, and being a doctor she had gotten an eyeful on more than one occasion. She wondered at the size of Adam's hoard. She knew some men had more family jewels than others.

Oh, why had she let him kiss her? She wasn't a stupid woman. She knew that curiosity had killed three of Bluebeard's wives, and that was something she didn't want to mimic.

As Adam noted his wife's reaction, a secret thrill shot through him. She was such a passionate little thing, which boded well for the years ahead in their marriage bed. Managing an expression of contrition, he hung his head and looked suitably disconsolate. "I take that to mean no."

Shaking with rage, she lost control. "I'm warning you, stay away from Fester! Stay the bloody hell away from my patients! And most of all, stay away from me!"

"But, darling, I can't. I'm over the moon about you. Besides, my little beauty, you've got your hands full. You need me. I want to help. I *need* to help. I'll carry your load, carry your books, carry a tune, carry on and carry forward—anything, if you'll just let me. But most of all I want to carry you off into the sunset."

Truly, the maddening man did look sincere. With his commanding air of devilish tomfoolery, Eve found herself intrigued in spite of her better judgment. But despite his being the best kisser she had ever known, Adam Griffin's good intentions were nothing more than an illusion as false as Fester's gold.

"I mean what I say, Adam. Stay away from Fester. You're not a doctor." She added with angry dignity, "And this is an insane asylum, not a 'loony bin' or 'a house for crackbrained idiots.' I must insist you watch your wording. Some of my patients are sensitive to slurs cast upon their conditions."

Adam sighed. "You lecture me like a naughty school-boy, but I shall contrive to remember your advice. But you must not forget that I know a few things. Remember, I cured a vampire of his oral fixation."

"In your dreams," she snapped. As if he knew anything about oral fixations. Surely he didn't know enough. He didn't know about her wicked dreams, how she had awoken in a panic. Her fantasy had seemed so real, her nipples ached. Adam had been sucking them while fondling other parts. What a wanton hussy she was! And her thoughts af-terward? Now *that* was an oral fixation. She blushed, hating how he'd burst into her life, intruding upon her world and dreams. It sucked. Though not literally.

Adam laughed, noting his wife's blush. "In my dreams? No, I believe in yours. And, by the way, I haven't thanked you yet."

She didn't want to ask; she really didn't. She really wasn't curious. "Thank me for what?"

"For having given me such an interesting profession. I'm so glad you didn't make me a lawyer." He shuddered theatrically. "All those nasty judges to deal with. Or you could have said I was a man of business, and I'd have had to spend all my days crunching dusty old numbers. But thanks to you, I'm a doctor of the mind. I use my mouth and my head to help people. Oral fixations? I know about all things oral, as a matter of fact. Why, the things an educated man can do with his tongue are just amazing," he added outrageously, a wicked grin on his face. "I'd be happy to show you a trick or two, if I could just get you onto a couch."

"Argh!"

"You sound just like your father when you do that." He laughed. Then, moving to stand below her on the staircase and seeing her look of outrage, he added, "Don't blame me. After all, you invented me, not the other way around."

She glared at him and stormed up the stairs. He counted to five, but had only hit three when another "Argh!" followed closely on the heels of the last. He also heard words that sounded suspiciously like *fickle fake* and *pretentious prick*.

"Don't forget that tonight we're guests of the Earl of Wolverton and his wife at Vauxhall Gardens," he called up to her. "We will more or less be onstage as the happily married couple only recently reunited."

From the vulgarity of her reply, he doubted there'd be any reunion in the marital bed anytime soon.

CHAPTER EIGHTEEN

The Three Faces of Eve
and the Great Pretender

Romance was in the air, which was not surprising, since midnight in the Garden of Vauxhall was always conducive to love. In the dark blue heavens above, fireworks lit the sky with brilliant patterns of flowering yellows, greens, and reds. Couples strolled the dark, twisting pathways to quiet spots in the shadowy world of unlit paths. Inside the pavilion, brightly dressed couples were waltzing together in gay harmony.

Yes, everywhere it appeared that Cupid's little arrows were flying, but nowhere more than in the Earl of Wolverton's private box. The earl and Lady Jane had been the perfect hosts for the past several hours, yet once the firework display began, the earl turned his attentions to his wife. And Lady Jane was not much better; she had eyes only for her husband.

Eve suffered a moment's pause, an unaccustomed stab

of envy for the besotted pair. Every once in a great, great while, Eve dreamed of inspiring such a love. It wasn't often, since she had much to occupy her time, and truth be told, she had never been terribly romantic or whimsical. She had often thought her lack of romantic notions was due to growing up aboard a pirate ship. Such ships were filled with pirates, of course, which tended to make a person focus more on the realities of life than the sentimental. Like never having enough freshwater for a bath, or fresh fruit for eating. Oh, yes, and all those smelly boots. Since freshwater was ofttimes scarce, pirates were a ripe lot, and their feet the worst of all. It didn't matter, Eve supposed; even now she didn't have the time for romance. Her work was too important. Her patients were too desperate in their despair, and if that meant she missed out on love, then so be it.

"They look very happy." Adam had been silent the last few minutes, but now he spoke up. "Very much in love. Was it love at first sight?"

Eve snorted. "Anything but."

She sneaked a peak at Adam. To be honest, it was somehow quite thrilling to be sitting in the shadows with him. Since the brigand had barged into her life, he had made himself all that was amenable in a husband. And tonight he was in exceptionally fine looks, dressed all in black, very restrained yet quite elegant. His Hessians were polished to a gleam, and his cravat was tied in the plainest of styles, with only a modicum of starch.

Again glancing furtively out of the corner of her eye, she was faintly amused at her dithering thoughts. Yes, her husband was every bit as good-looking as the Earl of Wolverton, without the vampire's aristocratic hauteur.

Adam had a commanding presence about him, but he lacked the pomposity that Eve disliked.

Adam glanced at the other couple. "They're lucky to have found each other," he whispered. "Fate was kind to them."

"I wouldn't actually call it fate," Eve, remarked. She thought with amusement that they'd both had a stake in the outcome.

"Fate comes in many forms. Look at us," Adam suggested.

Eve did. And it gave her an idea. "Speaking of fate, how would you feel about dying?" she asked.

He glanced at her sharply. "Unhappy."

She snorted. "I mean, you could pretend die, just like my father's plan, only it will be my plan. Instead of faking death for him, you can fake it for me."

"So, you want me to pretend to die before your father even wants me to?" he asked. His tone was cold. "Have I got that right? Why? So you can go merrily on your way to marry Captain Hook? Surely I'm a better husband than he!" He hated to admit it, but her plan hurt his pride.

"Hook is quite the rat—and I've never been partial to rodents," she admitted reluctantly. She thought about what he said. He was right. If he died sooner rather than later, her father would still press her to marry Hook. "I guess I'll have to reevaluate my plan," she said.

He retorted, "I guess."

Catching a glimpse of his expression, Eve imagined that Adam's feelings were hurt. If only circumstances were different. She might have been proud to be sitting at his side if they were truly man and wife. Instead, she felt like a character in a farce, especially since Adam had been pressing his thigh against hers and drawing little circles on her palm, pestering her, no doubt in an attempt to try to stir her senses. He was succeeding. He was too near and too disturbingly male for her peace of mind. She was not used to having her palm caressed tenderly, or having someone bewilder her with heated glances and wicked winks. But things were how they were, and she would not—could not—find him even a little bit enchanting.

"May I have my hand back?" she asked. Her voice held a husky little shiver.

"I don't think so. I love the way it feels. And you love the way this feels. Relax and enjoy your husband's lovemaking."

The sneaky scalawag was attacking from the stern, trying to weaken her defenses, she thought warily. He was just too dashing for his own good. And hers. "Rubbish," she said. "We aren't making love, and we won't."

"Give me time. Love isn't a disease, Eve; it's a miracle. It soothes us in our times of trouble and lends us strength. It can move mountains. And a helpmate can lighten any load by adding a strong back and caring arms. They can bring affection, humor, and passion to everyday life. So, what are you afraid of?"

She sniffed, sitting more stiffly with a prim pout plastered upon her face. "Bluebeards fear nothing!" she growled. "We are notorious scourges of the seas. Men quake when they hear our name."

Adam grinned wickedly. "Temper, my little admiral. Temper, temper."

She narrowed her eyes, assessing him. "You are goading me on purpose."

"How astute of you to notice." A lazy smile crossed his lips.

"I can see that you are determined to be difficult," Eve remarked stiffly. Why couldn't he move farther away? Why did he so stir her blood? He was only a corsair after her treasure and her virtue.

"Only with you, my love." His eyes roved over her, absorbing how lovely she was in that amber gown. It did wonderful things to her fiery hair. The fabric cupped her breasts like a lover's hands, clung deliciously to her delightful form. "Have anyone else's kisses ever made your toes curl?"

"You presume too much. And my toes don't curl," she stated emphatically, her fingers crossed behind her back.

"Yes, they do. And, I imagine, much more," he replied, his voice husky. Leaning toward her, he couldn't help but place a brief but tender kiss upon Eve's lush pink lips. He definitely wanted more, but restrained himself. He understood implicitly that all good things came to those who wait, if they weren't stolen first. He intended to be victorious.

Adam's gentle kiss stirred Eve's senses, sending her into a tizzy. *Enough!* This impish Irish impostor had been playing the tender lover since their arrival over two hours ago, and it had to cease. "Stop being so familiar with me," she hissed.

"If you keep whispering in my ear like that, you little enchantress, I shall ravish you on the spot," he warned.

She quietly and inconspicuously kicked him in the shin.

"Come, now, my little admiral. You must pretend a modicum of civility. Dash it, Eve. A husband can never be too familiar with his wife. Look at Lord Asher and Lady Jane. They can barely keep their hands off each other. How would it look if I ignored you? Think of the scandal! And your funding—we must present a united and loving front as the most devoted of couples if you want it."

"Hmph."

"It's not just your reputation at stake, but my own," Adam continued. "Just because you won't allow me to take you to heaven doesn't mean people should think I can't. Like the Earl and Countess of Wolverton."

Inching back, Eve slowly shook her head, his audacity infuriating. But at the same time, the nearness of his body made her breath quicken. His kisses were addictive, lethal, and made her heart dance. He had the look of a Gypsy and the heart of a rogue. But she was a psychiatrist and made of sterner stuff; she would not be led down the garden path. At least, not while in Asher's private box.

"Why should I care what the earl thinks about you?" she asked.

"A wife knowledgeable about the paranormal world should always care if a master vampire thinks her husband is less than a man. I don't want to be shown to disadvantage," he remarked stubbornly. Before Eve could argue, he added, "Shush. Besides, as my wife you have an obligation to me."

She drew back, astonished. "Your pretending to be my absentee husband obligates me? How dare you, sirrah!"

No matter what she did, she couldn't seem to make a dent in his strategy to act as her spouse. "Surely you must be getting bored with this!"

He bit back a chuckle. "With you, my dear, I could never be bored. That's why I'm crazy about you, crazy for you, crazed to have you. And I must confess, I am ready, willing, and cleverly able to do crazy things to keep you by my side."

"Oh, go and sell your craziness somewhere else," Eve said. "I bought at the office." This bounder was forever teasing, testing, and tormenting her, and the worst thing was, she was never certain whether he was maddeningly sincere or a compulsive liar with lucre or lust in mind.

Adam chuckled. The time for action was here. He placed a hand under his chin and lifted her face to his, and with determination and tenderness he kissed her.

Eve would not be seduced so easily. With pure indignation she fought the feel of his lips, paying no heed to the small, secret place within her that rejoiced in triumph. But after a few moments passed, his lips caressing hers, his fervor had her opening her mouth to protest—only to be routed as Adam quickly took advantage, his tongue dueling with her own.

Heat flooded her system, and Eve felt tiny butterflies in her stomach. Deep, deep down, she felt the stirrings of a hunger long dormant. And good grief, she could feel her toes start to curl from the heat of the kiss. Why, oh, why, did this man stir her senses to insensibility?

Breathing harshly, Adam reluctantly ended the kiss, his bones aching to the very marrow as he leaned his forehead against hers. He had almost lost his head, the kiss affecting him to such a degree that he wished to lower her to the ground and make mad, passionate love to her here, in public. Yet his self-control had resurrected itself.

"No more. Please, no more," she beseeched him breathlessly.

Reluctantly he drew back, not trusting himself. Her lips were swollen, and she was staring at him in a bewitching manner. There was a candor in her eyes he had not seen before.

"You're much too dangerous to be my husband," she said. "Too unpredictable. I hate to admit it, but you run circles around me. It's quite disconcerting."

"I vow I'll be a wonderful husband," he said.

"No. You're too great a risk. Too much the rake, the adventurer. A lady could never risk her heart upon you."

"It's true that I'm drawn to adventure," he said. "But the only adventure I seek is in your bed. The risk for me is already taken, for I fear you have stolen my heart."

He sounded so sincere . . . but then, con men usually did. Yet, Eve heard at least a grain of truth in his words, which caused her to recognize a fundamental truth: the man in front of her—Adam Griffin—had been going through a change since he first opened his mouth—from nobody to somebody. How disturbing. Worse, she was coming to admire him. But how could she ever trust him? She had to remember that he was a clever conniver who could convince anyone of anything, even someone as grounded in rational thinking and the sciences as herself.

She sat back rather weakly in her chair, her sensibilities strained as she tried to articulate her feelings. "I don't trust you. You're too wild to be reliable. Too much the roving schemer."

"So, tame me. You're a special woman, capable of achieving the improbable—even the impossible. Cure my wanderlust and let me love you, be loved by you."

"Poppycock, pure wishful thinking."

"Is that a medical opinion?" Adam asked. He fought off surliness. He was revealing bits and pieces of himself, yet she refused to believe his sincere intentions. He had met hardheaded people before, ogres being notoriously so: even when hit over the head with a tree, they often failed to fall. But Eve was more stubborn than most.

"Adam, admit it—you don't really want me. You took this scheme for the gold." She stared at him, as if trying to guess his thoughts.

"It is true that wealth was the draw. The gold is the reason I became your husband—but my staying is your fault. I can't leave you."

"It's only your libido speaking. You desire me; that's all."

"Ah, libido. I love it when you talk doctor talk."

Eve couldn't help it; she found herself giggling like a schoolgirl. But before she could do something totally stupid, like kiss him, Lady Jane and Asher joined them and interrupted their conversation. She said, "I'm finding myself feeling quite silly, and I need to apologize. I've been a terrible hostess. It's just that Asher has been gone the past few nights, and I've missed him terribly."

"It's been a wonderful evening—truly," Eve replied.

"I'm sure you understand," Asher added. "You two have been apart much longer than a few nights. I must commend you, Adam, on your forbearance. I must admit I would miss my Jane too dreadfully to be without her for years."

"Sitting beside my lovely wife now, I can't imagine ever being without her again," Adam responded. Eve kicked his ankle with her dainty slippers, but that didn't stop his grin. Turning his eyes to the earl, Adam asked, "How did you meet?" He liked both the Wolvertons. They seemed such an unlikely pair.

"You might say our courtship was rather unusual," the earl admitted. "She doused me with brandy and tried to stake me. It's that Van Helsing blood. Rather a violent lot," he teased his wife, his blue eyes sparkling.

Jane snorted, and Asher's chuckle turned into a heartfelt laugh. Eve giggled.

"And I thought our courtship was strange," Adam remarked thoughtfully.

"How?" Lady Jane asked.

Taking a chance, Eve replied, "Adam can be so elusive. At times I felt I was being wooed by an invisible man."

She didn't have long to wait for Adam's reaction. He looked stunned, then barked out a laugh. Glancing at the earl, he remarked, "The little admiral likes to run a tight ship."

"I have to, in a lunatic asylum," Asher said.

"Quite so," Adam agreed.

Suddenly Lady Jane dropped her fan, her attention caught by something along one of Vauxhall's many scattered pathways. Eve and the rest turned to see.

"Why, it's Frederick," Eve said, watching as Frederick Frankenstein loped up to a tall woman with an extremely complex hairdo. She was rather attractive, with remarkably large, expressive gray eyes. The lady was with three female companions, and was surrounded by young bucks. Apparently she was enjoying her conversation with the young men. She was unaware of the monster who was hurtling her way, his greenish skin touched by pink.

"I do hope Frederick slows down. He can be so clumsy when besotted, and besotted he is!" Lady Jane worried. "I only wish I knew more about Miss Beal. She appears nice enough, however. Her father is the Marquess of Cleese."

Asher nodded. "Very high in the instep. Soul of propriety and that sort of thing. Might not look too kindly on a match between a Frankenstein and a Cleese."

From the earl's private box, they all watched in concern as Frederick approached Miss Beal, his grin wide. But as he made to bow before the cherished lady, his very big feet got in the way and he tripped. He knocked Miss Beal's hand—the hand holding her punch, which sprayed all over her white silk gown. Hissing at Frederick, she fled with two of her female companions, leaving only the young bucks laughing uproariously and mocking Frederick's courting technique. Their mockery was too much for the gentle giant. Frederick fled, his back hunched and his big heart breaking.

"We must find Frederick at once!" Eve exclaimed. "I can't believe this is happening to him." Knowing the severity of his inferiority complex, she knew she must soothe him before he had an extreme attack of nerves.

Lady Jane rose to her feet with alacrity. "Yes. Let's go at once. I don't understand why some people must hurt others to feel better about themselves. Why did they all have to laugh at him? Oh, I wish his cousin Clare were here."

"History repeats itself," Eve replied. Then, seeing Jane's distress, she added, "I never understood why some people kick dogs, gossip to no good, or make others cry. It's a defect in their character—or rather, lack of character. They are missing something vital within, and because of this, I fear they will never truly be happy."

"If I know Frederick, he'll try to drink himself under the table in some run-down tavern," Lady Jane stated.

"Can he find a table that big?" Adam asked.

"Let's just hurry. I must find Frederick," Eve said. "I imagine he is experiencing a rather abrupt case of melancholia." She hurried out of the box, urging Adam with her.

He caught up, handing her the shawl she had left behind. "Don't worry, Evie; we'll find him. How hard can it be to find a six-foot-eight monster?"

CHAPTER NINETEEN

Hooked!

Their initial search for Frederick Frankenstein was to no avail, though they covered over a dozen paths in the gardens; they'd sent Lady Jane to start searching taverns. Far overhead, the stars were tiny diamonds, glittering. Wisps of smoke from the last of the fireworks still hung in the air, and the golden glow of lanterns and the moon above made the shadows mysterious and romantic. Any other time, Adam would attempt to ravish the lovely woman beside him. But rogue though he was, he also recognized Eve's concern for her patient.

Wearily Eve shook her head. "I fear Frederick has long left," she said. Her voice broke suddenly, and she lowered her head. "My feet hurt. If I had known I would be walking for hours on end, I would have worn my walking boots."

"I believe you're right. Frederick's not here," Adam agreed. "Why don't you send a note to Dr. Frankenstein?" He reassuringly patted Eve's hand.

"I will. And I'll let Dr. Frankenstein know that I must

see Frederick as soon as possible. This debacle tonight has probably set back his treatment by months. If I had been able to see him straightaway, I might have been able to defuse some of his embarrassment. He has such a big heart. Unfortunately, his feet are bigger," she remarked.

In spite of the seriousness of the situation, Adam found himself smiling. "He's lucky to have you. You care quite deeply for your patients. You don't believe in unfair restraints, even for Hugo. You don't put your wards in pits or treat them harshly. So many fear those who are different, but you care for and about them."

Gazing into his eyes, Eve felt her breath hitch. He had such compelling eyes, which had suddenly had grown heavy-lidded with desire. His compliment might not fix everything, but it certainly lightened her load. "Thank you. I try so hard. Hours of therapy and evaluating—but I rarely am certain of the results."

Releasing her hand, he paced. "The point is, my dear, your patients can trust that you'll never give up on them."

Tilting her head, she studied him. It was as though a warm sea breeze trailed over her soul, and suddenly she needed to be held in his arms, to feel secure and warm . . . maybe even a tiny bit cherished. She nodded, feeling a marvelous sense of safety and comfort, knowing someone cared and understood.

"Yes, that's it exactly," she said. "And I must confess that you have been rather good with my patients, too."

"My aunt. She was a gentle lady with a loving soul. She lived with us. In her later years, she suffered delusions."

"I'm sorry," Eve responded, feeling more of a connection with Adam than she ever had. The man had befuddled, badgered, and butted heads with her, and now he was slowly bewitching her. The hint of true vulnerability beneath his charming facade had touched her soul. "What happened?"

The expression on his face showed that these memories came with a cost. Watching him, Eve felt the strongest urge to lay her head upon his breast and ease his pain—a most wifely thing to do, she noted absently, and most assuredly absurd.

"My aunt heard voices. It was not unusual to see her carrying on a conversation with no one, or with a tadpole in a pond, gesturing and grumbling. She would talk to a blank wall, or to a piece of lint on her sleeve. Her favorite conversationalist was a duck in our pond. She died when I was twelve. My mother—her sister—never gave up hope that she would become herself again. She combed my aunt's hair at night while listening to her complain about how the rocks shouted at her. Even after we lost my father, my mother was kindness itself."

"Your mother sounds like she was a remarkable woman," Eve said.

"Yes. She was one of the best of ladies. And she knew that love is not bestowed on the basis of merit or wealth. Love endures."

Eve took a few steps closer and placed her hand upon Adam's chest—her first really spontaneous gesture toward him.

Adam responded by leaning forward to kiss her lush lips. He felt desire swamp him, as much as when he was a lad of fourteen and had been given his first real kiss by a lusty milkmaid. A grand and glorious tupping had followed, and Adam was still known to look appreciatively at a mug of milk.

He groaned in anticipation as Eve abandoned her reserve, clutching his jacket and pulling him hard against her, fiercely kissing him back. For once, they were two minds meeting in perfect accord under a star-filled night in a garden of paradise and pleasures.

He began to deepen their kiss when he found them interrupted by a loud, obnoxious laugh.

"Why, you sly boots! Lassie, what are you doing out here in the dark corners of Vauxhall, kissing yer husband like any common wench?" Captain Bluebeard asked with a wry grin.

Both Eve and Adam drew back, Eve with chagrin, Adam with annoyance.

Repressing the urge to curse a blue streak, Adam clamped his teeth together and tried to ease the ache in his groin. The next time he attempted seduction, he would definitely plan more cautiously. He certainly couldn't call her father out for protecting Eve. And he currently wasn't foolish enough to do it, since the Captain was known to be expert with both pistol and cutlass.

"Father, what are you doing here?" Eve gasped, watching her father's swagger. Unhappily, he was with one of his more unsavory boon companions. She'd wanted to groan out loud when she recognized the rat. His hair was black and unruly. He had one beady eye—a very dark brown one, the color of sooty walnut—and a black eye patch on the other. His lips were rather sensual, but he had a long blade of a nose with an arched ridge.

"Hook." Eve gave a curt nod, her facial features tightening, and without really thinking she reached out her hand to find Adam's, giving him a speaking glance as Hook took her other hand and raised it to his lips.

"Eve, the gods must be smiling on me to find you here tonight. You look enchanting, as always." Lowering his lips Hook softly caressed her hand. He lingered a bit too long, his one good eye lit with desire as his nostrils flared.

Jerking back her hand, Eve found herself suddenly quite tired of men slobbering all over it. Wrinkling her nose, she addressed the pirate captain by his first name: "Ben." The word was said with an obvious lack of courtesy.

Adam protectively circled Eve's waist with his arm, sending a challenging glare at the one-handed buccaneer. "I'm Adam Griffin. Dr. Adam Griffin. Eve's husband." His last two words were not only possessive; they were clearly a threat. Hook was said to be ruthless in getting what he wanted. His crews were the dregs of the rodent world, a scurvy sort made up of full-blooded wererats and wereweasels. So Adam's hackles rose along with his combative instinct.

Hook sent a malicious look at Adam, then stepped back, his one good hand clenching into a fist. His one good eye was shimmering with malice. "Ah, the missing husband. The husband who left his wife alone for, what—more than two years, isn't it? How smitten by her charms you must be."

Answering the verbal insult with an arrogant tilt of his head, Adam smiled grimly. "Grave responsibilities kept me from my beloved. But now, I'm here and I'm staying," he warned.

"How unfortunate," Hook snarled, his sharp teeth glistening. "Most unlucky. You see, I've been at sea the past two years, but I too am back. His words were a challenge I've missed you, my Eve. I've thought of you often."

"I've not thought of you," she replied, glad for once to have a husband by her side, pretend or otherwise. "And with Adam's return, I have been happily involved."

Captain Bluebeard watched silently, a thick dark brow cocked, his eyes fairly dancing with delight. Resolutely he managed to remain quiet—not an easy feat for one of his nature. His plan was working wondrously. Eve, in spite of her fierce independence, was clinging to her husband, while the great pretender was not pretending at possessiveness.

Yes, Bluebeard nodded to himself, all was going according to plan. The young privateer was a good man to have for a pirating and drinking mate—and even better as a son-in-law. Hook was a ruthless foe, a man after Bluebeard's own heart, but he was too wild and too much a womanizer to be wedded to his daughter. Evie needed a man who would understand her mind and cherish it, and who would let her dictate to him some of the time. Well, Bluebeard thought, *most* of the time. Hook would never be that man; his temperament too fierce, his nature too domineering, and his fidelity too doubtful. Adam however, would.

"Adam, me boy, 'tis good to see ye again. How is married life treating ye?" he asked in his booming voice. "With the grin on your face, I am guessing ye aren't feeling leg-shackled."

"How could it be anything but perfection with an enchantress like Eve for a wife?" the young pirate replied, caressing Eve's shoulder. "How fortunate that I was able to claim a wife like my Eve. She is everything I ever wanted in a woman, and she's mine alone. Beware, Captain Hook, I'm an ill bird for plucking."

Captain Bluebeard ignored the tension between the two men, threw back his head, and laughed. "Never thought I'd see the day when me own daughter was brought to heel. Love does work wonders."

"Why are you here, Da?" Eve asked, glaring at her father.

"Me and Hook were just in the neighborhood. Course, it took us three fancy carriages to get here," he added with a chortle.

Eve was not amused.

"Come, Ben, me boy," he coaxed, grabbing the other captain's arm. "I know when I'm not wanted. Let's leave the lovebirds to their nest."

His words caused Eve to grimace, while Adam grinned wickedly, which caused Hook to mutter a curse.

Hook gave Adam the evil eye—an eye as dark and foreboding as the heavens above. "This isn't over by a long shot. I saw her first, when she was barely a girl of fourteen. Even then she was a temptress, with her glorious hair and those lips red as apples. I knew then she would one day be my own."

"Over my dead body," Adam responded. Deadly menace was written across his features.

"Exactly," Hook replied, his voice hard. He raised his gold hook to gesture. "Exactly my point."

Before a challenge could be issued and a duel set up, Bluebeard threw a heavy arm around Hook and began dragging him away. Both Adam and Eve watched silently, half-listening to Bluebeard's chastising. A few threats for Hook were thrown in as well, threats to leave his favorite son-in-law—his only son-in-law—alone.

Eve stamped her foot. "Oh, how I despise that great hooked lout! I would dance a pirate jig if he'd be lost at sea! The man is a nodcock of the first degree if he thinks I'd ever marry him. I wouldn't have him on a solid gold platter—a *hundred* platters."

Watching her stomp her foot in ire, Adam could only be glad that this time Eve's temper wasn't directed at him. Still, she was a beauty. "How fortunate for you that you can't marry him, because, my dear, sweet wife, you're married to me." *And, by God, you're going to stay married to me.*

Before she could say the usual words of outraged protest, he grabbed her and kissed her silly. He was going to tame this woman or die trying.

Her breath coming in spurts, Eve looked up at Adam, her blue eyes afire with passion. "This can't be happening," she said. She needed to refute him, to rout him, to rattle him—even to riposte him—but not stand here and let him drive her senses mad. His nearness and his hot, sweet kisses made her toes curl to such a degree that she was in danger of tearing her slippers.

"Oh, my love, it is," he replied, stroking a curl that had come loose from her topknot. "Your hair is like a burst of flame flickering about your soft cheek. Such lovely hair. It begs me to free it." So saying, he snatched the pins from her hair while she stood there stupidly.

"I prefer it loose," he continued. "You'll have to wear it that way in our bedchamber." And without further ado, he kissed her again, a kiss that was fierce with need.

Her scent was so tantalizing: a blend of fresh spring breezes, with the heady scent of gardenias mixed in. Her firm breasts pressed against his chest, making him want to rip off her bodice and suckle to his heart's content.

Again, Eve found herself responding to the passionate possessiveness of Adam's kiss. Her heart beat wildly. It was more than obvious that the scoundrel wanted her, but there was more to his touch than mere seduction. When he wrapped her in his arms, she felt a tender regard. His eyes were large and expressive. They revealed a need for her, and admiration. She felt her universe shift, as if the moon were eclipsed and the earth shook. Adam truly did care for her.

So, he was more than fond of her, but how did she feel about him? His touch sent her senses scrambling, and when she looked into that gleam of unbridled passion in his eyes, she felt desired and special. She loved that. But was this only desire? No. She knew now that, in spite of his teasing ways, she liked Adam, really liked him.

Eve's passionate response to his desire was temptation itself, causing Adam's hands to begin a quest. As he trapped her firm breasts beneath his palms, she gasped and he smiled against her mouth. His wordy wife was a hot handful, and she was his forever, even if she didn't know it yet. Perhaps tonight was the night she would learn.

Tugging down the neckline of her gown, he kissed his way across her silken chest and began to feast on her ripe breasts, the nipples puckering under his assault. He drew back for a scant few seconds to appraise her bounty. Her breasts were softer than the back of a baby duck, and the nipples like plump raspberries.

Adam's tugging on her nipples aroused her desire, and Eve loosed a heartfelt groan. She was burning up inside. How could she even think when his elegant fingers were doing such magic? Her back arched, and the place between her thighs was aching. She had never felt like this. "Oh, Adam . . ."

Eve's arching her back cast her more in the lantern light, and Adam lifted his head and stared down at the firm orbs that had been plaguing his dreams at night. They were as perfect as he had dreamed, all white flesh and deep coral nipples. Underneath those breasts her lacy white slip had bunched, causing the breasts to plump together. Adam sighed lustily. She was his for the taking, and he would take her again and again until he had her with child. Then she would truly be his, he reasoned dazedly. Captain Bluebeard could not object nor expect him to disappear into deathly obscurity if he had fathered a child with Eve.

She moaned, and Adam tugged on her lacy slip, trying to pull it lower. "Lovely. You're beyond beautiful, my dear." He tugged harder on the slip.

Ever practical, even in a dense fog of passion, Eve knew she needed to protest. Breathing rapidly, she gasped, "Careful, or else you'll tear it, and it's too costly too replace. It's one of Mrs. Freud's."

"Ah, a Freudian slip," he growled. He had heard of this from a courtesan or two: that Mrs. Freud from Bavaria was the most sought-after undergarment maker for the ton. She was also the costliest. "I'll buy you another—ten others."

Those words were like throwing cold water upon Eve. This time her gasp was not passion-induced. "With my father's gold."

Adam's lust had slowed his brain to a dull plod. "Of course," he replied, continuing to cover her neck and breasts with tiny nibbling bites. She was the queen of all temptation, his Eve. "I'll buy you a hundred of Mrs. Freud's slips," he remarked fervently.

Eve seethed, her passion turning to anger. Adam would buy her costly slips when the Towers might be closing down? *What an idiot!* She shoved him away. "You're nothing but a rapscallion and a rogue."

"And you are a tasty handful," he responded, his eyes glittering in the moonlight.

Adjusting her gown and costly slip, and stepping back, she glared at him, noting that once again she had failed to discourage him. Just what did it take? He was like some craggy mountain peak: always there, a force of nature to be reckoned with.

He took two steps forward, advancing on her, his erection more than apparent from the tight fit of his trousers. He ached from unspent passion and wasn't ready to admit defeat. However, he readily admitted he was a fool for having mentioned money. Eve desperately needed funding for her asylum, and he, beset by lust, had stupidly reminded her of the treasure from her father.

Momentarily, he thought about lying as he stared at her passion-plumped lips and her slightly askew décolleté. He could tell her that the chest her father gave him was now hers. Except the chest now held only a few precious stones, the rest having long been sent to Ireland to buy back the old family estate. Besides, he wanted Eve to love him for himself, not for wealth. He was just arrogant enough to want Eve to want him because he was the only man for her, the only man who would love her forever, warts, Hooks, lunatics, and all.

"You have absolutely no scruples," she accused.

"I have scruples coming out my ears. Just none where seducing my wife is concerned. And now, having seen the bounty that awaits, I don't know how I'll survive without tasting you further." He sighed. "And you desire me too, Eve. You can't deny it."

She gave him a look as she walked off, clearly affronted.

CHAPTER TWENTY

Swinging in the Rain

The next day found Eve anxiously waiting to hear from either Frederick or Dr. Victor Frankenstein. At noon she received a note from the doctor telling her that he'd sent out some of his servants to try to find his adopted son. Dr. Frankenstein had admitted that sometimes Frederick got a screw loose, especially when he was drinking. He feared that, after such an embarrassment, Frederick would most likely go to some of his favorite taverns, and was probably dipping into his cups rather heavily.

Noting Eve's distraction, Adam had volunteered to go out and search Frederick's favorite haunts. He still wasn't back, and neither had she heard from Frederick.

Hours had passed since Adam left, and Eve found herself fretting. When he volunteered for monster retrieval, she had gratefully accepted, thinking at the time that having a helping husband wasn't such a bad thing, even if he wasn't real. She had even thought that perhaps Adam would give to her the gold he'd been given by her father. Eve had twisted that thought around in her mind, knowing that he cared for and was crazy for her. The same thought filled her mind now as she started down the hallway into the patients' ward. Would Adam give her his ill-gotten gains for her asylum, or he would keep it all for himself?

She sighed as she walked down the corridor. The asylum was unusually quiet today, with the exception of the rain that was thundering upon the roof and clinking into the gutters. Many people felt gloomy when it rained, but Eve loved the sound. She also loved the scent of freshness that each storm brought. Many of her patients despised the rain, especially the wereboar's widow, Mrs. Monkfort, who wanted to scrub each drop. Eve chuckled at the notion.

She had been summoned by her staff earlier to attend to one of Mrs. Monkfort's cleaning tizzies. Eve had put aside her worries and concentrated on helping the poor widow overcome her compulsive behavior, but after a good hour spent talking Mrs. Monkfort out of cleaning her shoes and watching her crochet that huge, white lace monstrosity, Eve had finally sighed in defeat. And when it started raining and Mrs. Monkfort opened her window and began cleaning the drops that landed on her arms, Eve's patience ended along with the session.

Glancing down at her sparkling clean slippers, Eve couldn't help but shake her head in amusement. Never had the asylum halls looked so clean. Even her footwear was—enough to eat dinner upon. Well, since her feet were so small, you could only fit a snack. The latter thought made her laugh aloud. Perhaps she should just hire Mrs. Monkfort as her housekeeper and relegate Mrs. Fawlty to nursing duties.

Crossing to the library, Eve jumped as the long mullioned windows shook with the force of the wind, large

raindrops beating against the stone house in a loud tattoo. She hoped Frederick would be found soon. If he was
indeed falling-down drunk, he could become quite ill if
he collapsed in a gutter. Inflammation of the lungs—
especially such expansive lungs—could be deadly.

She found herself startled again as she heard the sudden banging of doors. Since she'd left Teeter upstairs attending Mrs. Monkfort, she cautiously entered the
library . . . and found the French doors not only open, but
also banging against the walls. The curtains were billow-
ing in the breeze, soaking wet.

She quickly crossed the room to shut the doors, wondering who would be crazy enough to go outside in this
downpour. Then, as she realized what she had just
thought, a bark of laughter flew from her lips. "Anyone in
this place," she answered herself.

As she grabbed hold of the French doors to shut them,
she happened to catch sight of a flash of color. Curious,
she leaned out the door and looked outside. To her dismay, she found none other than Jack the Rip, tearing off
his clothes in frenzied anticipation. Throwing down his
shirt and stomping on it, he began to dance a merry jig in
front of her rain-drenched rosebushes.

She shook her head, annoyed. Jack was such a thorn in
her side. "I suppose I'll have to send Teeter and Totter to
go and haul him in," she muttered to herself. And Mrs.
Fawlty would be pulling thorns out of his backside again.
And other places, she thought with a shudder.

Observing Jack bowing to the Marilyn red rosebush,
one of her favorites, she sighed in resignation. The werefox was demented. She doubted he would ever get well.

Planning to summon Teeter, she'd hastily begun to
close the door, when suddenly she stopped, her jaw

falling open. Then, mindless, Eve walked out into the rain to get a better look.

She closed her eyes.

She opened her eyes.

She closed them again.

When next she could look, the sight remained: Jack the Rip was not the only lunatic out swinging in the rain. Frederick was there, too, naked as the day he was created, dancing a jig in the downpour, his big body swinging here and there and everywhere. *All* of it.

Eve gasped. Never had she seen a man's nether parts so big. Talk about being cock of any walk! Frederick was enormous, and it also appeared that he was blotto. He seemed to be yelling something, but she couldn't hear what.

Running back inside, she swiftly grabbed an umbrella. She dashed back out, and icy cold raindrops ran down her neck as she hastened to where Frederick was dancing and singing. Eve could hear him now, three sheets to the wind, singing in a loud baritone. His was actually a very beautiful voice.

As she ran toward Frederick, she didn't realize that her jaw dropped open again and she gaped like a fish. The gentle giant was not alone! Oh, no, Adam was singing and dancing right alongside the merry monster. And while her husband's voice was not as deep as Frederick's, it had a nice husky quality that she admired. Fortunately for her sanity, he was not dancing in the altogether. He was garbed in a pair of doeskin breeches, molded completely to his skin by the pounding rain, revealing his taut muscles and an interesting bulge. He also had on a water-logged hat, the brim dripping rain.

"They are totally without the sense God or Victor Frankenstein gave them!" Eve chided, feeling some measure of annoyance. At the same time, she wanted to whoop with laughter.

She approached, Frederick jumping in rain puddles while Adam swung around one of the tall Grecian columns, his hat pointed at a jaunty angle. Adam was sopping wet, the water droplets covering his chest and gliding down it. Eve found herself licking her lips.

As Adam swung and Frederick splashed, dozens of frogs joined in their cheerful song, hopping this way and that. Surprisingly, the frog's croaks seemed to harmonize. Eve stifled a giggle.

Staring at the huge, naked Frederick and her wayward spouse, she shook her head. She really had to run a tighter ship. But then, what fun she would miss. Again, a few giggles slipped past her lips.

Spotting Eve, Adam let go of his column and splashed toward her, while Frederick began to spin on the opposite column. The heavy marble wobbled with his great weight.

"Good afternoon, my love!" Adam said, tugging at the brim of his soaking-wet bowler.

"What are you doing?" Eve schooled her expression to one of mere curiosity, hoping he couldn't hear the amusement in her voice. The silly man was adorable even wet.

Adam shrugged, a grin on his face. "Nothing important. Merely making a fool of myself," he replied.

"Oh, what a surprise. I thought you might actually do something different today," she replied. He wasn't falling-down drunk, but he had definitely tossed back a few. She grinned. Why did the very nearness of him make her heart leap? She could not account for it, exactly. Especially since the feelings Adam engendered had sprung up in so brief a time.

"I see you've found Frederick and some friends," she noted. Her eyes darted to the frogs, which just happened to be happily hopping and croaking, living the high life.

Adam choked back laughter, but when he spoke his voice was still full of amusement. "Yes. When I found him, he was drowning his sorrows in the Old Kelley Inn."

Eve held her umbrella over her head and gestured for Adam to share. "It appears Frederick is *still* drowning his sorrows. I take it you helped?"

Adam bent down and took the umbrella from her, holding it above both their heads. "So I did—and I must confess I might have had an ale or two myself."

She raised a skeptical eyebrow.

"Or perhaps three."

"Perhaps," she said. "But why didn't you bring Frederick inside when you first got back?"

"Have you ever tried to get a giant to go somewhere he doesn't want?" Adam asked. "It's a very tall order."

Eve giggled and shook her head. "You are the most exasperating man I know. Well, come—we need to get both Frederick and Jack inside before they catch their deaths of cold."

He nodded in agreement, and they started toward Frederick, but before they could reach him the giant fell backward with a splash. He lay there in the middle of a huge rain puddle, arms outstretched. As they hurried over, a big bullfrog hopped on top of Frederick's knee while another, even larger than the first, perched on his giant green head.

Eve knelt beside the big lout. "Are you all right?" she asked. When Frederick grinned stupidly she sighed. "He's still sloshed to the gills."

"That's an understatement," Adam said. "Hard to believe that any monster can't hold his liquor, but Frederick here is absolute proof." Casting down their umbrella, he knelt and placed an arm under Frederick's shoulder, coaching the man to his feet. "I want you to sit up."

Frederick managed to do so, barely.

"Now, I want you to stand on your own two feet," Adam encouraged in a stern tone. Frederick looked doubtful, but Adam continued pressing. "You can do it. You can do it."

Eve got on the other side of the huge monster. "Men and their bottles and broken hearts," she grumbled half-heartedly. Really, she was finding the situation too amusing for words. But as Frederick's doctor, she must show disapproval.

"I'll be all right, Dr. Eve. Dr. Adam put me on the straight and . . . narrow," Frederick said. "I'll be better in a bit. He said I mus . . . must take disappointment with a quiet dignity. After all, I am a Frankenstein. We may be . . ." He hiccupped, gave a great loud belch, then managed to finish: "Frankenstein's are eccentric and scary and sometimes downright mad as hatters, but we do have our dig . . . nity. Dr. Adam reminded me." He added another loud hiccup.

Eve was impressed, truly impressed with both her patient and faux husband. She glanced over at Adam. He should have looked foolish in his soggy trousers and dripping hat, but the knave looked dashing and heroic, and she felt quite fond of him—perhaps even greater-than fond.

"What else did you tell him?" she asked as they began to carefully guide Frederick back to the house, the giant balanced between the two of them.

"I told him that every man makes himself a fool over some woman, often more than once. The trick is to give things your best shot, and if that doesn't work, go on about your life, even if you leave a bit of your heart behind. Crying over spilt milk never proved the pudding."

"What a crusty thing to say."

"You should trust your husband more—a lot more," Adam said. "That's what a good husband does: cossets and takes care of his wife. And she cossets him, especially in the boudoir. That is the secret to wedded harmony."

Frederick groaned beside her, his weight causing her back to ache, and Eve thought of what had just been said. She had never really thought all that much about husbands or what she wanted in one. That was, until Adam had stuck his nose into her life and asylum. One thing she did know, however. Well, several actually. If she were thinking about husbands—which she really wasn't—she would want one who loved her. He would be her helpmate within the asylum, and would think of the members of the Towers as an extended family—an odd family, but a family nonetheless. Strangely, Adam fit most of those requirements.

With the rain pounding down upon her head and soaking her to the skin, Eve groaned as the soused Frederick stumbled, almost bringing all three of them to their knees. She wished the castaway creature were at least four feet shorter and easier to help along.

Reaching the terrace steps to the balcony, she sighed in relief. They'd soon be inside.

"I love Miss Beal, and I'll show . . . shower her roses," Frederick slurred. "Shower with roses."

Eve stuck her head around Frederick's belly, looked at Adam, and said, "Shower with roses?"

"I told him to send over four or five baskets of flowers

for Miss Beal, and apologize in person for his clumsiness. If she doesn't accept the apology, then she isn't worthy of such a fine fellow as Frederick."

"My, my, Dr. Adam, you do surprise me," Eve conceded graciously as Teeter and Totter came bounding down the terrace steps to help. Relieved of her burden, she stared in admiration at Adam. He might not be trained in psychiatry, but he had a good head on strong shoulders, and a fine instinct about people.

Frederick stumbled less as her butler and gardener half carried him up the terrace steps. "Dr. Eve, I didn't even get to l-look at all those inky pictures of yours." He finished his complaint with a series of loud hiccups.

Adam chortled, saying, "Don't worry, the results are spotty anyway."

Eve scowled. "My ink test is being touted as highly effective, thank you very much."

Wisely, the butler, the monster, and the gardener all kept quiet.

Jack the Rip, however, did not. He let loose a sudden bellow of both pain and outrage. Glancing back over her shoulder, Eve sadly shook her head. "Totter, go and get Jack untangled. It appears everything's coming up roses."

"How very gothic."

CHAPTER TWENTY-ONE

Take Two Glasses of Port
and Call Me in the Morning

Eve's carriage was filled with laughter and off-key singing, and the creature crooning was not only slightly off balance but off his rocker as well. Frederick was still sloshed to the gills, and he wasn't even part merfolk! Luckily, Adam had some experience with drunks; after all, he had once worked in a tavern in Paris. So while they traveled along the rutted roads, making their way through the London streets to Dr. Frankenstein's, he restrained Frederick from bellowing at the top of his lungs.

As they approached Mayfield Square, where only the bluest of blue bloods lived, along with a few vampires, Frederick, his damp hair sticking to his scalp, began to sing a bawdy song. Adam intervened, saving not only Eve's eardrums but her pride as well. She had no desire to make a scene.

Twilight was falling, the sky shrouded in dim gray and

black, as Eve asked Adam more about his tavern experience. He told her that his job had been to roust drunks and keep the tavern from being torn to shreds during shape-shifter fights. His stories were enthralling, and Eve clearly saw that wherever he wandered he made an impression—and left one as well. Her hypothetical husband had done so many things in his life. He was a jack-of-all-trades, a chameleon, blending in perfectly with his surroundings no matter where he laid his head at night.

She smiled at something he said, thinking about what an odd man he was. Adam was composed of many parts, not unlike Frederick. She hadn't even known the man a full week, and yet she found it difficult to imagine that he'd once been nothing but a figment of her imagination. He had come into her life and made it better with his presence.

He smiled back at her, patting Frederick, who was now waxing rhapsodic about Miss Beal's attributes. Eve rolled her eyes. If Frederick wasn't singing some horrid song, he was writing odes to Miss Beal's beauty. If she heard one more word about the woman's dainty elbows, she would go mad herself.

The carriage stopped. Catching Eve's expression, Adam helped a lurching Frederick into the house, along with her driver, James. Inside, his creator and Clair both scolded the wayward giant.

Adam returned to the carriage and climbed inside. Once settled comfortably against the seat, he crisply rapped on the roof. "Home, James!" he called. Then, turning to Eve, he smiled a slow, crooked smile, which left her slightly breathless. "I'm so glad that your driver's name is James. I've always wanted to say that."

Eve laughed, surprisingly happy. In her wildest dreams,

she would never have imagined loving the devilish glint in a husband's lovely hazel eyes, or recalling fondly the way his broad shoulders looked while he was shoveling dirt alongside Fester.

Adam winked, his manner quite merry for someone who had been singing in the rain with a nude monster a short while earlier. His humor was infectious, and she found herself giggling for no reason at all. Her feelings for him were becoming rather warm, even though she knew that he was calculating, cagey, cunning, and probably as crooked as the day was long. But he did make her toes curl when he kissed her. Maybe even more important was the fact that he made her laugh.

As the carriage took them back along the muddy roads to the asylum, he and Eve talked more about his past. Adam found her questions to be a dashing good sign. To his way of thinking, her curiosity indicated interest, and interest could be turned into lovemaking, if a man were both cunning and intrepid. Adam was nothing if not intrepid.

As they talked, Adam stared at Eve. She was his guiding light, his shining star. When he was younger, he had stood alone on jagged peaks in distant lands, and below he would watch the world go by without him. Now the world was a different place, and his participation in it began with Eve.

She was telling him something about her past, and he commiserated, noting appreciatively how the soft glow of the carriage lantern set off her creamy complexion. The reddish-gold strands of her hair were highlighted, and glistened like flame.

"What about your early life and family?" Eve asked. "You've mentioned them little."

Adam sighed. "My father, before he lost the estates, was a jolly fellow, always laughing. He taught me to love nature, to ride, to hunt, and he always had a good story to tell." His father had also taught him pride in his heritage. "He was a good father. He chased away the monsters in the dark when I was small."

He stared into the flickering fire of the lantern, his surroundings fading from view. Bravely he summoned memories of things long left buried, and he looked back across the years.

"I remember him fondly. When we were small, my father used to throw me and my little brother into the air, laughing the whole time. My mother would scold him and kiss him on the cheek, while she combed our mussed hair. Mine was always tangled. I was quite the little scapegrace."

Eve noted the slightest curl of his lips, and the faint smile sent her heart pitter-pattering in her chest. "You had love and affection in your childhood," she said. "I wish all my patients could say the same. With love as a foundation, most people can make a decent life. It gives them strength to avoid temptations and wrong roads. It gives them a reserve to draw upon in times of trouble."

He nodded. "We did have love—and wealth and a general gaiety of life. Until the betrayal."

"What happened?"

"My father invested with a distant relative. The venture failed, and we lost almost everything. To recoup his losses, my father gambled at a very high-stakes game at a party thrown by that same relative. Needless to say, my father lost the rest of our fortune. He retained his title, but the baronial estates were unentailed and therefore forfeit. We were left with a small cottage located on the coast of Ireland. Our distant relative, who'd won everything, moved into our ancestral home, and my father never seemed to regain his balance. Not long after, he began to drink."

"I'm so sorry, Adam." Eve touched his arm, her concern clear in her blue eyes. "What of your brother and mother?"

"My brother died six months after our move. My father had been drinking heavily and took him out sailing. The boat capsized and my brother drowned. My father became very ill. He blamed himself and died a scant two weeks later. My mother followed a little over a year from then, with inflammation of the lungs. I've always believed that it was due to our reduced circumstances, and the loss of my father and her youngest child."

The flickering light cast half shadows upon his face, yet Eve recognized courage when she saw it. Yes, courage. This man had dropped his barriers enough for her to see beneath his bold and droll exterior to a sensitive, kind, and wounded soul beneath. It was a view, she instinctively knew, that Adam kept hidden from others. Yet he had revealed it to her, which meant more than a hundred flowery compliments.

"I'm so very sorry for your tragedies," she said. "Life is never quite what we expect, is it? We hope for rainbows and merry memories, but we end up with stormy skies, sad inclinations, and, if we're lucky, we have only a trickle of hope left to begin again. I hate to think of you left alone at such a tender age."

Eve's sincere response and compassion caressed Adam's lonely heart. It also eased the long-buried ache. Placing his hand over hers, he stared into her lovely pale face, and the rustle of past ghosts seemed to fade like dust in the wind. "And yours, my sweet? What was childhood like on a pirate ship? Merry, scary, or rather bawdy?" He hoped to lighten the somber mood in the coach.

"All three and more," Eve answered. "There was freedom, yet no room to explore it. So much water surrounds you, and yet there were times when the freshwater was so low that we went without bathing for weeks on end. I climbed ropes instead of trees. My playmates were a scurvy lot—Peg Leg Peggins, who taught me to dance, and One-eyed Jack, who made me a doll out of rope. And I wore breeches and practiced with cutlasses. I saw whales in the Atlantic with their blowholes spouting, and pink dolphins off the coast of Asia—along with a mermaid or two."

"Did you play pirate?" he asked mischievously.

She laughed. "I imagined tea parties at the queen's, and I played doctor. I doctored cut fingers and sword wounds, and treated rum poisoning. Why, I even tried to fix Peggins a new leg! Unfortunately, a shark ate that one as well. When I dressed up and decked myself out, I had the help of my mother's treasure chest. I did so at least once a week. My father thought me quite unnatural."

"Though I do admire your father, at times he can be thickheaded," Adam remarked gallantly, placing a kiss upon her wrist.

"You don't find me a bit unusual?" Eve tried to ignore the heated tingle beginning in her belly.

"Is this a trick question?" Before she could reply, he leaned over the carriage seat and began to kiss her eyelids, lingeringly and with soft adoration. He placed feathery kisses across her lips. As she clasped her arms about his neck, he moved his mouth to hers. His arms tightened possessively about her. She was absolutely perfect.

Closing her eyes, Eve felt as if a hurricane had swept her away. Her body came alive, responding to Adam's passion; she was tingling and quaking all over. Her toes curled at the heat shooting through her, making her grind restlessly against the soft cushions of the carriage and his hard body. Her fingers eagerly roamed his chest, delving into his jacket and beneath his white shirt, and she gloried in the feel of his chest's strong muscles and its mat of crisp short hair. Lower, she felt the hard bulge in his trousers.

Pure heat shot through Adam, and his caresses became more desperate. He trailed tiny kisses along Eve's throat, wanting to eat her alive. His arousal throbbed in his breeches.

In the blink of an eye he'd urged her back against the cushions. With an expertise born of years of experience, he released her breasts from their confinement. His breath rasping, he managed to relieve Eve of her gown to her waist. As her chest was revealed, his body burned. Her nipples were erect and reminded him of hard, dark garnets. The most wonderful treasures ever.

Catching his breath, Adam groaned. Eve was some pagan goddess come to life. *His* pagan goddess. And he wanted to worship.

Exercising strict control, he forced himself to move slowly when all he wanted to do was ravish her on the spot. "How beautiful you are. So lovely, so divine." He bent to lick and suck her breasts. They were so very soft, and he nipped at them lightly, listening to her soft moan. "The great treasure of Bluebeard revealed."

Pressing her even farther back upon the carriage seat,

he slid his fingers under her gown, caressing the white flesh of her thighs. She gasped loudly. The breathy sound stirred his already overheated senses as nothing else could, and his nostrils flared as he breathed in the scent of her arousal. She was all hot female and silky skin. His blood was racing, and his heartbeat quick. He felt more alive than he ever had. This was the grandest adventure of his lifetime.

It was several minutes before Eve's rational mind offered protest. Her wits had gone a-begging, disarmed by his masterful seduction. But . . . "No, Adam. We shouldn't be doing this," she protested weakly. He made her feel so wicked, so desirable, as if her skin were on fire. Her breasts ached, and the place between her thighs was burning. Embarrassingly, she could feel wetness there, as if her womb were weeping for something that only Adam could provide.

His arousal pressed against her hip, and she moaned again. His effect on her was devastating, like a typhoon in the tropics—and she was now about as wet as one. That last thought had her nails sinking into his shoulders.

"This is wrong. I'm an unmarried—well, married in a way—but a virgin. Our wedded life is a fantasy. A fantasy growing on me, but a fantasy nonetheless. Besides, we can't make love in a carriage. It's so unladylike."

Adam argued by kissing her nipples. Then he said, "Making love in carriages is all the rage. Why, a duchess I once knew—" He fell silent as her eyes popped open and she hit him on the arm.

"I don't need to hear of your past conquests!"

"Of course not, my love. But I swear on my sainted grandmother's grave that none of them compare to you. And I haven't even gotten you to bed yet. See what a little temptress you are?"

"Adam, you're not stopping," she remarked. "I can feel your hands." His fingers had skimmed the tops of her thighs and pressed into the slit in her lace drawers. The spot he touched was virgin, and the sensations shocking and yet seductively wondrous. "Oh . . . oh . . . oh, *Adam*."

"My love, my sweet. I adore you," he whispered, kissing his way across her flushed and heaving chest. His fingers were as busy, playing lovingly between her legs.

"Argh . . ." This time, Eve's exclamation was whispered in wonder and not in annoyance. The blue eyes staring up into Adam's were heavy with passion.

Eve knew somewhere deep inside that she should stop this foolishness, but then his fingers teased that perfect place between her thighs, and the tingling there grew to a fierce, overweening need that eclipsed all else. He began a fiery stroking. At last, he touched a spot that had her muscles clenching. It was surprising, delicious, and made her yearn to know all love's many splendors. After all, she was twenty-seven years old.

"I adore you," Adam gasped, his breathing heavy as he slid two fingers into her. She was tight and wet. The pearl of her passion was plump and juicy with need, yet another treasure for him to plunder. He needed her. He wanted her with an intensity that bordered on madness.

"Feel how much I desire you," he moaned, releasing himself from his trousers, his face dark with desperation. "I think I shall die if I don't have you right now."

My, *my*, Eve thought in stunned amusement. From what she could see, her husband was walking proof of Dr. Sigmund's theory of envy. And he wanted to share that magnificent specimen with her! She shivered—whether in anticipation or appreciation, she wasn't sure.

He had just begun the lengthy entrance when outside

the carriage a loud shout was heard, and the galloping of horse hooves pounded the earth. "Halt that carriage or I'll shoot!" came a voice.

Adam's muscles bunched, and his face became a study in pain. The shout had caused him to halt his advance. With a ruthless gleam in his eye, he raised his head, and Eve tried to sit up, saying urgently, "It's a highwayman; I need to hide my jewels."

Glancing down at where they were half-joined, Adam winced and licked his lips. "That's what I thought I was doing," he muttered. His passion was overwhelming, and yet they could be in danger. He must protect Eve at all costs, even his own desire. Sighing, he added, "I suppose a different cache is in order." Once again, his seduction had been sabotaged. *What rotten luck.*

"I can't believe I don't have a pistol with me," Eve said. "But I don't!" Their carriage was slowing, and it hit a rut, knocking her head back against the cushions.

"What kind of pirate's daughter are you, no pistol?" Adam's expression was beyond grim. He ached with need and unfulfilled lust.

"A reinvented one," was her firm answer, and she stuck her pert little nose in the air.

Again a shout sounded outside the carriage. This time the robber's voice was much nearer, and recognizable. "Stop, ye bloody English. I know ye are carrying the king's gold. Ye think to fool me by traveling in disguise, but you shan't or my name isn't Napoleon Bonaparte. I'll have yer gold for me army. Charge!"

Startled, Eve managed to partially lift herself so that she could see through the carriage window. Despite the darkness of the night, there was enough of a moon to il-luminate a horse and rider. The rider was perhaps four feet behind the carriage, and there were two men following him at a small distance.

Her expression filled with steely determination. "Bloody hell! That's Major Gallant playing highwayman! Where's his bloody keeper?"

Glancing over Eve's head, Adam retorted, "I do believe that's him 'galloping' up. He's as slow a top as that nag of his." He reached out a long arm and knocked on the carriage roof. "Don't stop, James. We'll haul in the loonies later. Much later—maybe never." The last was said with heartfelt disgust.

Glancing back outside, he noted that the third rider was sitting sidesaddle, without a stitch of clothing on—although the nude cuckoo was wearing his Hessians. "Oh, dear. I believe I see Jack the Rip riding along as well. What's next—Lady Godiva?"

"Is Jack dressed?"

"Is the moon pink?" Adam replied, lowering his head from the window and leaning it back against the seat. He shut his eyes tightly, his mouth a slash.

Taking one look at his agitated expression and general disarray, Eve glanced down at herself. The picture she presented was not a dignified one. Half sprawled across the crimson seat like the veriest wanton, she noted that her gown was bunched around her waist. She had one shoe off, and Adam's huge erection was bobbing at her like a Frenchman's salute. She shook her head in disbelief. A week ago she would never have been caught dead in such a compromising position, but here she was. Her giggles turned into heartfelt laughter, her husky voice filling the carriage with her mirth.

Adam's eyes popped open. Eve's eyes were dancing on his erection. "Well, this is a new experience. Women have swooned when I've revealed the family jewels. Some have dropped to their knees in adoration. But I don't recall a single one being struck with hilarity."

Eve couldn't help herself; his words made her laugh harder. Major Gallant's antics had drawn her back to her senses just in time, keeping her and Adam's Bonaparte. She pulled up her gown and began to fix the bodice. She knew better than to make love to Adam. She wasn't married to him, even if she felt as though she were.

Another shout outside the carriage door drew Adam's attention. In a black mood, he stuck his head out and yelled, "Get the bloody hell away from this coach, or I swear I'll stop and tear you up with my bare hands."

All shouting stopped, along with the sound of horses in hot pursuit. Eve continued to chuckle, half sitting and half reclining, her back shoved into the corner of the carriage.

Adam moved swiftly, placing both his hands on either side and trapping her between them. Growling low in his throat, he lowered his head to kiss her again—which she gently but firmly rebuffed. Placing her hands on his chest she shook her head, her curls bouncing.

"I don't think it would behoove me to take this lying down—or sitting up. Most especially since we are but a mile from the Towers."

Knowing the game was lost, Adam sighed. He would accept defeat for now, though not for long. Growling, he fervently wished that he could clip Jack's prickers and rip that would-be Napoleon a new Trafalgar. What infernally lousy timing! But then, the real Bonaparte had been known to spike a cannon or two himself.

The moment was fraught with sexual tension and unrequited desire, and he inhaled audibly, deciding humor in this instance would get him farther than petulance. Reluctantly he pushed himself back and plopped down on the opposite seat. "If your sensibilities are too proper to try it in a carriage, perhaps we could adjourn to your bed—or that nice Persian rug before the fireplace in your study?"

She still had a grin on her face, but said, "Don't think to end on top of this situation. I've come to my senses." Yes, she longed to broaden her horizons, but she didn't want her waist broadening with an illegitimate child. He had introduced to her the spicy taste of passion—a taste she would not forget anytime soon—but a full meal was a long way off.

"Come to your senses? Oh, no, my dear, you've surely lost them," he replied, wincing as he shifted and sat back against the seat. His trousers were definitely too tight. "Do you know, I believe I will shoot Major Gallant when we get back to the nuthouse. I've always disliked the French, and you can't trust a man who hides his hand. I mean, where's he been sticking it? And what can I say about Jack? He'd better be nimble; he'd better be quick—or else he'll get a nasty stick. Right up the backside," he added ineloquently.

Running a hand through his hair, he gazed at his wife with focused intent while she righted her clothing. His heart rate was beginning to slow, and his erection was now at half-mast. "Do you know, Eve, I have a reputation to consider. I don't like this one bit. If we don't relieve this sexual tension between us, soon I'll be howling like a mad dog. They'll think I'm one of your patients! Perhaps I'll join the major and Jack and take to the highways."

Eve swallowed another laugh, even though the weepy place between her thighs was still sensitive and felt hollow. Strange, but she had never noticed it much before his arrival. "We always seem to be at cross-purposes," she remarked. Buttoning her gown, she felt remarkably strong and regrettably stupid. Still, when all was said and done, she couldn't allow this to happen. Could she?

"Truer words were never spoken. I try to make love to you, and find myself constantly interrupted by your demented patients. I'm not teasing, my little pearl; if I don't have you soon, you'll have to lock me away. By the by, if you have to take that drastic step, I do hope you'll let Dr. Sigmund visit me. After all, he understands this thwarted-libido stuff."

Eve's mirth spilled forth again, filling the carriage, which pulled up to the Towers, the horse's hooves ringing on the cobblestones. In the background she heard Sir Loring say, "Stay away from my coffin! I'll have no Englishmen and mad dogs disturb my eternal resting place. Do you hear that, Totter? Don't let Mrs. Monkfort touch my soil!"

Adam shook his head balefully. "Spring cleaning . . . in the fall."

Eve's eyes narrowed. "They may be loud, they may be mad, and some may even be a bit perverted, but these are *my* raving lunatics. I happen to be quite fond of them."

Adam shook his head in mock disgust. "But not as fond as you are of me. No need to deny it, Eve. You're falling in love with me, and I couldn't be happier."

Her eyes assessed him with a sharp gleam. She hated to admit that his words held any truth, but they did. She was fond of him, although she certainly wasn't in love with him. She would never be that stupid. Adam whatever-his-name-was was too wild, too witty, and much too mischievous. Furthermore, there was another damning fact: her Adam had accepted gold to care for her. Even if he really loved her, such a disgraceful beginning couldn't have a happy ending. So without another word she pushed past him out the carriage door, and hurried up the stone steps to the front door.

Behind her, she heard Adam mutter, "A chest, a chest—my kingdom for Eve's chest."

CHAPTER TWENTY-TWO

Sense and Sensuality

It was the days of autumn rain. Outside her bedchamber, Eve could hear the splash of raindrops and tree branches scratching against the windowpanes. She barely glanced at herself in the oval mirror as she put on her pearl necklace. Nor did she note the tiny frown lines around her mouth. Instead, her mind was consumed with Adam, just like in her dreams and daytime fantasies. Ever since Adam had helped Frederick come to terms with his social gaffe, all lingering anger she felt at his deception had slowly bled away, leaving her longing to be with him.

Yet, four days had passed since the aborted assault on her virginity. Days in which she'd considered and reconsidered her choice. Anticipation and angst had been Eve's daily companions, for her husband had been the perfect gentleman. To say that was surprising was an understatement, Eve thought disgustedly. And she should be hopping up and down with joy. Instead, here she was, staring into her mirror, seeing nothing but Adam's face, and wondering when he would make a move to seduce her again. His lips were so soft and hot, making her tremble with need. Placing several drops of perfume beneath her breasts and finishing the last of her toilette, she stared at her reflection. She was in fine form tonight. Her gown was fitted tightly at the waist, and it showcased her figure. The décolletage was lower than she usually wore, revealing the curve of her breasts. Adam would notice those—breasts that had begun to ache at night from wanting his mouth fastened to them.

Eve frowned, questioning her sanity. She couldn't really want to bed the man, could she? Just because he was devastatingly handsome was no reason to lose all sense. And why had he stopped tempting her and trying to get her alone? She knew he wasn't the kind of man to be stopped by repeated failures. He was too strong for that, and too virile.

"Of course," she said to herself, "if I were being absolutely fair, I must admit we've been busy here." With the full moon only a night away, the lunatics had been a rowdy bunch. They had kept both her and Adam busy soothing anxious nerves and calming turbulent water beds.

Giving one last look in the mirror, she nodded. "Let him ignore me *tonight*," she dared. And with those words she left her room to descend the stairs, her mind finding explanations for Adam's disinterest in her boudoir.

"Three nights ago," she said thoughtfully, "we had to track Mr. Carlen through the London stews. That certainly wasn't a picnic." Mr. Carlen had reverted to gargoyle form and flown the coop. Out of necessity, she and her husband had become a team, afraid that if the gargoyle went into a catatonic state he would be discovered. Humans would just not understand a gargoyle in the flesh. Therefore, Adam and Eve had tramped around until near dawn, when they had luckily spotted him. He was perched on the roof of the Birds of Paradise club, which Adam had seemed to think was a good sign. The flying monster was clearly looking for a feathered mate—or at least an evening with a soiled dove.

"And last night our patients and staff played cards," she mumbled as she crossed to the dining room. It surprisingly had been an enjoyable evening that Eve would long remember. Adam had patiently explained several games to a few of the patients and staff, while Mr. Pryce had explained the finer points of gin rummy to Mrs. Monkfort. Even Sir Loring, who had been hiding in the draperies and playing dead, had finally joined in the fun and games, and he'd won more than a few hands after having a cup of his native soil delivered under his chair. For good luck, the lanky vampire had explained.

Adam entered the dining room and greeted his wife cordially, his hazel eyes twinkling as he took in her dress. How he managed to act nonplussed, he didn't know. Tonight she was dressed in a rich royal blue, the color of the icy Atlantic. Her bodice was rounded and revealed her ample charms. And no doubt, he thought lecherously, underneath was her Freudian slip. The gown was cut lower than she usually wore, and he would bet all of Fester's gold that she had worn it to show him just what he was missing. The little corsair was adorable, but he would not play into her hands.

Before Eve could fully evaluate her husband's reaction, Pavlov claimed her attention with a compliment. Dinner then proceeded, and Eve scrutinized Adam then, although in a secretive manner. Just because she was becoming besotted with her spouse was no reason to let him know it. Why weren't those fingers stroking her at night? She took a sip of her soup, smiling slightly, watching as Adam dangled his wineglass from elegant fingers as he spoke with Pavlov.

"Tell me about the time you found yourself locked in a wine cellar with a thirsty vampiress, *n'est-ce pas?*" Pavlov cajoled, requesting one of Adam's more lurid adventures.

Eve tilted her head, listening vaguely to Adam's story while secretly pondering their problem. Adam was excellent. Despite her initial protests, she knew when to give praise. Adam visited with all the patients now, listening with the air of one really interested. His remarks were well thought out, almost as if he could see deep into the hearts of their darkness. The patients listened to his advice with wide smiles, and appeared to feel better after talking to him. Adam had told Eve that he preferred to call his sessions chats, rather than Verbal Intercourse, since he was saving that for her alone. Once she would have been incensed, but this time she found him amusing.

Actually, the past four days had seen many revelations for her, giving her new insight into Adam the man. Yesterday Mrs. Monkfort had even gone so far as to drink a glass of water without washing it first. She said Adam had convinced her that the water in the deep well behind the asylum was clean. And Jack the Rip had honored his wager to Adam after losing a game of piquet last night; this afternoon when Eve was called out to halt Jack from flashing her roses, his trousers had been off but his undergarments were firmly in place.

And the staff adored Adam, she mused. It was obvious. Collins—a sometimes footman and sometimes member of the serving staff—had noticed that her husband had finished his sautéed mushrooms, and he quickly dished out another serving. Of course, the trollish fellow managed to appropriate a few for himself, but Eve didn't begrudge them, since those with troll blood were notoriously fond of truffles.

Taking a bite of braised rabbit, Eve listened to Adam's response to one of Pavlov's remarks. Eve's lips twitched into a smile as she noted that even her assistant seemed impressed.

Pavlov began laughing at something Adam said. He did have a dry, wicked wit, she admitted, and he obviously relished playing doctor. She just wished he'd play it on her.

Watching his handsome face break into an engaging grin, Eve realized that she was more than fond of him. Until this dashing rogue had burst into her life like a Nosferatu springing from a coffin, Eve had preferred her heart just where it was. Life had been much simpler then, but it was so much more fulfilled now. Was this love, this awakening of the senses whenever he was near? When he was gone, she felt a hollowness inside. At times like that, she found that she had to actually resist the temptation to go running to find him.

As Collins sidled forward to pour her more wine, she pondered this marvelously scary feeling, and what would happen if love blossomed full force. Adam was an adventurer, an ex-privateer. If he got the urge to wander again, what would she do? What *could* she do? If he chose to someday leave her, whom would she tease about digging holes with Fester? Who was brave enough or foolish enough to dance and sing in the rain with frogs and Frankensteins? Who would wink at her over Mrs. Monkfort's shoulder? And how in the world would she live without Adam's impassioned kisses? Yet an adventurer was an adventurer, and prone to wander. She had to beware.

Adam choked back laughter. His wife's glances were quite different now from when he'd first arrived. Thank goodness he had always been difficult to discourage. She was everything he could have hoped for in a mate—a feisty little autocrat, yet tenderly concerned with her patients. She was a kind commander, but also managed to be firm. Coming to know her had been one of the high points in his life. He had formed a great respect for her accomplishments. She had become a psychiatrist at a time when most women were content to be put upon a pedestal and endlessly admired and feted for their great beauty. Not Eve.

It was beyond strange, Adam thought, that as lovely as she was, Eve was one of the least vain women he had ever met. It was due, he reasoned, to the fact that most of her time was taken up with helping others—which had ironically made her even more beautiful.

Her kind nature had actually worked against him recently, as she'd been tending to her patients. But he had a battle plan. Eve was a Bluebeard: deny her something she wanted and she would fight to the death to get it. She wanted him, and was just now beginning to realize it. His feigned disinterest should drive her mad with desire, and by the look in her eyes it was working. He was more than relieved, not knowing if his passion for her could go another unrequited night.

Pavlov concentrated on the cherries jubilee, but Adam sipped his wine, leaning back in his rose brocade chair. His eyes fixed firmly on Eve. His grand battle plan would come to an end tonight; it had been decided when she walked into the room in all her glory. She was ripe for the plucking. He would have her in bed and on his body or beneath his body, crying out in ecstasy. Theirs would be an earth-shaking release. Tonight he would get his cock in a position to be envied.

Her husband's heated eyes burned into her, causing Eve to blush. Flustered, she glanced at the grandfather clock on the wall. "We have an hour to reach the Scientific Museum of Supernatural Studies," she said. "Dr. Sigmund's lecture starts then. We can't be late."

"*Absolument.* Dr. Sigmund would have your head, Dr. Eve. He hates tardiness," Pavlov agreed. "My friend will arrive soon to take me with him. I dare not be late either. Those troll eyes of Dr. Sigmund's can be intimidating when burning with anger."

Adam grimaced. "I know we are engaged to attend, but I must confess that I hope this lecture isn't on chamber pots."

Eve sighed. "Since he is the head of the funding committee, I can't risk not attending." She added with a conspiratorial smile, "However, I feel we are both in luck. Tonight his lecture is not about chamber pots. He and Dr. Hartley will be discussing the treatment of bizarre behaviors of the chaos-ridden mind. Also, there's something about some werewolves named Petersen and Borden, and how multiple personalities can manifest with lycanthropy."

"Sounds riveting," Adam replied. But still. What could a troll really know about a werewolf?

"Fraud. I thought you *enjoyed* playing doctor," Eve said—so softly that Pavlov wouldn't hear, her teasing words fraught with fondness.

This, Adam understood, was a good sign. Eve was coming to value his talents, and to trust him. Both qualities he felt were essential in a truly harmonious and loving marriage.

Leaning toward her, he tenderly lifted her hand to his mouth and stared with heavy-lidded eyes into hers. "With you there, my dear, it will be highly entertaining. If nothing else I can absorb your beauty. Besides, I live in hope that Dr. Sigmund will mention his rooster theory again, as I do find that quite interesting. Perhaps you and I might discuss the applications of it later." Yes, from the look in her eyes, she was ripe for the plucking. And once Eve was plucked, they could settle down and nest for life. By thunder, how he loved her, even with her lair of lunatics.

Eve stifled a groan and felt another blush flushing her cheeks. Adam was such a little devil when he wanted to be.

Pavlov, missing the undercurrents of sexual tension, remarked thoughtfully, "*Oui*, I've taken several of his classes. His barnyard begrudgement is a more recent theory, however, and I feel that it is not that impressive. I believe my behavior patterning will someday overshadow it. Everyone will know of my bells. Still, I am interested in his theories on multiple personalities. I've always felt that shifting from animal to human form must take a toll on the psyche. So many werecreatures are insane."

Adam studied Eve's assistant, then turned back to her. "Do you agree?" he asked. "Do you think that all werecreatures are likely to be demented?" He didn't believe she felt that way, but he needed to know. He had thought to reveal his paranormal nature tonight, after they made love. But if she thought shape-shifters were basically unstable, he might think more about his confession first.

"Of course not," she replied, cocking a brow at her assistant. "Really, Pavlov, I've told you that your theory of rampant insanity among werecreatures is a fallacy—with the exception of wererats. I've always felt that they are a bit off balance."

Adam grinned, remarking, "Probably because of their tiny little feet." He knew she was talking about Captain Hook.

Pavlov looked surprised, then joined in Eve's laughter.

A loud noise shattered their mirth as bells began to toll, their loud peals filling the air. In unison, all three turned toward the huge stained-glass window, and they stared out at the bell tower. In unison, all three growled, "Hugo."

The bells continued to ring, and Pavlov's obese dog came flying through the dining room doors. With practiced ease he leaped onto the brocade chair next to his master. His expression was blissful, his speckled tongue hanging out, and he waited to be fed, panting and wriggling. Pavlov had trained him perhaps too well.

"This is *folie*—madness! It's a disaster," Pavlov cried, patting his mutt's head. "Once again, my beloved dog answers the call of the bells—just what I wanted when I began my behavior patterning. But with that *fou* Hugo ringing bells at all times of the night and day, *mon chien* is becoming *un cheval!*" Junger just whined.

Suddenly, the doors to the kitchens slammed open and Teeter lurched into the room. "You rang, Dr. Eve?"

Adam's bark of laughter could be heard over the bells. "God, I love this place."

CHAPTER TWENTY-THREE

As Good as It Gets

Several hours later found Adam and Eve listening to Dr. Sigmund's lecture, which was now coming to a close. Eve glanced around at the wash of present faces. They were many and varied, but then, the older psychiatrist had always commanded great respect. Beside her she felt Adam's restlessness, and he shifted a time or two in the hard-backed chair.

"Multiple personalities have been found in some werewolves. This can lend itself to blood savagery when they are moonstruck. Therefore, in treating them, one must use extreme caution. I must urge all of you not to forget that werewolves often bite the hands that feed them." Dr. Sigmund's closing words were met by loud applause.

The clapping grew, began to reverberate through the room, becoming thunderous. Leaving the sound behind her, Eve escaped to the ladies' lounge to freshen up, while Adam waited to speak with Dr. Sigmund. Hopefully the doctor would have news of the funding committee's decision.

Before the lecture began, Dr. Sigmund had signaled to them. He had specifically asked that Adam meet with him afterward, which had left Eve silently fuming. She was just as worthy as Adam to hear whatever Dr. Sigmund had to say. Even more so. Yet, now that Adam was supposedly returned from the great Transylvania, she was again ignored and regulated to the petticoat line.

Inside the lounge, Eve straightened her hair and tucked on her bonnet, wondering nervously what the committee's decision was. The Towers did so need the money.

Her mind on her worries, Eve took little note of her surroundings as she walked back to the lecture hall. As she was passing a darkened alcove, a golden hook appeared from behind the deep crimson curtains and grabbed her by the long puffy sleeve. Suddenly Eve found herself being reeled in like a fish on a line.

The curtains dropped back behind her, where she found herself in an enclosed small space with the one pirate she certainly had no wish to encounter or encourage. Immediately she took up a militant stance. Glowering up into the face of her abductor, she lifted her nose and looked down it at him—not an easy feet for one of her stature. Stubborn, strong-willed, and courageous, somehow she managed. It never entered Eve's head to cry out for help, even when manhandled by a tall, thin, partial wererat. "Unhand me at once! What effrontery is this to waylay me here?"

Hook laughed, holding her tightly with the fingers of his good hand curled around her neck. His hook was now caught in the skirts of her gown. If she moved, he would tear it. He had a dark look and steely determination in his good eye.

"I've waited a long time to have you near me, Eve. I

don't want to let you go too soon. We need to have a few words." It was a bold statement with nefarious intent.

"You know I desire you," he continued, grinning in lusty amusement. Behind his words lay a world of want. "I've *always* wanted you, Eve. And I intend to have you—as soon as I've disposed of your husband."

Jerking her head to the side and trying to be rid of his foul touch, she railed at him. "Such presumption! I have not encouraged you, and well you know it!" She was worried about him hurting Adam. She wouldn't let him.

"Liar," he announced. "You loved me when you were fifteen. That summer you spent on yer father's ship, you gave me your kisses . . . and a bit more."

She couldn't help but blush, because that summer the tall, thin young man had spent several months on her father's *Jolly Roger*, learning the pirating, plundering, and pillaging business. At the time Ben had been twenty-one and filled with lusty intentions.

"You were to be mine!" he cried.

"I was young and foolish. That summer, you were the closest in age to me and the most gallant. But I must point out that that's not saying much on a pirate ship. Even seagulls are more gallant than buccaneers."

"You were a vision then, and have grown into a goddess," Hook remarked, his dark brown eye alive with long-repressed desire.

That burning gaze was intimidating. Talk about repressed libidos! Eve scowled. She knew she had been in the wrong all those years ago, allowing him to believe she was hooked, but that was all she had done. Guilt had dogged her for years afterward, and that summer her eyes had been opened to the more nefarious part of his character, like women, wine, women, and song. And women.

"I can't believe I lost you. You were always meant to be mine, sweetling," Hook said.

"I disagree," Eve replied. But it appeared Hook was back and determined to force his hand—onto her. Eve found his intentions reprehensible. She shoved the black-hearted villain back, hard, but to no avail; Hook didn't budge an inch, and all she managed was to rip her gown.

She tried abusing him verbally: "Oh, go boil yourself in oil, and leave me be. I'm a happily married woman." She didn't like the look in Hook's eye or his threatening stance. She didn't think he would rape her, or even abduct her from the museum, yet she was afraid for Adam. Something fierce had grabbed her savagely by the heart, rolling her toward love like the crashing of the ocean's mighty waves to shore. She couldn't stand the thought of her Adam's much too early demise. It was strange, she knew; just last week she would have danced upon Dr. Griffin's grave. Well, maybe not danced . . .

"You'll be a happy widow, but not for long. My waiting days are over. I've waited for you longer than I have for anything, and I intend to have you. Yer husband will be wondering where you are. When he comes, I'll see to his death."

So that was Hook's game. "If you hurt my husband, I'll kill you!" she vowed. "I swear it on my mother's grave! I don't love you, Ben. I'll *never* love you. If you hurt my husband, I'll see to it you walk the plank of one of my father's ships—but not before you're keelhauled once or twice, you dirty rat!"

Eve had taken the wrong tack; she recognized that fact as soon as Hook's face turned red and his expression filled with malice. So much for the truth. Eve shoved him hard, hearing her gown rip further. "Leave me the bloody hell alone!" she cried.

Fortunately, her gown was made of strong stuff, and basically held, but his gold hook still captured a thick piece of her skirt.

Hook leaned in so close that Eve smelled the rum on his breath. His one eye glowered at her with frustrated desire and hatred. "You bitch! Love him, do you? Well, no matter. I'll serve his liver to you on a platter!"

Eve tried not to shudder as Hook's mouth took possession of her own. It was a brutal assault, leaving her lower lip cut and bruised. His hook pressed hard into her back, and his other hand still held her neck in a death grip.

She gagged and bit down on his tongue.

"You vicious bitch!" he accused, and his hand moved to her breast and squeezed cruelly. "You'll pay for that!" He squeezed again, with malicious intent, smiling grimly when he heard her whimper. "I hadn't planned to tup you here, but your razorish tongue has decided your fate. You'll learn obedience to me on your knees, like the bitch you are!"

Realizing that the situation had gone far beyond her control, and not wanting to have her virginity forcibly taken, she opened her mouth and yelled, "Adam!"

Hook laughed wickedly, crushing her breast again and tearing at her gown, the tiny pearl buttons popping. As a portion of her chemise and breasts were revealed, Eve again called Adam's name.

Hook silenced her with another ruthless kiss. His arousal was thick and hard against her stomach, and the feel of it was so different from Adam's seductions that she cringed. But her subsequent effort to free herself only made the kiss turn brutally savage.

Hook's attention was so focused that he missed the ripping open of the curtains. Cold fury filled Adam's face as he took in the despicable situation. His heart was racing and his throat felt tight. Hearing Eve's call had filled him with fear. He had died a hundred deaths racing to her aid. Now, with lightning-quick reflexes, he ducked low and flew at Hook, taking the pirate captain down with a crash.

Eve stared, unable to believe her eyes. Her savior had arrived. It was Adam, so quick on his feet that he was like the winged god Mercury. She clapped her hands in admiration and joy.

Adam punched Hook in the face. There came a crack, and Hook's nose flattened. Blood spattered him and he swung at Adam with his hook, missing flesh but gouging the flap of Adam's jacket. His attack also caught the draperies, tearing them the rest of the way open as the two men crashed out into the hallway.

Eve followed, a smile forming on her lips. Adam was fighting for her honor just like every husband should do for his wife. *What an amazing man!* she thought with bemusement. In some ways he was an impostor, but he was also a prize.

"Watch out for his hook," Eve warned, making a fist and holding it up in front of her, giving an imaginary jab.

"Ouch!" Hook had just slammed a fist into Adam's face.

The hallway was now cluttered with people from the lecture. Dr. Sigmund came to stand beside Eve, taking in her torn clothing, and he scowled at Hook. "Hit him a good one, Adam!" he cried.

The bent Hook swung again, but Adam dodged the assault. As his opponent redoubled his efforts and managed to kick him in the thigh, Adam retaliated by ducking low and swinging hard. His punch caught Hook's shoulder, and as Eve cheered him on, along with Dr. Sigmund, Adam's foot next connected with Hook's groin. The pirate fell to his knees, clutching his privates while blood trickled down his face.

Several of Hook's crew barged into the hall and shoved Adam back. One of them grabbed their captain, while two others held threatening pistols at the crowd.

Glaring at the doubled-over villain, Adam snarled, "Leave my wife alone or I'll kill you, you son of a wharf rat! I'll tear you to pieces bit by bit and feed you to the sharks!"

Hook glowered, blood covering his face and his clothes. "I'll see ye in hell, and I'll be the one sending ye there," he vowed. But with those words, he and his men disappeared down the hall.

"Should we follow them?" one of the onlookers asked.

Adam and Eve both shook their heads. Adam quickly assessed her appearance, looking closely for serious damage. "No, we wouldn't be able to catch them," he said. "Wererats."

Several of the gentlemen nodded, while Dr. Sigmund said, "Ah, that explains the remarkably quick escape. Dr. Griffin, are you all right?" he asked Eve.

"I'm fine, thanks to Adam. But I thank you for your concern."

"I think I should take my wife home now," Adam spoke up.

Dr. Sigmund nodded. "We should attend to other matters right now, ourselves," he said with some perspicacity. He rapidly ushered the rest of the group down the hallway.

Eve glanced at the departing crowd and then at Adam. The look in his eyes was one of concern, yet it also held a glint of fierce triumph. He had fought for her and won. Eve recognized the expression instinctively, a very primitive reaction that had her heart speeding up and her breath hitching. Adam cherished her and valued her, and she trusted him more for it. She now knew that he wanted to add to her life, not take from it, and he wanted to walk by her side and not before or after her. He would dry her tears when life's great tragedies befell them, and cheer her up too. In essence, Adam would make the everyday extraordinary.

She paused to tenderly wipe the blood off his cheek. She saw so much that was new. Her husband was a strong character, and dependable, a man who hid much of himself behind a sharp wit and droll humor. But what lay underneath was a man to lean on, a man to trust. In short, Adam was a man for all seasons. And her father—her horrible, meddling, obnoxious, assertive . . . wonderful, wise father—had sent him to her.

Glancing down at his beloved, Adam was struck by the look in her eyes: Eve had stopped running. Wanting to throw back his head and bellow in triumph, he restrained his urge. Finally, the love of his life was beginning to understand the depths of his affection.

Taking her hand, he pulled her toward a back exit. Once outside, he again examined her closely, making sure she was uninjured; then he kissed her tenderly while lifting her into their carriage. He followed, saying, "Thank God you're safe." Rapping on the carriage roof, he shouted, "Anchors aweigh, James."

"You were quite the hero in there," she replied. "But you made a deadly enemy," she fretted, her eyes worried. He had a bruise on his jaw and a cut cheek, but he looked dashingly disheveled. And the fierceness with which he had defeated Hook had roused her passions. Her hubby had been adamantly protective, and he had won. And while she knew it was a shallow thought, something in her Bluebeard heritage loved and needed a winner. "I guess I should admit that I was a tiny bit awed by that rousing display of manliness."

Grabbing her hand, he squeezed it enthusiastically. "Only a tiny bit? And I thought I was quite the knight in shining armor, riding in to do battle with your dragon—"

"Wererat," she interrupted.

Adam chuckled. Then he leaned closer, his voice a soft whisper against her face. "At last, my strategy is working. In spite of our inauspicious meeting, you admire and respect me. At long last."

"Not that long," she replied, her voice teasing. "You are all right, aren't you? You're not hurt badly?"

"No. And you?" he asked tersely, studying her cut lip.

"No. I must admit I was worried there for a short while, but you came to my rescue."

"You're an amazing woman, Eve Bluebeard. Most women would have fallen into a fit of vapors or crying hysterics. Not you. But then, you are made of sterner stuff. You didn't even fly off into a tizzy."

"No, I'll leave flying to Mr. Pryce."

Adam laughed. Lust rushing through his blood, he began nipping at her neck. Then, with great confidence, he kissed her cheek. Tonight he would be victorious, and this pirate's daughter would be trimming his sails. At last the family jewels would be buried by a Bluebeard.

"Adam?" Eve asked.

"Yes?" Minutes earlier she had looked happy, but now he saw she looked worried.

"Did Dr. Sigmund tell you the committee's decision?"

Adam thought about lying to her, but he found he couldn't do that. "Yes. Eve, it's not that bad, but . . . it's also not the best of news."

"What?" Her voice was filled with trepidation, and she gazed anxiously at him.

"They are giving us the fourth grant."

"But that will barely last six months," Eve complained. "How could they do this? The Towers needed the first grant—or at least the second one. Even the third would have been better."

Adam drew her into the sheltering circle of his arms, holding her tight and intending to offer her comfort. They rode through the dark night. The sounds of the wheels filled the silence, but as time passed, temptation raised its swollen purple head. The scent and feel of her was too much, and Adam forgot his decision to leave Eve alone until her disappointment was not so keen. He began to kiss her cheeks, her nose, and her lips, finally moving to the silky smoothness of her neck.

Encased in misery and feeling sorry for herself, Eve suddenly found her attention caught by Adam's tender ministrations. He began to kiss her neck, and her insides began to tingle. Warmth invaded her body, and her toes curled in her slippers. Fickle toes! They certainly hadn't curled when Hook mauled her. But as Adam slipped his tongue into her ear, she began to shiver in delight.

"You need me, Eve," he said. "You want me, darling. I bet you're wet with desire."

Her blue eyes were glassy, and his words sizzled through her. Rot the blighter if he wasn't right, for she felt a gush of liquid between her thighs. "How could this happen so quickly? I am a rational person, a doctor," she said. "One doesn't just snap her fingers and find love knocking at her door."

"I didn't knock," he managed to growl, the warm tenderness in his eyes becoming blazing-hot desire. His arousal pressed against her, showing his attraction, and he leaned over and suckled on her breast. Lifting his head, he begged, "Darling, let me love you."

The sound of crunching gravel and James's shout interrupted, however. Eve quickly pushed against him. "Adam! Stop that. We've arrived back at the Towers. We can't do this on my doorstep!"

Adam groaned, his blood burning, his manhood literally ready to explode at any moment. "Then for pity's sake, let's hurry to your bedroom."

Eve's heart was thundering in her chest as she straightened what she could of her gown. Need was riding her shoulders, for she indeed wanted this man to take possession of her, to introduce to her to the delights of the marriage bed. She had waited too long, and this would be a night never to forget.

The driver had opened the door and placed the steps for her to get down. Adam followed, then grabbed her hand. Together they ran up the steps to the asylum, laughing merrily. They took the stairs two at a time, and Eve hadn't felt so carefree since her days on the *Jolly Roger*.

No sooner had they burst through the front door, than the towering Teeter grimly greeted them. "The little bald fellow has been digging holes again, the fanged gentleman is most upset about his dirty bed, and the buggy patient has flown himself into a web," he reported.

Things were generally crazy, Eve knew, but for a grown

man (or werewolf) to be caught in a trifling spiderweb made no sense at all. She narrowed her eyes suspiciously. "Teeter, have you been drinking?"

"Oh, madam, if only I had," he replied.

Through the window, Eve saw Mrs. Monkfort waxing some fronds near the pond. Sir Loring was there, too, pacing frantically in the conservatory, looking for dirt, which Eve assumed Mrs. Monkfort had removed.

Adam glanced at Eve. Apparently his desires were to be thwarted once again. He asked in a voice filled with irritation, "I don't suppose we could just get back in the carriage?"

Eve narrowed her eyes in weary resignation, then dutifully followed Teeter into the conservatory.

Adam sighed, reluctantly trudging after them. He knew patience was a virtue, but he'd never been very virtuous. He was the conquering hero, but with no reward.

Shrugging with ill grace, he grumbled, "Somewhere tonight, people are happy and laughing. Perhaps they're at a ball, or a musical, and they are sharing heated glances and secret assignations. Somewhere tonight, young lovers are lying entwined in each other's arms, but it bloody well isn't here."

And was this as good as it was ever going to get?

CHAPTER TWENTY-FOUR

Oh, the Webs We Weave . . .

Adam's eyes widened. Sir Loring was dashing about the conservatory, crying mournfully and tearing out fist-fuls of his hair. "That woman! That maddening mad-woman has thrown out my native soil. The native soil that filled my coffin. What shall I do? I'm doomed—doomed!"

Mrs. Monkfort peeked over the fountain. The garden room was filled with a dense array of foliage and colorful flowers. It was an exotic jungle with the rich scents of earth and hundreds of flowering plants. Normally it was a place of sanctuary and serenity. Not today.

"Oh, dear," Eve remarked, a frown furrowing her brow. This was serious. Vampires had to have their native soil close at hand in case of accidents, since native soil aided greatly in their regeneration. It also helped vampires who had a tendency toward hysteria, calming their over-wrought nerves. Sir Loring, more than most undead, was particularly grounded in his soil.

Turning to the culprit in question, Eve leveled a stern look at her. "Mrs. Monkfort?!"

The woman pointed an accusatory finger at the vampire. "I won't have all this dirt in my house. It's disgraceful and so, well . . . dirty!"

"Mrs. Monkfort, it wasn't your dirt, and this isn't your house. It's mine. You had no right to throw away anyone's dirt, or even to touch another patient's belongings," Eve replied. "Where is the dirt?"

"Where you'll never find it. Never."

Sir Loring continued to whine.

Teeter groaned. "It's an orchard in here, I tell you. Every day, a veritable new treeful of fruits. I must insist on higher wages. I can't take much more. Especially if I'm to do this sober."

Adam silently seconded the butler's thoughts.

"There's too much dirt," Mrs. Monkfort continued. "Too much nasty, nasty dirt. And naughty little bugs crawling around in it. We're got a long, long way to go before we're clean. And that bloody leprechaun isn't making my task any easier," she added, pointing.

Eve glanced over to where Mrs. Monkfort was motioning, where Fester was digging up the flower beds. "Fester!" she yelled in outrage, spotting two very large holes near her orchids. "How could you?"

At the sight of Fester's panicked face and his wife's fury, Adam couldn't help but laugh.

Eve put her hands on her hips, incensed. Adam should be helping her halt this nonsense, but instead he was hysterical. Well, she would have a long talk with him and remind him of a husband's duty—both to a wife and to her mad patients.

Fester turned a guilty glance their way and set aside his shovel. He knew better than to dig a deeper hole for himself, especially when Dr. Eve was wearing her little-admiral look. His ship was sunk.

Placing a hand on his wife's shoulder, Adam narrowed his eyes in speculation. Could Fester's gold finally be here? He hoped so. What Captain Bluebeard had paid him had been a great help, but a man could always use more. Especially if he were to do what he truly wanted.

"Fester, I think you should stop. You've upset Dr. Eve," he said with a hint of steel in his voice. "You're about to make her check herself *out* of a loony bin. We'll hunt down your gold later. After all, two heads are better than one. Right, old man?"

The chagrined leprechaun thought about it a moment or two, then finally nodded and threw down his shovel.

Eve shook her head, annoyed. But before she could begin a reprimand, a tiny voice from behind the Venus flytraps rang out: "Help me! Help me!"

Both Adam and Eve glanced at each other, shock on their faces. The leprechaun shrugged. "Me hearing ain't what it used to be," he said. "I never heard no cry of help before."

They cautiously made their way down rows of towering green plants and dense foliage, and Mrs. Monkfort scurried behind them. She wore a slightly guilty look. Ahead, half-hidden in shadow, three massive Venus flytraps rose from the corner of the room. Mr. Pryce was entwined in what appeared to be a large spiderweb, his hands outstretched and wrapped in white tendrils. He was staring in sheer terror at the large gaping mouths of the flytraps.

But there was a bigger surprise. The spiderweb was the giant lacelike thing Mrs. Monkfort had been crocheting.

Eve's jaw dropped open, her eyes round in patent disbelief. "Really, this is simply too much, Mrs. Monkfort!" she cried.

The pitiful Mr. Pryce tried to flap his pretend wings, buzzing and shrieking in a high voice, "Help me!" He indeed looked like a desperate housefly.

Everyone turned at once to glare at Mrs. Monkfort, who began dusting a massive fern next to her. Glancing up, a haughty expression on her countenance, she asked crossly, "What? I did only what needed doing. We don't need such fake flies in our home, especially not going around and buzzing respectable people who are hard at work. Yes, I wrapped him up in that lace cloth and set him in front of the flytraps, but he's the one who froze like that. It's not like the demented man is stuck. He could be free if he wanted." She waved a dismissive hand at him.

Eve said frostily, "Mrs. Monkfort, this is cruel. Mr. Pryce is terrified of flytraps. How could you do this?"

Noting Mr. Prince's dejected, desperate expression, and Mrs. Monkfort's blush, Adam suddenly had a brainstorm of epic magnitude. The puzzle pieces clicked together all at once. "Mrs. Monkfort," Adam addressed the odd lady, "I do believe I know what's happening. Mr. Pryce is courting you in the only way he knows how."

Surprise replaced the woman's arrogant demeanor. A slight smile crossed her thin lips; then she remarked, "No. I don't need a man buzzing about me, a fly in the ointment. Besides, he's got the personality of a gnat."

"He doesn't have to bug you," Adam suggested. "He's not always hieing fly."

Eve, catching on quickly, took up the reins. "No, he isn't. And Mr. Pryce is not just any man. He's quite wealthy in his own right, the third son of a marquess. So he sometimes needs a good swat. But how could you blame him for being taken with your charms? You know what they say about flies and honey . . . But he's also a werewolf, and wolves are noted for their faithfulness—as well as keeping themselves and their dens clean."

Mrs. Monkfort stood quietly, preening at the mention of a clean den. "I should quash his pretensions," she remarked, stealing a glance at the trapped bug-man. "After all, Mr. Pryce lives *here*. It's a lunatic asylum, you know," she confided.

Adam whispered to Eve, "No place else could these two meet."

Mrs. Monkfort cooed, her gaze going all coy. Behind her, Teeter untangled Mr. Pryce from the crocheted web.

Adam chuckled, and Eve shot him a speaking glance, but before either could talk, a loud rasping and banging drew their attention. Sir Loring the vampire was quietly but methodically beating his feet against the floor. He had lain down under several exotic ferns and vivid pink orchids, and was sniveling.

"My poor soil. It's gone!" he moaned.

The vampire was truly pitiable, and although Adam had never cared for bloodsuckers personally—due mostly to having been on the business end of several pointy teeth a time or two—he couldn't let the poor old fellow suffer.

Leading Mrs. Monkfort quickly to the fly-man, he cajoled hurriedly, "Just think: Mr. Pryce is mad about you. To celebrate this momentous occasion, we should do something a little special."

"What?" the washing widow asked. She fluttered her eyelashes at the flyboy.

"Let's find Sir Loring's dirt—so he can be jolly too,"

Adam explained in his softest, huskiest voice. He didn't really expect the morose Sir Loring ever to be jolly, but he hoped for an apparent mild contentment. "You can take the dirt, but can you dish it out?"

Mrs. Monkfort looked strangely thoughtful, then finally agreed. "All right. Perhaps I can wash it for him. I threw it in Fester's hole. The one over there by the orange tree."

Giving her a quick peck on the cheek, Adam thanked her, and Mrs. Monkfort blushed becomingly. Unfortunately Mr. Pryce took exception to the kiss, and he took his new lady's hand and firmly walked out the door, the large spiderish blanket trailing behind the odd couple, still entangled about his waist.

Adam just grinned.

Soon afterward, Sir Loring's dirt had been restored to its rightful owner and Eve and Adam soaked in the calm after the storm of insanity. Eve shook her head and glanced around the garden.

"Sometimes my patients do things that fly in the face of all reason. Imagine Mr. Pryce being held captive by that crocheted blanket!"

Adam chuckled. "The imagination is a powerful thing," he said. And he should know—he'd been imagining the things he would do to Eve all night. Clasping her hand, he teased, "Alone at last. And in a place like this, crawling with manic monsters, solitude is not easy to get."

Admiration lit her face, and she stared up at him. "You were marvelous. You really should have been trained as a psychiatrist. I've been amazed that you instinctively know how to treat the patients, or at least help them with their troubles," she confided, staring at him with wonder. "You have hidden depths, my pirate husband. I do believe they are deeper than the Atlantic Ocean."

Her admission stirred Adam deeply. He needed Eve, like his biblical namesake must have, for this woman was clearly made especially for him. His yearning for her defied all logic and physical boundaries. Somehow Eve had become everything wonderful and delightful to him, and she gave him determination to beat all of life's challenges. She was the laughter of a child, the cooling wind on a hot Caribbean beach, and the brightest star in the heavens. Infinity was found in her smile, and true goodness in her desire to help those less fortunate. "I adore you, my love, and I always will," he vowed.

In Adam's eyes, Eve could see her beauty, her desire, and . . . yes, perhaps her destiny. She was all things to him, and that was a heady thought. Especially to a scientific-minded female who had not thought to marry.

Eve smiled. She was through fighting against overwhelming odds, against Adam's dashing nature and wit. The time for pretense was over. Adam was like no one she had ever met. He was better even than her imagined husband, and that was saying something.

"Such hidden depths," she marveled. "I knew you were trouble the minute I laid eyes on you. But aren't I the fortunate one?" She touched his cheek, her eyes misting with love.

"Hidden depths, eh?" he remarked wickedly, smiling, keeping her tears of happiness at bay. Pressing her hand up against his suddenly painful erection, he said, "I have a feeling you have a few hidden depths as well. Depths I'm well ready to plumb. Do you feel what you do to me?"

Eve suddenly felt feverish. Placing her hand on her chest she said, "I feel what you do to me." Her heart was beating madly, her breath coming in soft gasps. She wanted this man, wanted him with an intensity that was almost ludicrous. "What would you recommend, Dr. Griffin?"

"Complete bed rest, with lots of Verbal Intercourse to keep you sane. And we must not forget good old-fashioned regular intercourse. Every night for at least a year or two—or perhaps even a lifetime," he suggested.

"I concur, Dr. Griffin, with your treatment." And with that, Eve wrapped herself around him and hung on for dear life.

CHAPTER TWENTY-FIVE

The Doctor Is In

As she stared into Adam's eyes, the last of Eve's defenses came crashing down. She sighed with pleasure. She knew some women felt that losing their virginity was a dreadful experience. She knew some women hated to "do their duty" and let their husbands lie with them. But that was not the case. Not with her. Her body warmed at the thought of what magic they were about to make.

Gazing down at Eve, Adam admired how her eyes sparkled like blue diamonds, how her nostrils were flaring with passion. His blood was surging, and the conservatory felt as though it had risen several degrees in temperature.

Surrounding them were deep green foliage and brightly hued flowers. Eve lay upon his jacket beneath a massive fern near the Venus flytraps. Her rich auburn hair was now in a tangle about her shoulders, a visual feast. He had unbuttoned her bodice and her breasts spilled free. So firm, the coral nipples beckoned his lips to suck and cherish. Her gown was raised to her thighs and her skin looked very soft and pale. A sprinkling of freckles lay high near the nest of springy auburn curls. He wanted to kiss every adorable mark.

Lowering himself hastily beside her, he moved his fingers quickly. Caressing her leg, he savored the way she moved, restlessly, shifting her weight from side to side. In a sense, this was a first for him: to truly make love to a woman, to love a woman with all his being. His other encounters had been lusty affairs of the body, but never had his heart been involved. "My treasure, my little jewel. I adore you."

"I'm mad about you, too." His hands were wandering heatedly over her body. The touch of his fingers and the wonder of his mouth had Eve eager and hungry—hungry for experience, hungry for passion, and hungry for her handsome husband. She gasped with wonder as he suckled her breast. "Oh, Adam!"

His kissed her hard, and her toes curled. Running her fingers up and down his back, she gloried in his body's strength. "Don't you need to be undressed for this? It seems I remember you promising something about burying the family jewels."

In Adam's haste to undress, his trouser fly lost two buttons. His arms got tangled in his shirt. It was ridiculous, Adam thought; usually he was a master of seduction, yet tonight he was like an untried schoolboy. He admitted it to her. "You don't know how I've longed for this moment. I almost can't believe it's here." And at last he stood nude before her.

Eve's body clenched in instant appreciation at the sight before her. Forget the fig leaves or modesty; she found herself unable to tear her gaze away from his proud form. He had powerful shoulders, the muscles of which rolled and bunched as he lowered himself to the floor beside her. He was tanned a deep golden color to the waist, and his leg muscles, though not large, were well defined and wiry. He was like a Greek statue come to life, a magnificent specimen.

Slipping a finger inside her, he found her wet and creamy, causing him to groan at the sensation. She was tight. "You're so hot, darling. Just for me."

She felt so many different feelings, actually: hot and yet clammy, tingling and beginning to ache. His fingers were long and well manicured—they were beautiful hands, pushing her thighs apart. It was shocking to feel his finger inside her, to feel his thumb pressing on the little nubbin of pleasure down there. But it was even more shocking to look down and spy his arousal, which jutted proudly out of a thick nest of dark brown curls. Soon it would push its way inside her.

Eve had seen men's members before, unexpectedly sometimes on the *Jolly Roger*, when the pirates relieved themselves. Also, she'd seen them when Jack the Rip stripped off his clothes, or that time with Frederick in the rainstorm. There had been cadavers and patients in medical school, too, though usually she had not given them the same attention. But the truth was, none were as impressive as Adam's display, and she would just have to revise her opinion on Dr. Sigmund's theory.

She lovingly touched the tip of his penis and watched it jerk. Giggling, she glanced up to see Adam giving her a tight little smile. "Hmmm," she said. "You look like a pirate bent on plunder."

"I am," he replied, his voice taut with unleashed passion. "And I can't wait much longer. But darling, if you touch me again it will all be over before it begins."

He leaned down and kissed her, his eyes heavy-lidded with passion. "Oh, Eve. I've been waiting all my life for you." Not only was he physically involved, but also spiritually. It was almost unnerving to realize it.

Running her fingers over his buttocks, Eve arched against him, feeling the tingling inside grow quickly into a rush of pleasure as he settled his weight between her thighs. Then she felt him at her entrance, probing and hard and hot. She gasped.

Adam plunged deep inside, breaking through and into his wife's virgin's sheath. Somewhere deep within his sensual haze of possessive delight, he heard her shocked gasp. She was his! Glancing down, he saw her wince and bite down on her lip. Though he wanted to pump fast and furious, he patiently waited, watching, buried deep inside her. He wanted to cause her pleasure, not pain.

Eve opened her eyes to find him staring down at her, an expression of tenderness in that burning gaze. "I think I could do without that last part," she managed to say.

He lowered his forehead to hers, groaning in agony. "I'll never willingly hurt you again, my love." His flesh twitched within her, and his primal instinct urged him to thrust. But no. By a slender thread, he held on to his willpower to wait until she was ready.

She moved just a bit, her muscles relaxing. The burning was gone, replaced by wanton need and lust.

"I love you," he said.

She moved again, and her breath came whispering out, her eyes steady on his, a wicked smile on her face as she said one word: "More."

Adam found himself laughing, and he withdrew, then plunged again and again into her. Tiny shocks radiated outward like a raging storm-tossed sea. Bracing himself upon his arms, he flexed his buttocks, surging deeper within her. He groaned, "Oh, my darling!"

Hearing Adam's husky words made Eve experience a whole new sensation: feeling uniquely feminine. She had driven Adam almost insane with lust! It was a heady notion, and it deeply stirred her. She could feel something tremendous building within, too. She breathed deep, smelling his skin, a scent of earthiness mixed with musk. His flesh was filling her to overflowing, and she felt her wetness became a liquid gush. Spiraling skyward she felt herself swept under in a huge tidal wave of pleasure. Her toes curled until she felt that they would touch her heels.

"Adam, my love!" she cried.

The tremendous force of his wife's release had Adam clenching his teeth. His body tightened as he surged to follow. He thrust hard and deep, marking her as his mate. She was whimpering in delighted abandon, thrashing her head from side to side. At last he thrust hard and came with a lusty piratical shout. Deep within her womb his seed spurted, over and over until he felt the last shuddering release. Breathing harshly, he sank down upon her in sated weariness. And a beautiful thought came over him: Perhaps they had made a child this night. A child of love.

He finally managed to muster enough strength to roll over, taking her with him, kissing her. Gazing down at her sweet expression, he managed an impish grin. "You're mine now, my love, forever. No matter what, come hell or high water or captains with hooked hands."

Drowsy, feeling as if she had touched the stars, Eve laid her head against his chest. After tonight she wholly trusted her heart in his steadfast care. At one time she might have wondered if he would wound or break it, if he would be faithful. At one time she might have thought it better to remain alone. But love's grasp had set her free, and tonight she had become a woman.

"Is it like this often between a man and a woman—this miraculous journey of the senses and the heart?" she asked.

Leaning over, he tenderly kissed her forehead. "No. What we just shared is very special. This is what love-making is *supposed* to be, but rarely is." And he began to prove it to her again, pushing inside her welcoming warmth.

Eve had been thinking. She had wanted to speak with him about the funding for her asylum. Now that she and he were joined as man and wife, Adam could help her with her financial woes. But his deep thrusts had her mind spinning, and Eve forgot her patients and the committee's decision. Everything was Adam. And afterward, she fell into a gentle slumber.

Staring at the sleeping woman by his side, Adam ran his hand through his hair. Eve was more than he had ever dreamed. He never wanted to let her go. Although replete from his spent passions and the warm glow of love, he was still restless. He felt the increasing pull of the moon. Tomorrow it would be full. He felt a twinge of guilt, wondering if perhaps he should have told Eve about what he was before they'd made love. He had intended to reveal his shape-shifter ancestry, but his mind had been too occupied with enjoying this. He hoped they wouldn't regret it.

Slipping on his trousers, he walked over to the large window of the conservatory. Pushing aside a fern, he looked outside, his mind hard at work. Eve had taken the committee's decision better than he had anticipated.

How he had dreaded telling her. She loved her asylum and her patients, but he'd been able to cheer up her disappointment. This thought pleased him immensely, and had him smiling.

Rubbing the back of his neck, he thought about the gold Bluebeard had given him. He had already used much of it to buy back the Hawkmore estate in Ireland. It was impossible to help Eve from that particular chest. But perhaps they could move to his ancestral home. Although the estate wasn't as large as the Towers, it was a nice-sized manor and had no bell tower.

Speaking of the bell tower, Adam found himself staring at a dim light near it. Someone was out there. Was it Hook? Would the pirate captain try again so soon? Surely not, Adam reasoned. He hoped not.

He knew Hook was going to be a formidable enemy, but he would never prevail. The quicker Hook realized that pertinent fact, the better for all concerned. And if the one-handed pirate didn't agree, then a dawn meeting with pistols or swords could easily be scheduled.

Throwing on his shirt, Adam went to investigate the dim light. It was Fester, busy digging another hole. Adam shook his head. He had begun to doubt that the leprechaun had any coins at all. He certainly had no sense, as he was breathing heavily, his shirt covered in sweat.

"Fester, let me help you dig."

The crusty old leprechaun nodded, a sly grin on his face. "I found me treasure map, I did! Forgot I stowed it in a ship's bottle over a hundred years ago. But I found it tonight." He chortled gleefully. Then his grin faded and his brows furrowed with a scowl. "That daft widow woman cleaned me bottle of its ship tonight. I can't get it back in! I guess it was fortunate, though, since the map was tucked in the sail."

Adam shook his head in amusement. "Thank heavens for small favors—and deranged widows. So, you hid the gold here? But, a hundred years? That's a long time, Fester. How could you have a map of this place when you lived in Ireland at the time? And all those years ago? It doesn't add up."

Chortling, the leprechaun pointed to the new hole he was digging, one just to the left of a massive chestnut tree, which was centuries old, its trunk enormous. Inside the large hole was something that glinted.

Fester swung his lantern over the hole, explaining as he did, "A hundred years ago, I had come to England as a young lad following me rainbow. I met and fell in love with a lovely lass, an elf, and was to be married. Unfortunately, her father was a grand ol' earl and didn't want his daughter marrying anybody who wasn't an elf. He especially didn't want an Irish leprechaun. He had me imprisoned and stole me pots of gold." Fester began scraping the dirt from the glinting object while Adam helped by shoveling the hole wider.

"I escaped and rescued me gold. But they were hard on me trail, so I buried me pots by an old church and a house with a bell tower, and I drew a treasure map. I got away, but was cursed on me way back to Ireland. That blasted bloody earl hired some wayward witch to do the evil deed, and I ended up asleep for sixty years. For a long time I forgot the gold."

"And you remember it now?" Adam asked, eagerly lifting what seemed to be several pots out of the ground. His breathing hitched and his eyes had a glazed look, and he stared down at what seemed to be many more pots still in the ground.

"Right. I remembered only recently about the gold. And I couldn't for the life of me remember where I'd put it. Still, I remembered enough to find me way back here to the Towers. Luckily I'm a little bit mad, so Dr. Eve took me in. She even lets me dig, although it drives her crazy." And with those words, the lucky leprechaun pulled up two more pots and wiped away some of the dirt. Underneath were golden nuggets.

Adam burst out laughing. The little pots were all filled to the brim with golden coins! He must be living a charmed life—he'd not only found Eve in Eden; he'd discovered the pots of gold at the end of the rainbow.

CHAPTER TWENTY-SIX

Flee-Adam Had-Her

Eve awoke alone in the conservatory, her toes nibbled by the Venus flytrap. Swatting the always ravenous plant, she sat up and noted that she was wrapped in Adam's jacket. She could tell by the sun filtering through the windows that it was probably midmorning. She stretched, then realized that she was wearing Adam's jacket and nothing else. And she recognized another pertinent fact: Adam was nowhere in sight.

"Why didn't he wake me?" she asked the nearby plant, but it merely shut its trap.

Finding her discarded clothes, she quickly dressed. Frowning, she shook her head. She could have been caught in the altogether by one of her staff or patients! "Like a regular little trollop," she muttered. Surely Adam had considered that before leaving her. The patients here had enough problems as it was; they certainly didn't need a loose woman for a doctor.

After such a wonderful night together, and Adam's whispered avowals of love, she had thought she would be kissed awake by a stiff and sexy husband. Instead, she was stiff and sore from sleeping on the ground.

She sneaked up to her bedchamber to get dressed, then went back downstairs and asked everyone—even Junger—if they had seen Adam this morning. No one had seen hide nor hair of him. Eve began to worry.

Before she could get overly nervous, she became downright concerned, though for a different reason. Fester ran into the room. He was shouting at the top of his little lungs that his gold had been stolen. At first she listened to the leprechaun's rant with half an ear; Fester's gold was always stolen. Then Fester related the story of his map, and how helpful Dr. Adam had been in helping him dig up the treasure. After all that digging, the leprechaun said, he was mighty thirsty, so he had left Adam guarding the gold while he went into the library to pour himself a drink. He had been so merry that he had drunk the whole bottle of whiskey and fallen asleep. When he awoke, he'd found both Dr. Adam and his gold gone. His face a mask of pure misery, the belabored leprechaun held up a handful of gold coins. Old golden coins, Eve noted vaguely. Then her world collapsed. Fester's gold was real. She was the fool.

All Eve could do was stare at Fester with a dead expression on her face. Her brain refused to accept that Adam had made love to her and then left to steal the leprechaun's gold. That betrayal was too ugly, and it was breaking her heart into a thousand tiny pieces—pieces of her loving nature, her pride, and her trust, which would never be completely put together again.

Her fierce Bluebeard pride reared up. She was going to *kill* him when she found him, and she would leave no hiding place unsearched. The lying libertine had not only stolen her virginity but her heart. And apparently he thought that gold was more important than spending their golden years together. How could she have fallen for his polished charm, and how could she have polished his family jewels so lovingly, so trustingly? She would never forgive herself.

She indulged herself by throwing a temper tantrum— and about fifty pieces of her favorite porcelain. The display made Teeter vow the younger generation was cracked, and Eve stormed off in a huff to lock herself in the cellar. There she screamed until she was blue in the face. It felt remarkably freeing. She marked down the process as the I Scream, You Scream, We All Scream for Iced Dreams treatment.

After her hysterical fit, she sat down on a barrel of ale and wept until her eyes were red. She wasn't getting enough funding for her beloved Towers, and now this? How could Adam have done it to her? What an idiot she'd been.

Sniffing, she sat in the dark cellar and found that she hated him. Yes, she despised him almost as much as she did herself for trusting him. She had known just who and what he was—well, maybe not exactly who, but definitely what. The crook had always been enamored of wealth, yet she had been in a stupid, romantic haze, believing that he had grown more enamored of her. How foolish!

Wringing her handkerchief, she got up from her chair but snuffled some more. She was pathetic. She hated him; she loved him. He had betrayed her and the Towers. It was unforgivable, unforgettable, and just plain despicable.

The hours passed, and just as the afternoon was about

to be put to bed, her fiendish father called on her. It was an inopportune call—for him—for Eve was still in her nasty mood. She had cried until waterlogged and screamed until hoarse. She had bemoaned Adam's betrayal with a shattered heart and wrung hands. Her feelings were bloody, raw, and aching as she left the dark cellar, and everyone in the asylum was walking on eggshells—with the exception of her father, who came strolling into her study with a happy swagger.

Captain Bluebeard stopped in the doorway, instantly noting the redness around his daughter's eyes. Her despair reached out and grabbed him by the throat, and he felt something he hadn't felt in a many a year: guilt. He didn't like it one bit.

"You cutthroat privateer! You meddling menace! How could you? You saddled me with a husband whom I didn't want and I didn't need. Only to find out that I *did* need and want him, wanted him more than anything, even my degree in psychiatry. And you know how hard I worked for that. I'd like to shove your blasted boots down your throat. I hope your ship capsizes in a maelstrom!" She wanted to say more, but felt that if she did, tears would come again. Adam was gone, along with her dreams and trust. "I tasted heaven in his arms. He made me laugh. He helped me and listened to me. He complimented my life and my work. But then he left me and stole Fester's pots of gold."

Her father donned an aggrieved expression. His expression was one of humility, a look he wore uncomfortably, his legs braced apart, his hands useless at his side. "Now, Evie, all's not what it seems."

"I was perfectly fine alone. I didn't know what I was

missing, but now I do. How could he barge in here and upset my apple cart, only to desert me when I just discovered how much I needed him? My patients love him too. He not only betrayed me; he betrayed them! Poor, poor Fester. How can I ever forgive that?"

Bluebeard sighed. "So, lassie—you love him," he remarked. Then he opened his arms for his much-beleaguered daughter. After a slight hesitation, she ran into them.

Her father's arms and stocky body were warm. He smelled of wintergreen pipe smoke and the salty sea. It was a comforting memory of childhood. "How could he leave like this?" she asked. "How could he betray me? I thought he loved me."

Yes, she had given her mind, body, and soul to Adam. His betrayal would destroy her. Not literally, because she wouldn't lie down and die, but the woman she was—or rather, had been last night—was right now struggling in her death throes. Gasping her final breaths. And what would take her place would be bitter and distrustful, perhaps too mistrusting ever to seek love again.

"Oh, Da—why?"

Shaking his head, Bluebeard held her tightly. Awful as it was, it was better to let Eve know the truth than imagine Adam would betray her. "Buck up, lass. Adam hasn't left you. And he didn't steal the leprechaun's gold. Ben's got his hooks in him, I'm afraid—along with the gold."

Startled, Eve pushed back and stared at her father. "How?"

The Captain shook his head. "Me spies told me that Hook left his ship last night with a motley crew of wererats. Not long ago Mrs. Holly, the bartender at the Neverland Tavern, came to see me. Her house is near where Hook keeps his landing boats. She saw Hook and his crew hauling a bunch of little pots and a man aboard. Then they rowed out to his ship. The man was bound and gagged, but she saw his hair color. Brown like the earth, she said. She knew they were kidnapping him. Didn't concern her much, since she's seen it before. But something about the man stirred her memory. She said that she thought she'd seen us together at her tavern a few weeks ago."

Eve's soul filled with worry, despair, hope, and fear. "Hook? This isn't good at all. He'll maim him or kill Adam to pay me back for scorning him—and to pay Adam back for their fight last night."

"Aye," Bluebeard agreed. "And I'm afraid I'm much to blame. I pushed the competition between the two. I told Hook that Adam might not be the man ye needed, to not lose heart until I could judge. I lied to Adam, telling him that I intended to have him disappear from your life so that you could marry Hook—after a decent mourning period, of course. Afraid I've been hoist by me own petard."

"*Why?*" Eve asked, confused, gritting her teeth against the urge to give her father a well-deserved boot in the arse. She pushed away from him, her eyes narrowed in suspicion. "Why both men?"

"I've known Adam for a long time. He comes from a fine family that was destroyed by betrayal and tragedy. Many men wouldn't have survived. Others might not have survived with honor and a sense of humor—not to mention courage. I wanted him for you. But knowing how stubborn ye are, I decided to throw a little smoke into the mix. I also knew Adam is about as stubborn as ye be. If he knew I wanted him in wedlock with ye permanently, he might not have been so willing. I used Hook to make him jealous. And it worked."

The captain began to pace as he tried to explain. "I always intended for Adam to be your husband, not Hook. Ben would make a bad mate for any lassie, since he can't keep his breeches closed. And his temper's too fierce. I thought it was a sound plan."

"Aye, such a cunning plan that the love of my life may soon be out of it," she growled. "I never thought the serpent in my own home would be my father!"

"You wound me, lassie; you truly do. I had only your best interests at heart. I can't believe Hook turned on me like a rabid dog! 'Tis mutiny, I say, mutiny!"

Eve could tell through his bluster that her father was deeply hurt. He valued loyalty highly, and Hook's betrayal was quite a blow.

She headed toward the door. Hook was an insane monster—and not because he was hairy or liked to clean too many things, but in the bad way, like being cruel, ruthless, and hating anyone to best him. She had to act.

"Where be ye going, Evie?" her father called.

Glancing back over her shoulder, she snapped, "Hurry up. I know you must have some plan to rescue Adam, since you came here. Well, don't you?" she asked in exasperation, her legs braced, her hands on her hips.

"Aye. That I do, that I do," he agreed.

"Then let's ready the deck, for this is war!"

Opening the door to her study, Eve was surprised to find a row of faces. The owners were all milling about the hallway, both staff and patients looking to her for answers. Evidently they had been eavesdropping. She really should scold them, but she didn't have the heart.

Fester cleared his throat, looking both apologetic and

guilty. The guilt was for blaming Dr. Adam, she supposed, not for digging holes in her cellar.

"We want to help you rescue Dr. Adam," the sometimes starched butler stated emphatically, his head tilting up and down.

Fester nodded with a grunt. "And it's me gold. That dastardly Hook ain't got no right to it—or to our Dr. Adam."

"Why did you all eavesdrop?" Eve asked, her eyes narrowed.

"Because Adam would have never disappeared without somebody taking him," the somber Teeter replied.

"He lovezzzzz you," Mr. Pryce buzzed, still not quite used to his voice. But then, he had been playing a fly for a long time. "He lovezzz us too."

"Aye, and he loves ye in his bed, Dr. Eve," cackled Mrs. Fawlty. "He'll have forgotten them foreign women, he will. A fine man he is. A fitting mate for our Dr. Eve. All bite and no bark."

Eve blushed, thinking of her husband's mouth. As she took a quick peek at her father, he seemed to find the statement good news, for he was grinning cheerfully. Oh, yes, he spotted grandkids on the horizon. He was as happy as a pig in filth.

"All bite, eh?" the Captain asked. "I thought he might be. Faithful, too—unlike that cur Hook, who I thought was me friend."

Eve would have felt sorry for her father, but his meddling could cost Adam his life. She would forgive the Captain later, when she knew just how much she had to forgive. Turning her attention back to her patients, she used her firmest voice. "Absolutely not. None of you may come. The rescue will be dangerous, and I don't want any of you hurt. My father and I will rescue Dr. Adam, along with his crew. Only Totter may accompany us." Looking each of her patients in the eye, she stared them down, praying they would do as she said and stay put. After all, they were under her care.

Spotting her assistant, she swiftly advised him to watch the patients, putting him in charge. "Fester, you can come. It is, after all, your gold," she conceded to the little fellow. He was jumping up and down, hopping mad and not just madly demented.

Pavlov frowned. "I think I should come too."

"No," Eve said. "We'll have enough help with my father's crew. Now come on, Father; let's go a-pirating."

"Er, Evie," Captain Bluebeard mumbled, putting a forceful hand to her arm. It stopped her from storming outside and down the front steps. "Me crew took the *Jolly Roger* out for a turn at sea. I've only got Stinky Sam and Peg Leg Peggins for help. They're out watching the docks and keeping an eye open for Hook's ship."

In other words, they were in deep barnacles.

Eve frowned. "It's just us, then? Us against Hook and his whole debauched crew? Blister it all!" Sparing a glance at her butler, she reorganized her thoughts, planning the rescue operation. "Teeter, you're tall and strong. You come too—and Pavlov." She nodded to the housekeeper. "Mrs. Fawlty and Collins will be in charge here." And so saying, she hurried out the door with the captain right behind.

Totter had to duck his head as he followed them into the carriage. Teeter and Pavlov soon appeared, while Fester swung himself up on top to ride by the driver.

"Put 'em to it," Bluebeard shouted, and the horses clattered off. Eve looked back to see all her patients standing and staring, not realizing they were plotting mutiny.

CHAPTER TWENTY-SEVEN

Hook and All

The light of a dozen lanterns lit the deck of the *Tiger Lily* and the bruised and bloody man tied to one of the ship's masts. A crew of bloodthirsty pirates surrounded him. The night was windy and his shirt fluttered in the breeze. Again, Adam jerked as the cat-o'-nine-tails bit into his skin. The whip drew blood, and he bit his lip to keep from making a noise. He wouldn't give Captain Hook the satisfaction of knowing how much it hurt.

The pain eased after a moment, and Adam breathed better. He had been in hundreds of tight spots before, and had always gotten away. This time, however, he felt he was in too deep. Behind him he heard Captain Hook raise the whip.

"Eve's mine! She'll always be, you misbegotten cur. You dared touch her, but now I've got you in my hands and you'll rue the day," Hook ranted, his expression filled with loathing.

Lifting his head to judge the moon's ascent, Adam

bided his time. Soon he would be able to transform. Then there would be hell to pay.

"Eve's mine. She loves me," he replied.

The taunt infuriated Hook further. Growling, the captain struck with his whip again, the lash biting into Adam's back. Adam cringed in pain. He was weak now, as he had only barely survived the keelhauling this afternoon. Only his supernatural strength and stamina had kept him alive, but survive he had, because he now had a life to live for, complete with his true love and a family. Okay, an odd sort of family, but a family just the same, where he was needed and respected.

He groaned, waiting for the whip to fall again. The full, round moon was creeping ever closer to the midpoint in the sky, when all shape-shifters would shift into their secondary forms. He wished it would move faster. Captain Hook was in for a big surprise.

"I love Eve Bluebeard. I've always loved her. When you're dead she'll marry me, and together we'll sail the oceans and spend her father's fortune." Hook was laughing maniacally as his nose began to twitch, catching the scent of all that lovely blood on Adam's back. His fingers elongated as claws burst through the skin. He snapped his cat-o'-nine-tails. "I intend to eat most of you, but I'll leave your head so that people will know you're dead."

"Over my dead body," Adam replied. The pain in his back was amplifying, causing him some dizziness. Yet beyond the pain he could feel the moon's power tightening his muscles and making his blood hum. He could feel the change coming upon him, which meant that the wererats aboard ship were feeling the moon's call as well. He hoped he could overcome them.

"Precisely!" Hook replied, laughing demonically.

Adam started to protest, but a sudden sound of scrambling and noise on wooden planks had him lifting his head off his chest. He couldn't believe his eyes.

"Well, laddie, I'm afraid you'll have more to eat than you bargained for. You'll have to add me own fine carcass to the mix." It was Captain Bluebeard, who snarled as he stepped into the lantern light, clutching a pistol in each hand.

"And mine," Eve shouted, appearing from behind a stack of barrels. "You dirty rat!"

"And mine," Sir Loring cried, the glow of the lanterns shining red in his eyes, making his sharp fangs glint.

"And mine," came a chorus of the Towers' patients. They stepped up behind the Bluebeards, along with two of Captain Bluebeard's original crew and Junger.

"You rotten rodent! You stole me gold! A pox upon yer blighted head!" Fester was hopping mad, and what little hair was upon his baldpate stuck straight up as he shouted at Hook.

"Ye double-crossed me, laddie, and ye know how I feel about mutiny. I can't let it go," Bluebeard chimed in again.

Whip still in hand, ratlike claws extending, Hook froze, his dark eye showing astonishment. "How did you get here? We're two miles out to sea. How could ye find us?"

"We rowed," Bluebeard replied, a brutal grin on his bearded face. "And ye forget yourself, boy. Remember, I've werewolf blood flowing through me veins. I sniffed ye out, you and your ratty crew."

"I didn't hear you come aboard," Hook said, his tone one of cold curiosity.

"We were quiet as mice." Bluebeard laughed. "Didn't think ye'd be setting out cheese plates in welcome."

Hook snarled, his beady eye dark with fury. "It's a shame. All this folderol over a nobody."

"Not a nobody anymore," Eve cried. "He's somebody, and the only anybody I ever want. He's Adam Griffin, my cherished husband." Eve stared at her beloved, processing the bloody welts on Adam's back. How she hated Hook. Thank goodness there was a plank nearby.

Staring hard at Hook, Bluebeard shook his head. What a waste, what a tragedy. Men would die tonight—good men, bad men, and many, many rats.

"Ye didn't think I'd let ye kill me son-in-law," he said. "Not when he's just shown up and hasn't had time to get me daughter with child—did you? Especially not when I handpicked him meself."

Dropping the whip, Hook began to snarl, his mouth protruding slightly as his canines finished their transformation. They looked extremely sharp. His shoulders hunched slightly, and a scattering of coarse fur began to grow upon his body. Behind Hook, the sound of clothes ripping and shredding filled the night, along with the squeals of men becoming giant mice-men.

Rats, thought Eve.

"You think to stop us, Edward? I don't think so. Maybe you and this mangy crew might have had a chance on another night, but tonight the moon is full, and you aren't a full shape-shifter. Most of my crew are full-bloods. Tonight you are food for us rats." Hook paused. "Leave now, Bluebeard, and I'll let you live. If not, I'll have your liver for supper while your daughter watches."

"Not full shape-shifters?" Mr. Pryce called out, stepping to the front of Bluebeard's band. "I am." Everyone gave a gasp of surprise, except Mrs. Monkfort, who remarked with adoration, "My hero."

Jack the Rip growled and stepped forward, red fur sprouting on his foxy face, and revealing sharp little teeth and pointed ears. "I'm looking forward to a little snack," he said.

Hook's laugh was razor-sharp. "I have thirty crew members, and twenty-three are wererats," he said. The sounds of claws and paws filled the air. Time was up. Hook's crew had finished their transformations, and their heads had reshaped into those of giant rats. Long tails protruded from their hairy buttocks, and extremely wicked-looking teeth were bared in anger.

Suddenly Major Gallant charged out of nowhere, in Bonaparte style, an imaginary sword in his hand. The mutt Junger was nipping at his heels and barking frenziedly. Eve gasped, then watched in stunned disbelief as the nimble Hugo also appeared, leaping from the rigging to the crow's nest. From there he swung across the yardarm, his little face twisted in gleeful madness. He pelted the pi-rats with marbles, causing them to slip and slide as if they were learning a new kind of jig.

Jack the Rip charged forward, caught sight of one crewman's tattoo—a rose—and, just as the pirate drew his blade, exposed himself. "Take that!" he yelled to the stunned pirate. Before the man could reply, he was knocked overboard by Hugo. The splash he made started the battle.

Adam stared in astonishment, for Eve's patients were out in full force, the whole mad lot. And this time, it was to his benefit! He loved the whole scurvy lot. He would have laughed at the absurdity of it all if Hook weren't leering at Eve.

"Soon you'll be mine," the wererat captain snarled, then he turned to attack Adam.

"Never!" Eve retorted.

Adam saw dark figures sneaking up behind her, and he yelled, "Darling, there!" He pointed.

Grabbing her pistol, she spun and fired. The shot hit one rat bastard right in the eye. He fell and did not rise.

Adam grinned, admiring his wife's deadly aim as she dodged another wererat and fired at close range, blowing out its brains. Fester jumped upon a nearby pi-rat's back with a shout of rage, his little face red. "I want me gold!" he cried. And two more of Hook's crew jumped overboard to avoid his maniacal charge.

As Hugo sailed past on a rope, Adam admitted, Yes, the lunatics were in full swing. And those like Gallant and Fester were in charge.

He turned to find Eve, sniffing, intending to use his keen sense of smell. She had disappeared far into the maddening crowd. The foolish woman had risked her life to save him, and surprisingly so had Captain Bluebeard. He had to save her. He had to break free before Hook returned.

Blood loss slowed Adam's shape changing, but finally he felt the tremors begin and the skin on his back and shoulders stretch. He fought, working hard not to transform completely; he wanted to be able to explain his shape to Eve. But his eyesight became sharper, and the raw, ravaged flesh on his back slit open for massive wings to emerge. Talonlike hooks burst through his toes and fingertips. He used those to rip free of his bonds.

Throwing back his head, he stretched, feeling strength course through him as the ropes fell away. Long, brownish-gray wings had erupted from his back. A dusting of feathers now covered his chest and arms, while a short beak had formed—a very sharp, slightly curved beak. A beak that he would soon use to good advantage, for he was immediately confronted by none other than Captain Hook himself.

"Damn you to hell! You're a werehawk," the head pirat hissed between his daggerlike teeth. He raised his hook to the sky and shook it, raging at heaven and hell and everything in between. Adam valiantly faced the monster.

In the process of reloading her pistol, Eve glanced over at Adam to see how he was faring. Gasping, she was shocked into stillness at the sight of her lover. Adam was a werehawk, and his wings were magnificent!

"Blast me to smithereens with a bottle of rum," she mumbled, appalled at the fact that she hadn't even known this part of his nature. He must be of a royal lineage to be able to blend into humanity so smoothly.

Off to her side, she heard Major Gallant charging up and down the deck, yelling, while she finished loading her pistols. She shook her head grimly. Major Gallant should show more fangs and less dash, and Adam shouldn't have kept his heritage a secret. But while she ought to be furious, she found she was not. He was such a splendid specimen, in the prime of life, and with such magnificent wings and glorious feathers. . . . He was also battling for his very life.

As her two supernatural suitors clashed, Eve held her breath, praying that her beloved would prevail. Hook *couldn't* win. She winced as he clawed Adam across the chest, but Adam struck back and slashed Hook's face with a talon. Rivulets of blood filled the wererat's good eye. And though the fight turned bloodier from there, Eve was forced to turn her attention back to her own precarious situation. She was surrounded by three of Hook's goons.

She immediately shot one of them with a pistol, but her second shot was delayed as the firing pin jammed. She threw the pistol aside and reached for her cutlass, feeling the wererat's fetid breath on her shoulder. In the nick of time, she was saved by Teeter, who grabbed the rapacious rat and threw him over the side of the ship. The last rat attacking Eve saw that he was alone and turned to scurry away. But he lost the race as Mrs. Monkfort set him on fire with a torch, screeching, "Rats! Dirty, nasty little buggers! Off the ship, I say— off the ship!"

The wererat obeyed, jumping into the water with the smell of scorched hair trailing after. The intrepid Mrs. Monkfort was encouraged by the result, and began to shove her torch at two more nearby wererats.

Observing Mrs. Monkfort's success, Pavlov stepped up. He urged the others to pick up torches—with the exception of Sir Loring, Jack the Rip, and Mr. Pryce, who, being werecreatures, had a fear of fire. Rapidly Bluebeard's crew began forcing Hook's over the side. Soon only a small contingent remained, encircled by the Towers lunatic army.

"Deserting a sinking ship?" Eve called out to the fleeing wererats, and managed a shaky laugh. "Bravo! Bravo!" Then, feeling a whisper of wind behind her, she turned to find Adam. His chest was bleeding slightly, but behind him Hook lay dead.

Eve shook her head. Evil would always come to an end, and good would always triumph. Or so she wanted to believe.

Adam's breathing slowed as he saw that Eve was not injured. She might be a bit of a mess, what with her hair waving in the night breeze and gunpowder on her clothes and cheeks, but didn't she look lovely? He would never forget the way she looked tonight. The wind whipped through her hair, and the cool sea breeze brought a rosy hue to her cheeks. He wanted to enfold her in his arms—wings—forever. Yet, in spite of the almost irresistible urge to clasp her close, he remained motionless, trying to judge what she was feeling about his ancestry. His heart pounded in his chest. Her grandparents had been a mixed couple, and he hoped Eve had no prejudices.

"Eve?" he said.

His fears were swiftly displaced. She gave him a blinding smile and rushed into his arms, clasping her hands around his neck, holding on for all she was worth.

"Oh, Adam—you could have died!" she cried, breathless. "What would I have done without you?"

"Have an empty bed again." Mrs. Fawlty just had to put in her two guineas.

A few chuckles were heard, but Eve lovingly touched Adam's feathers. "My, my. I must say that you are a fine-feathered figure of a man. Adam, you're a werehawk! Why didn't you tell me?" she asked. "Mmm, soft."

"Darling girl, *you* could have been hurt!" Adam countered. He wrapped Eve in his wings. She was smiling up at him. Apparently his supernatural heritage hadn't shocked or repulsed her. And she didn't appear to be mad at him for keeping the secret.

Glancing around at the crowd of the dotty and dithering, he crowed. Above, Hugo swung from the crow's nest.

Junger and Jack the Rip began howling in unison, raising their voices—and fortunately, nothing else—in triumphant song. Major Gallant charged up the steps to the main deck, calling, "The scurvy rats, they jumped ship! Charge, me buckos—once more into the breach!"

All Eve wanted was once more into Adam's breeches.

On the lower deck, Mrs. Monkfort was already busy swabbing, and Fester was busy searching out his pilfered pots. Sir Loring was petting some dirt he had brought with him, while Mr. Pryce was relieving himself on a railing. Eve was glad he was acting more wolfish than flylike.

As his wife broke out of his embrace and doubled over laughing, Adam quickly followed. Life had never looked better to him. Even Captain Bluebeard was chortling, his dancing blue eyes merry with amusement—and victory.

Several moments passed with the golden glow of the full moon shining down on the deckfull of merrymakers. Congratulations and praise were uttered. Everyone was in a gay mood, even those who had been wounded.

Suddenly, Eve stopped chuckling and narrowed her eyes at her impossible husband. Yanking on Adam's feathered chest, she spoke fiercely. "I was so mad at you when I discovered Fester really had gold and that it was missing. I thought you'd taken it. I was miserable. I thought that you'd betrayed me. Oh, Adam, I'm sorry. Can you ever forgive me?" She tugged again on the feathered chest. "How could you let me be so miserable? Next time you're kidnapped by a deranged rodent, leave a note."

"I will, my darling," he agreed, seeing how upset his dear wife was. He would promise her anything. And pulling her close to his side, he kissed the top of her forehead and chided her softly, "I don't know many women who would have risked their lives for me. You're a pearl, and the only treasure I'll ever again need. Your price is far above rubies. Now promise me you won't do anything so stupid again."

"Stupid?" she shouted in outrage. "Shiver me timbers. I was worried sick about you! Stupid?"

Taking in the scene, Bluebeard knew when to interrupt. Using a father-in-law's prerogative, he spoke: "Now, Evie, Adam's just worried about your health—as all good husbands should be. But, Adam, me daughter ain't got a stupid bone in her body."

Both Adam and Eve glared at him.

Bluebeard glared back. "It's me right to counsel! What kind of father would I be if I didn't?"

Eve stamped her foot. "The way I see it, you don't need to be giving advice but an apology to Adam."

"Now, why should I be apologizing when my little trick has given him the best thing he's ever had?"

"Father," Eve threatened.

"What apology?" Adam asked, noting how Captain Bluebeard avoided his gaze.

"It weren't *that* awful. I don't know what me daughter is carrying on about." The pirate captain looked abashed. "I might have played both ye and Hook against each other in me plan to see Eve happily wed. I always wanted ye to be the one to stay and be a true husband to me lassie, but I feared ye would balk at being permanently wed. And though I admired some things about Hook, he would never have made a good husband."

The Captain's comments took Adam aback. "Eve, do you see any planks about?" he asked.

Eve gave a startled gasp, half-amused by her husband's comment. But placing her hand on his arm, she gave a squeeze. "I've traded my fascination with planks for family harmony."

His gaze flicked between the two Bluebeards, and Adam thought hard. Then he nodded in acceptance of both the apology and the knowledge that the captain considered him a fitting mate for his beloved daughter. "You did what you had to do. And the result is paradise found rather than lost."

An amused smile graced Eve's lovely features; then she turned to her father, shaking her head slightly. "I should box your ears. Or at least scold you. But I find I can't. You made a good move, Father. One worthy of the Bluebeard heritage. Aye, you old scalawag, we all discovered treasure far from where we buried it."

Adam gave Eve a wink at her mention of buried treasure, then turned toward the others. "I want to thank you all for this gallant rescue," he said. "You've saved my life, and I am deeply in your debt. I have never been more proud."

"Hear, hear," Major Gallant cried. "But I was only one of your rescuers. I wish you the best."

Mrs. Fawlty seconded the major's speech. "Aye, you are a fine, lusty man, and a good master. We love ye, Dr. Adam—all of us. And Dr. Eve? Why, she loves ye best of all, and so she should, even if you are part foreign."

Eve giggled. Adam could feel her warm breath stirring against his chest feathers. He grinned at the tart housekeeper, and at Teeter, who stood beside her bloody and disheveled, nodding with stiff grace.

"You're family, Dr. Adam, just like our fine Dr. Eve."

Hugo swung by on a mainsail rope, cackling and trying to tinker with the ship's bell. He called out, "Ye climb the ropes as good as me. Ding-dong, the Hook is dead. The wicked Hook, he was a crook."

"Oh, get down from there, Hugo!" Teeter scolded. He didn't relish climbing the rigging to fetch the wayward dwarf.

Adam Pierce Hawkmore—alias Dr. Adam Griffin—did something he hadn't done in years: his eyes filled with tears. "Aye," he finally managed to say, swallowing past the lump in his throat. "I feel the same way. We're family." And so saying, he took three leaping steps and soared off into the sky.

"Adam! What are you doing?" Eve screeched. He had scooped her gently into the air, and she stared at the sea beneath her. She felt the fierce rush of his wings and heard a victorious cry from his lips.

"Taking you to heaven," he replied. "Or at least the heavens."

His words stirred her Bluebeard blood as the wind caressed her face. Glancing down, she saw the deck of the ship far below.

Noting her tension, Adam asked, "Do you want me to set you back down?"

She thought about it for only a moment. If pirates couldn't take risks, then who could? "No." She was amazed and afraid, but didn't want to return. Not yet. She'd spent too long trying to keep others grounded. "We're flying," she said, the words whispered in amazement.

Again, she looked to the sea below. Tiny lights from the lanterns were all that was visible of the ship. In the moon glow, waves crashed and crested. The world was so beautiful from this distance. The violence on board was now hidden, and peace surrounded her.

Breathing deeply, she simply enjoyed being alive. The strong wind was cold and smelled of sea salt. It was a whole new perspective. "I can't believe I'm flying," she repeated. She lovingly patted Adam's chest, snuggling closer to him.

He chuckled, leaning his head lower so that she could hear his answer. "It's what werehawks do."

"You take my breath away," she said.

"It's the height."

"You romantic feather-wit, you," she teased. As she laid her head against his chest, she found the feathers were soft as goose down. "How I love you."

"Thank you for taking a chance on me," he forced himself to say. "For taking that first terrifying leap of faith and giving me your trust. I know how difficult it was for you under the circumstances. But you are my mate. I knew it from the first. I'll always love and cherish you."

He could feel her tears wet his chest, tears that stirred his soul in a thousand ways.

"My beloved, where are we going?" she asked.

"Home."

Eve nestled closer against Adam's warmth, feeling stupendously weightless. Such a remarkable sensation, this flying. Far beneath her she could see tiny lights glowing. The wind was brisk yet invigorating. Her heart filled to overflowing with love.

Rubbing Adam's chest affectionately, she asked curiously, "What is your real last name?"

"Hawkmore," Adam replied.

"How fitting." And so saying, Eve burst into laughter.

She was indeed happy. She had a scoundrel for a husband, but if he was one who would fly away, she now believed he'd take her with him.

It's a wonderful life, she thought.

CHAPTER TWENTY-EIGHT

Two Flew over the Cuckoo's Nest

The flight to the asylum, holding tight to the werehawk she loved, was breathtaking. As Eve glanced below, the lights of London looked like tiny sparks. Fog covered parts of the city, increasing the fairyland effect. Above, milky clouds moved slowly against the deep black sky, and the full moon appeared close enough to touch. Eve would never forget.

Never had she felt so touched by magic. Not even when her father's seventh wife, who also happened to be a witch, had cursed her. She patted Adam's cheek in gratitude, his great wings beating fiercely against the cold night air.

"You were so brave tonight," she said, filled with love and admiration. "Like a knight of old." Her husband had rushed in where pirates feared to tread, and had won her heart completely. He was a man far above all others, even when he wasn't flying. And while he might not be perfect, he was perfect for her. "You certainly know how to sweep a girl off her feet."

Looking down at her face, he grinned. "I've told you before that I aim to please. And I'd do anything to keep you from harm. You're my life, Eve," he replied, soaring higher. He held her tightly, his mind replaying the battle. His darling could have been hurt, or worse! He hugged her tighter, his arms around her like bands of iron. He would never let her go again.

Nestling her cheek against his chest, Eve closed her eyes. She was growing sleepy, and the pitch-black of night was turning to the grays and pinks of morning. And even this high up, she had never felt so safe.

She sighed as rain began to fall, wetting their bodies and refreshing her. Just as Adam's love had done, she realized, renewing her life with a hundred little blessings—along with one or two big ones. She giggled, feeling ridiculously silly. As she kissed his chest, he groaned and shifted direction.

His big wings beating hard, he began to circle, gliding lower and lower in a tightening spiral. Over Adam's shoulder, Eve noticed an iridescent rainbow. How fitting. It was a day for new beginnings.

Landing on the balcony to her bedchamber, Adam gently set her down. Eve met his gaze and, seeing the raw lust glinting in his heavily hooded eyes, she smiled, certain that her own eyes were reflecting the same. Before her was her future, the alpha and the omega.

Indicating the rainbow, she said, "Look, Adam, our good-luck charm."

Adam grinned. "Thank heavens Fester isn't here. He'd be squealing with delight and trying to talk me into going and having a look for more pots of gold. But I have more important things to do this morning."

"Such as?"

"You want my body, you wanton wench, and being the wonderful husband that I am, I intend to oblige you until you're too tired to move," he teased. But he led her quickly inside.

Eve shook her head. "I don't know why I put up with you. You're much too impertinent," she grumbled good-naturedly.

A fire danced merrily in the bedroom grate, and the silken blue bedcovers had been turned down invitingly. Inside the cozy comfort of the room, Adam's wings descended back into the strong muscles of his back. Eve watched in fascination as a deep purple light surrounded him and he finished his transformation. The feathers receded into his skin like water evaporating from the ground.

"My grandmother Ruby's light was gold," she remarked.

Back in human form, Adam answered, "Werecreatures that aren't feathered have golden light, but birds tend toward purples. Now, enough talk!" Then Adam whooped and scooped Eve into his arms, his destination the big four-poster bed.

Eve laughed gaily as he threw her down on the mattress and landed beside her with a thump. He remarked, "I thought you might be a little upset. You got a husband you didn't want, and one who's supernatural in the bargain."

She replied softly, running a hand tenderly down his cheek, "A wild and winged wonder who has swooped down to steal my heart and mind and soul. I'd hawk your wares any day." And she winked.

For a moment the two stared at each other in rapt fascination. The looks of love in each other's eyes were stark and elemental, forming memories that would never grow old or fade as the years soared by.

A great peace descended upon Adam. At last, the bitter sorrow of yesterday was gone. Taking his wife's dainty hand, he raised it to his lips and kissed it. Afterward, he drew her into his sheltering embrace.

"Oh, my love, before you my days were long and my nights unending. I was a rover, never finding a home, restless and wandering. But you have broken me to your hand."

Her sigh was deep and fulfilled. "As you have broken me to yours." Taking his hand, she placed it above her heart. "In sickness and in health, and in feathered form, I pledge my love and troth to thee."

"As do I," he whispered, his voice fraught with passionate yearnings. He began to unbutton what was left of her torn gown, giving her a lusty look. "I've found my Eden."

Spreading the cloth wide, he gazed down at the thin chemise that barely covered her breasts. "I hope you don't mind, but I find myself fixated on your treasured chest again."

"I thought you'd never uncover it," she replied.

Nuzzling one breast, he began to suckle, and it spread fire up and down her body. Eve arched her back. She could feel herself growing damp in anticipation as his tongue and teeth tenderly nipped and swirled, and her fingers clutched at the powerful muscles of his back. He was very strong, and yet at the same time so gentle, making her feel like the most cherished of women.

As Adam's lust rose, his breathing became harsh. Impatiently he ripped at her chemise and then hurriedly helped her undress the rest of the way. Laughing, they fell upon each other, consumed by passion.

Eve opened her eyes to see the dark brown hair, the hawkish face, and the hazel beauty of her lover's eyes, which were at that moment all the more beautiful for shining with his love for her. His shoulders were extremely powerful, and they bunched and rolled as he caressed her body. She was breathless, hungry for him; never had she seen a creature more virile.

His fingers found the damp nest of her nether curls, found the little nubbin hidden within. He teased and caressed her, his fingers dancing in a rhythmic motion that had Eve arching and moaning.

Then, with a swiftness that both startled and excited her, he began kissing her there. His head was between her thighs, and his tongue was doing wicked things. At first she was shocked, but that quickly faded. His tongue was slightly raspy and very wet—just like she was getting.

"Adam! Oh, my . . . my goodness!" She screamed suddenly as the pressure inside her increased to a throb. The sensation was wondrous, as if she were back in the clouds again with the night breezes in her face and the colors of the night swirling all around. Deep hues of purple and indigo interspersed with flashes of bright golden light filled her closed eyes. "Adam," she moaned. "Please take me now. Now!"

Adam obeyed. The feel of her surrounding him, so hot and wet, almost drove him over the edge. Eve was so responsive and so uninhibited, a true mate for the wildness in his soul. How he loved her, he realized as he thrust inside her.

He groaned as he felt her muscles beginning to clench. "Eve, my darling!" Rearing back, he pulled her up and flipped her over, positioning her with her hands and knees on the bed. Her heart-shaped buttocks were in the air, a beacon beckoning him onward to glory. Leaning over her he pushed himself into her burning liquid depths, consumed by lust.

Eve savored the feel of his thighs against her. Again and again she reared back, urging him to thrust home hard and complete this mating ritual. Over and over he penetrated her, her inner muscles clenching around him like an iron glove. Eve felt each thrust all the way down to her toes,

"Come, fly with me now," Adam said. He felt his climax building. Deep in her honeyed warmth, he knew he'd found paradise.

Eve's muscles clenched violently around him. Once again, she was thrust high into the heavens. She screamed his name.

Her shout drove Adam crazy. "I love you, only you, always you," he whispered. Liquid warmth gushed down and around his member, and for a moment he thought he might actually expire from their passion. Being inside her and watching himself thrust over and over into her was his undoing. As she found fulfillment, he gave over to the most powerful climax of his life. It went on and on until Adam was boneless, and he collapsed beside her and kissed her neck. Some moments later, he managed to curve his arms around her, to hold her gently. "This settles it. We'll marry in three days' time."

Eyes still hazy with passion, Eve whispered, "But we're already married."

"No, Eve, you made that part up."

Thoroughly exhausted, Eve was more than a little foggy. But at last Adam's words made sense. "Argh, you're right. I did. But if we get married now, people will know I lied."

Putting a finger to her lips, he smoothed out her frown. "We'll say we're renewing our vows, since I was gone for so long a time. Everyone will be delighted—especially your father. He'll think you're the cleverest Bluebeard ever to stop sailing the seven seas."

She laughed. "That I am. And you can begin your psychologist training with me! I kept my university texts, as well as all the monthly Psychology Journals on the Supernaturally Insane."

"I'd like that. I enjoy helping the patients. It gives me a purpose in life that I haven't found in all my wanderings."

She kissed his cheek then caressed it with her fingers. "You have great instincts, and you've been a great help already, but think what you can do with more knowledge. You'll rival Dr. Sigmund himself!"

"I live to rival Dr. Sigmund," he said as he nuzzled her neck. "In matters psychological. But now let me show you where my real expertise lies." His eyes glinted with mischief.

Eve, the prominent and very rational psychologist, giggled like a schoolgirl. She soon agreed that in Adam's specialized field he was an unqualified expert, and he quite drove her mad.

CHAPTER TWENTY-NINE

A Bluebeard of Happiness

A rainbow graced Adam and Eve's wedding, and everyone who was connected with the Towers knew that somewhere over it, bluebirds were gloriously flying—and a crusty little leprechaun was looking for pots of gold. The guests watched Adam and Eve make their solemn vows. When the minister declared the bemused couple "man and wife," the rafters shook with cheers. Even Captain Bluebeard, for all his blustery ways, had a tear in his eye.

With the maddening din of good wishes ringing in their ears, Adam and Eve adjourned to the main portion of the asylum for the reception. Eve stood tall in the receiving line, her smile blinding, revealing to all the happiness that she was feeling. In this unstable and sometimes cruel world, such love as her husband's was as rare as a unicorn.

Yes, she was blessed. This man who had been a stranger to her so short a time ago was now the center of her life, filling a part of her she had never known was empty. He could fly her to the moon—or to the very heavens themselves.

"I'll never forget this night," she whispered. "Our wedding night. It's like a fairy tale."

"I doubt our patients or staff will forget it, either," Adam said. They both glanced around at the crowd of frolicking and laughing well-wishers.

Eve noted several of her father's crew talking with Major Gallant. The complex Napoleon wanna-be was standing against a column, hand in his stiff coat, and she heard a few of his louder remarks. Something about the rotten English. Her father's first mate, a true Frenchman—one who had seen the real Napoleon—listened impassively, a slight smirk on his face.

"I hope the major is content merely to plan a victory against Wellington and not enact it," she said. "It's too crowded on the stairs tonight."

Adam nodded and greeted another guest.

Sighing in deep contentment, Eve breathed in the fragrant scent of gardenias, orange blossoms, and roses. Tonight the asylum was filled with a plethora of flowers, their sweet scents filling the air. Eve's lips twitched into a smile. So far Jack the Rip, though foxed, was behaving himself. The man was otherwise occupied, flirting outrageously with one of the guests who happened to be wearing a very fetching bonnet with lush red roses placed around the brim. Pavlov, who was standing near the couple, gave Eve a nod, letting her know that he had his eye on things. Junger lay beside his master, and appeared to be hugely interested in the wedding cake. He was clearly waiting for the bell of the ball.

Teeter, beaming happily, approached with a tray of champagne in hand. "May I say the madhouse has never looked better?"

"Yes, it's breathtaking," Eve replied. "You've all done a

fine job, and I thank you for pitching in to help." Everyone at the Towers had shown their support. Early this afternoon Fester had generously gifted them with three pots of gold. Eve had cried in joy, and Adam had slapped the crusty little man on the back. Even Teeter had unbent a bit, and praised Fester for his generosity.

"The leprechaun cleans up well." The butler snitfed.

Eve smiled and glanced over to where Fester was standing. With his newly acquired wealth, he was now dressed to the nines in a velvet jacket of emerald green. Diamonds winked from his cuff links, and the diamond on his stickpin was as big as his thumb. He wore a black top hat and looked rather debonair as he argued with her father about some supposed triangle in the Caribbean where ships disappeared and were never seen again.

"That he does," she agreed.

"Of course, he would have done better to be less vulgar in his display of good fortune," Teeter remarked.

"I think he looks in fine feathers," Adam spoke up. "Besides, the old codger deserves to enjoy his spoils. He's waited a long time for them."

Frederick Frankenstein approached, with his escort—Miss Beal! Wearing a stupid grin on his face, the gentle giant congratulated the happy couple, followed by Lady Jane and the Earl of Wolverton, and all their other friends.

The newly married couple accepted all congratulations with happy smiles, though both were secretly wishing to be alone. They finally found their wish granted, as they stood off to the side by a large group of lush green ferns, just the two of them.

Adam smiled down at Eve, his arm about her waist. "You are the loveliest thing I have ever seen. When you walked down that aisle tonight, I thought I had died and gone to heaven. You looked like an angel. You don't know how proud I was to stand beside you and pledge my troth. Nothing will ever tear us apart." He quickly sent a swift but fervent look of thanks to the Almighty, who watches over the sparrow as well as the hawk, and who loves all things great and small. "God truly must love man. He must truly love me. I must say, he's a fine judge of character."

Eve cocked her head, curious. "Why?"

"He gave man woman, and he gave me you. I am the luckiest creature on earth."

Blinking back the tears that suddenly formed in her eyes, she replied softly, "No. I'm the fortunate one." She stood on her tiptoes and kissed him on the cheek. "You do realize, don't you, that most men would quake in fear of what you have committed yourself to." Taking her gaze off Adam, she glanced around the asylum. "When you took me on, you took on a daunting task. Many a sane man wouldn't want this bunch of lunatics."

"How could I not? I love you dearly and desperately. As for your flock—well, I know the lot of them. Yes, every batty, balmy, deranged, dotty, and stark-raving bedlamite in the world seems to have found their way here, but I have found that I like them one and all. Obsessive, delusional, fearful, hysterical—I fit in with them because I'm crazy about you. And since every one of them holds a tiny piece of your heart, they hold a part of mine."

Eve closed her eyes momentarily with joy: Adam understood. She nodded. "Everyone here is family," she said. And now they were also Adam's family. She said a heartfelt prayer of thanks to God for granting such happiness to mortals and paranormals alike. When He had given the heart the capacity to love, He had given mankind a blessing beyond measure. "I am more than fortunate."

Her father overheard her remark as he swaggered up to them. "That ye are, me daughter. It's a lucky thing for you that your dear old da is a crafty pirate with a devious, plotting mind. And a yen for grandchildren."

Eve chuckled and kissed him on the cheek. "You're never going to let me hear the end of this matchmaking plan being so utterly successful, are you?"

"It was inspired, and the results look more than promising. I'll soon be sailing the seas with a full crew of grandkids. What a lucky father I be." Then, turning his attention to Adam, he cocked a brow. "Well, what have you for me? Many a pirate would give their eyeteeth—or at least their eye patches—for me daughter."

"Your reward is my compliments. Your plan was brilliant and executed with a competence that I find remarkable. You are cunning, crafty, and devious," Adam replied.

Bluebeard preened. "And don't forget generous." His chest swelled with pride.

Both Adam and Eve laughed and agreed. "More than generous." After all, the Captain had been so pleased that his plan was concluded with such astounding success that his wedding gift had been two full chests filled with gold and jewels.

Eve said, "Now the Towers won't close down, and your generosity means that Adam can keep his family estate back in Ireland." She'd learned just how much that meant to him, and she had agreed to go to Ireland for the summer months. As she started to say more, she was interrupted by a loud knocking on the front door. "I wonder who that is. Everyone we invited is already here."

"Teeter will see to it," Adam said. He nodded to the butler, who was on his way by.

Teeter answered the knocking. Opening the front

door, he stared down at the three odd characters standing before him. One lady was talking to the air, calling someone Harvey. Another thin woman was hopping up and down, croaking. A third woman appeared to have a bit more dignity, though she was wearing an enormous monstrosity of a hat. She was the one who spoke.

"Good day to you! Isn't it a fine day? I got to wear my Sunday meeting hat, although it is Saturday. Fortunate, don't you think?"

Teeter ignored her chatter, quite used to the eccentricities of the insane. "Madam, who are you?"

The woman appeared flustered for a moment, then with a tiny smirk said, "I am called Lady Maddy Hatter, and next to me is Mrs. March O'Hare—she's speaking with her bunny. And this is Mrs. Bin. She's a leprechaun, who's quite gone round the bend and doesn't know how to get back. I am, of course, their keeper. We followed the rainbow here."

Teeter remained unruffled. He lived with bedlam daily, and the three glasses of champagne he'd drunk kept him feeling remarkably bubbly. The lady talking to "her bunny" was a handsome woman, but it was more than apparent that she was crazy. She was arguing quite rudely with absolutely no one.

"I see no rabbit," he pointed out, testing her.

"He's invisible," Lady Hatter explained in an aside. "He's a pooka."

"I see," Teeter said, and he did. He saw that they were all crackers. And they were just in time for the wedding cheese. "May I ask why you knocked?"

"We wanted to see the wedding. We'd heard it was Adam and Eve, but I thought they were dead. At least, it implies so in the Bible. We have also come to see about letting some rooms."

Teeter turned, anxious to get back to Mrs. Fawlty, who had been flirting with him outrageously earlier, when suddenly bells began ringing loud and clear. A loud scream sounded. He shook his head at the din, the gasps of shock, and Pavlov scolding his dog.

Mrs. Fawlty was screaming, "No, no! Not the wedding cake!"

"We're under attack from them scruffy English!" Major Gallant shouted. He ran out the door, imaginary sword in hand. Teeter barely managed to dodge him.

Mrs. Monkfort was wringing her hands and wailing, "My floor! There is icing on my spotless floor!"

Sir Loring passed by hurriedly, muttering to himself, "That madwoman is on a rampage again. I've got to hide my dirt. No one can get my dirt."

Teeter looked heavenward, as if for inspiration, then slammed the door in the surprised faces of Lady Maddy Hatter and friends, saying, "I'm sorry, but all our rooms are full. We've all the madness we can handle."

He turned from the front door, knowing Eve would be angry that he'd turned away the needy and neurotic. But still, this was her wedding day, and that of Dr. Adam. It was special, and didn't need to be sullied.

Feeling a slight wash of sentimentality, he glanced over at the newly remarried couple. They were indeed crazy—about each other. Dr. Adam was cradling his most prized possession—Eve—and she was giggling against his chest. As Teeter poured himself a whiskey, he said, "Yes, we're all full up on craziness here. But crazy is rooming with love, and that makes all the difference."